RENEGADE

BY
DONNA BOYD

Published by Blue Merle Publishing

ISBN-13: 978-0977329618
ISBN-10: 0977329615

This book is also available in digital format for your e-reader.

Cover art by www.bigstock.com

Also by Donna Boyd

THE PASSION
THE PROMISE

Dark...Dangerous... Powerful...

Rolfe straightened his cuffs in two curt gestures and returned to his seat, his expression now only pleasantly curious. "So tell me, these creatures of yours, these... what is it you call them?"

"Lupinotuum," supplied Emory politely. "It's from the Latin. It means 'part man, part wolf'."

He nodded. "So you would have us believe that they roam the world quite freely, and have done so for centuries."

Emory played the game. He had nothing to lose. Nothing at all. "Evidence suggests they are at least as old a species as homo sapiens. I think they may be older."

Rolfe laid a finger aside his lips, tapping thoughtfully. "And they walk about among humans unimpeded and undiscovered, even in today's world of sophisticated information technology – the internet, spy satellites--and no one has ever learned of their existence but you?"

Emory laughed softly. He couldn't help it. "First of all, they control the internet. They invented satellite technology. They could take down the entire human communications network with one keystroke if they wanted to. And I didn't say no one has ever known about them but me. Human history is filled with references to them – the wolf gods of the Mayas and the Egyptians, the myths of Greece and Rome. I know for a fact that other humans have lived within their households, and have known them for who they are. But I think I may be the only human who has studied them, and written their history down."

"Which of course is what makes you of such great interest to me," agreed Rolfe. "I want to hear the story from the source. How long were you with them?"

Emory glanced down at his nearly empty glass. "All my life," he said softly.

PART ONE

BEFORE THE FALL

A god is nothing without someone to worship him.

--Alexander Devoncroix,

werewolf

CHAPTER ONE

The Present

Emory had been imprisoned for a little under twelve hours. He knew this because the last thing he remembered before he lost consciousness was the face of his captor's Patek Philippe watch. It had read 1:45. Now that same watch, just visible beneath the crisp French cuff that rested on the surface of the black marble table top between them, read 1:00. It actually took Emory several moments to focus on the numbers, and to make sense of them. He was groggy, and his head throbbed with the rhythm of his heart.

"Welcome back," said the man with the watch. "I trust you had a pleasant rest." His voice was smooth, his smile cool. Dark hair, dark eyes; sharp, elegant features. Long slim fingers, with

1

nails that were professionally groomed. A custom tailored Italian suit, dark gray, pale blue silk tie. The watch.

Someone gripped Emory's shoulder from behind and pushed him into a chair that was drawn up before the marble table. His hands were bound behind him with rough plastic cable ties so tightly that his fingertips were cold. He could not remember how he got here. He looked at the man behind the table. Dark hair, blue silk tie. Patek Philippe watch. How did he know that?

The chair was upholstered in a green tapestry fabric, but its high back was uncomfortable and he had to lean forward to accommodate his bound hands. Seeing this, his captor gave a curt nod and Emory was shoved forward. A quick snick of a blade freed his hands.

Emory flexed his fingers and moved his arms in slow motion, eyes roaming around the room at the same heavy pace, focusing on one thing at a time, registering and analyzing with painful deliberation before moving on. His brain felt as though it were swimming in honey. The room was small, with carved panels painted cream. No windows. A large painting of a girl pouring water, framed in gold. A teardrop crystal chandelier overhead. A vase of fresh flowers on a cherry console. A wall of books, all of them with dark green leather covers. The black marble table. A pitcher with water and quartered lemons in the center. Next to it, a silver tray held a cut glass decanter filled with amber liquid and two glasses.

Emory said, "Where are we? Castle Devoncroix?" The hoarseness of his voice surprised him. His lips felt numb, his mouth filled with cotton.

The dark-eyed man seemed amused by this. "No." In a solicitous gesture, he poured a tumbler of the lemon water and

2

slid it across the table to Emory. "You must be thirsty."

Emory massaged his fingers, not trusting them to reach for the glass. "Is it drugged?"

The other man smiled. "Only a little. To help with your hangover."

Emory hesitated, then pulled the tumbler toward him. It was heavy cut glass, like the decanter. He had to use both hands to lift it. It would have made a good weapon, but he lacked the strength in his arms to use it. He drank the water down greedily and set the glass on the table, still thirsty. "It tastes like quinine." He had no idea how he knew that.

His captor politely refilled the glass. "It will counteract the effects of the drug you were given."

"Where are we?" Emory said. He knew he was repeating himself, but he could not seem to stop it, or remember the answer he had been given previously. The scientist in him was mildly intrigued by that. "Is this Castle Devoncroix?"

The other man just smiled, and poured himself a measure of the liquid from the decanter. "I expect you'll feel better in a moment or two. In the meantime, shall we get better acquainted? My name is Rolfe, and I will be your host for the duration of your stay here. Can you tell me your name, by chance?"

"Hilliford." Emory sipped the water, more slowly now. The throbbing in his head was beginning to ease. "Emory Hilliford."

"Excellent." He seemed pleased. "And what do you do, Mr. Hilliford?"

"Doctor," corrected Emory, frowning into the glass. "It's Dr. Hilliford. I'm a professor of ..." The word escaped him. "Something."

"Anthropology," prompted the man opposite.

"That's right. I have tenure at *l'Universite de Montreal.*"

"And what else do you do besides give lectures to anthropology students?"

"I write books."

"Is that all?"

Emory looked at him. "How long have I been here?"

"Three days."

Three days. Christ. He could not remember where he was three days ago, or what he had been doing. He could not even remember waking up, or walking into this room. He drank more of the water.

"You have several university degrees," continued Rolfe conversationally. "Do you recall what some of them might be?"

"No." *Genetics, history, molecular biology . . .* The headache was almost gone. His life was beginning to fall into place like pieces of a kaleidoscope, turning and tumbling and gradually forming a cohesive pattern. The picture that was being formed fascinated him.

Rolfe sipped his drink. "Let's make a deal, you and I, shall we? Let's not lie to each other. Things will go so much more smoothly if we don't."

"You kidnapped me."

"So I did."

"And I'm supposed to believe you won't lie to me?"

The other man gave a careless shrug. "As you please. But I will know if you lie, and please believe me, it is not in your best interests to do so."

"What will you do?" His voice held a surprising lack of interest. "Kill me?"

"No," admitted the other man equitably. "I'll merely make

4

you wish I would."

Then Emory smiled, and finished the water in his glass. The headache was gone. "Do you want to know what I do, Rolfe? Was that the question?"

"It was."

He leaned back in his chair, watching his captor without fear or curiosity. He supposed he had the residue of the drug in his system to thank for that. He said, "I am an assassin. That is what I was raised to be, educated to be, destined to be. And it is what I am."

Rolfe sipped again from his glass, his gaze thoughtful and unimpressed. Then he glanced over Emory's shoulder, briefly and dismissively. "Thank you, Cameron. I'll let you know if we need you."

Emory heard the door open and close. It was entirely too much effort to turn his head to see who was leaving. He poured more water.

Rolfe said, "Did you kill Alexander Devoncroix?"

"No. Where am I?"

"Someplace safe. Somewhere you'll not be found unless we wish you to be found. What about Nicholas Devoncroix?"

"I heard he was dead."

"Did you kill him?"

"No."

Rolfe lifted an eyebrow. "So far I find your skills as an assassin singularly unimpressive."

"Somehow I think you already knew that."

He smiled. "Ah. Feeling better, I see."

"Who are you?"

He sipped his drink, expressionless. "For now, you may think of me as the man who holds your future in his hands."

"What do you want from me?"

The other man was thoughtful for a time, regarding Emory with eyes that told nothing; cold, passionless, speculative. "It changed the world, you know," he said after a time. "Six hundred years of peace, the entire financial industry, science, technology, global commerce ... all of it collapsing in on itself like a slow-motion avalanche. It's been fascinating to watch, really. And it all began on a single night, in a single place with what should have been a single simple murder. You were a part of history, my boy. How very powerful that must make you feel."

Emory said, "I record history. I don't make it."

"Where is David Devoncroix?"

Emory looked down at his glass, lifted it, drank. "Dead." His tone was flat. "I killed him."

"Ah," said Rolfe softly, "now I'm disappointed."

Silence ticked away. Emory could feel the other man's gaze like physical thing, a heaviness in his chest, a hotness in his skin, a chill film of sweat at the back of his neck. He looked at the glass again, started to drink, and then did not.

Rolfe noticed. "Our chemists are quite brilliant," he remarked. "The drug we used to get you here is an amylase simulator that attaches itself to certain neurons that control short-term memory and renders the subject astonishingly compliant, yet it can be eradicated from the system completely in a few hours. We've already obtained twenty-seven patents on its variants, one of which has proven quite remarkable in the treatment of dementia. We're going to make a bloody fortune when it's released to the public."

Emory said, "Good for you." He blotted his forehead with

the back of his hand. His hairline felt damp.

"More water?" Rolfe lifted the pitcher, and when Emory just stared at him, put it down again. "Perhaps not. You've already had half a liter. Of course ..." He sat back again, and picked up his glass, smiling a little as he gazed at Emory. "It might be nothing but a cure for a hangover. Or it might contain a curiously effective truth serum that renders even the most taciturn of men quite garrulous. Or it might contain a slow acting poison that will eventually lead to a long and agonizing death – unless, of course, you receive the antidote in time. A bit pulp fiction-like, that one, but I confess I rather like it."

Emory met his eyes. His voice sounded as tired as he suddenly felt. "You should have done your research. Threats only work on men who have something to lose. Did it occur to you that I might not care what you do to me?"

"Oh, you'll care," Rolfe assured him. "Everyone does ... eventually."

He topped off his drink and pushed back a little from the table, crossing his legs. "You will pay for the lie you just told, by the way," he added negligently, "just as I promised you would. Shall we say ... one finger for each lie? Please be careful, I'm very good at keeping count and I am impeccable with my word. You've already lost one. But before I collect, you'll tell me your story. All of it. I want to know how this began, how we came to this, and I want to know the details. We've gone to a great deal of trouble to bring you here, for the simple reason that you are the only one who knows those details. So let's get started, shall we?"

Emory glanced down at his hands, and saw a fine ring of blood blisters had broken out beneath the skin of his right wrist. It might have been the result of his hands having been bound. Or it might have been the first sign of an internal hemorrhage. He leaned back in his chair. "I drank the water, didn't I?"

The other man seemed mildly puzzled by the non-sequitur, and he showed it in a small, querying lift of his brow.

"I drank the water," Emory repeated, "of my own free will. So you are wrong. I don't care. Not about what you do to me, or much of anything else for that matter. I'm a dying man, didn't you know that? And after the way I've lived these past ten years, any torture you can devise will be a relief. So you see I really do have nothing to lose. And that's why I'll tell you what you want to know. From the beginning, all of it. But will you tell me something first?"

Rolfe inclined his head politely. "If I can."

Emory studied him for a moment. "Are you human?"

That seemed to amuse him. "You surely don't mean to tell me that after all this time you cannot tell the difference."

"Humor me."

Rolfe regarded him speculatively for a time. "Suppose that I am," he said. "Would that make a difference in your story?"

"It might."

Rolfe lifted the cut glass decanter with a questioning glance toward him, and Emory slid his glass forward. Rolfe poured a measure of the liquid into Emory's glass, and then his own. Emory tasted it. "Armagnac," he said, and let the taste linger in his mouth, cling to the back of his tongue, take him home. "I haven't had this since Venice. It was a favorite of the prince."

"I know," Rolfe said.

Emory took another sip, and watched Rolfe silently for a time. He said, "There aren't many secrets left."

"So true," agreed Rolfe. "But, as ever, the most important

ones have yet to be told."

"And you think I know them."

Rolfe sipped his brandy. "Tell me your story, Dr. Hilliford," he invited. "If I were human, what would you want me to know?"

After a moment, Emory began to laugh, softly. "Everything," he said. "I'd want you to know everything."

CHAPTER TWO

Emory
1975-1992

I was raised on a diet of myth and magic in the city known for death, decadence and decay. Is it any wonder I became what I am?

And by that I mean, of course, an academic, not an assassin.

I was born into the household of Prince Fasburg of Auchenstein, where my mother was the executive manager of the Venetian villa in which the prince and his family spent most of their time. My father was a captain in Her Majesty's Royal Navy who died in the service of his country when I was still in my mother's womb. The Fasburgs, who owned the hotel in London in which my mother worked at the time, heard of the tragedy and brought her onto their personal staff in Venice. They had a reputation for such acts of generosity when misfortune struck one of their employees, and my mother, in this case, was their most grateful beneficiary.

It should be clarified here that the principality of Auchenstein had long ago become a republic, and that the title "prince" was an honorary one only. Nonetheless, could a boy have had a more exotic childhood? I lived in a palace where beautiful, elegantly clad people arrived via the shimmering purple waters of the Grand Canal at sunset in vaporetti or gold-painted gondolas, smoking cigarettes that smelled like perfume, tossing aside their furs in the grand foyer while their laughter echoed and bounced and magnified itself until it filled the vast, high-ceilinged chamber with its gay cacophony. I played beneath portraits painted by DaVinci, my running footsteps clattered down hallways where once the Medicis had roamed. I fell asleep to the sound of ancient waters lapping against the stone foundation, having no idea that everyone in the world did not live like this. Having no idea, certainly, that the keepers of this grand estate were not human.

The Fasburgs, most of their friends and many of their employees were, in fact, members of an ancient species known in Latin as lupinotuum. Occasionally they referred to themselves as *les loups garoux*, or, in the Italian familiar, *mannaro*. The English word is werewolf. And so adept were they at blending into the society of humans — at mastering that society, really — that I imagine, if it hadn't been for the tragedy that struck just after my fifth birthday, I might have gone my entire life without ever knowing what they were. Certainly, even after I learned it, the truth made little difference to me.

At least not then.

It was like living in a grand hotel, with constant comings and goings, banquets and masked balls and concerts and visiting dignitaries of one sort or another, for the Fasburgs were notorious for their hospitality and Venice is equally notorious for its festival atmosphere. Cordovan leather traveling cases in russet and burgundy and butternut appeared in the marble foyer on an almost daily basis, only to be whisked away to one of the opulent suites above. Sometimes I would hide behind the potted plants, as small boys are wont to do, and listen to the chatter of a dozen different languages, or watch the pretty women come down the majestic marble staircase in their shiny, form-fitting gowns and twinkling jewels. Their lips were always red, it seemed to me, and their fingernails sharp and brilliant, and even when they smiled at me I was too awed to smile back.

The ceilings in the public rooms were frescoed with cherubs and clouds and gilded gold; there were sixteen chandeliers in the grand foyer, all of them dripping in hand-blown Belgium crystal. The arched doorways that led from room to room were fifteen feet tall and painted gold, and the fireplaces, all of them large enough for a small boy to hide in, had carved marble mantles that depicted scenes from long-ago times, and stories whose heroes had names like Orpheus and Persephone.

There were indoor swimming pools tiled in blue glass, and sometimes the guests would swim nude, or sun themselves on the cushions that were scattered about beneath the high glass dome. This did not interest me as much as it would have had I been somewhat older. There were outdoor terraces and gardens where I would sometimes play with the children who visited the household, and where the adults would often lounge with drinks in their hands, watching us indulgently.

The massive front door opened onto a riotous garden of lilacs and climbing roses and wisteria vines that spilled down toward the Grand Canal, but the breadth of the house backed up against a smaller canal which was the entrance for the household staff and for deliveries. There was a set of stone steps that led down into the water, and there I would sometimes sit and try to catch water bugs with a long stick. I did not know until I was much older that the steps had once led down to dry land.

I had my own nanny and lived in a suite of rooms with marble floors and three television sets, for the Fasburgs were extremely generous with their employees and my mother, as manager of not only the Venetian villa but three other properties they owned, ranked high in their esteem. Until I was five years old I had no reason to suspect that the creatures with whom I shared this grand and glorious existence were anything other than as human as I was. Whether or not my mother knew I can't say for certain, but I doubt it. She might have observed a few small eccentricities, but she was certainly paid enough to keep her opinions to herself. The Fasburgs, as I was to eventually learn, were not like others of their kind. This was both to their advantage and their great detriment.

When I was five, my mother died of what I later would understand was ovarian cancer. She was sick for a summer, and sad, and I recall my nanny hugged me and wept a lot. Otherwise there is not a lot I remember from that time until the day we returned from the funeral, and the Princess herself came to my apartment.

Renegade

Nanny tried to keep me busy in the playroom, and to please her I solemnly sat on the floor in my scratchy wool suit and pretended to be absorbed in my building blocks, but I could hear what the others were saying in the room adjacent. They were women, mostly, who worked in the big house, whose faces I knew but whose names I did not. I was only a child whose world, until this point, had happily consisted of playdough and color crayons and storybooks with colorful pictures. I knew my mother for her goodnight kisses, but even the memory of those was beginning to fade. I was frightened, not by the loss which was, at that tender age, too big for me to comprehend, but by the sudden upheaval in my heretofore pleasant and predictable routine.

"Poor dear. She was a widow, you know. What will become of the little one now?"

"It breaks my heart. So young."

"No other relatives? What a pity."

"He'll have to go to an orphanage, there's no help for it."

"And I'll be out of a job." This was from Nanny, with a big sigh. And then she added quickly, "Not that that's important."

And suddenly the voices were stilled, as though with a single held breath. There was the clack-clacking sound of stilettos on marble. Someone murmured, "Signora," with a kind of reverence in her voice that made me pause in the building of my block fortress. Someone else said, "Princessa," in a voice that was barely above a whisper.

The authoritative click-click- clacking of sharp heels grew louder, and then was silenced completely as she crossed the carpet of my room. She stood before me, looking down. What I saw, from my position amidst the red and blue and yellow

14

building blocks scattered on the floor, were red shoes with open toes and high, high heels, as high as the Eiffel Tower, it seems to me in recollection, and legs clad in shiny stockings, and the hem of a narrow black skirt. And then suddenly she dropped to her knees before me, and I saw her smile, and her tender green eyes, and her dark hair, swept up into a knot atop her head with tendrils curling down around her face. She was, perhaps, the most beautiful person I had ever seen. She said, softly, "Well, look at you, little man. Aren't you the precious one?"

She opened her arms to me, and because I was young and she was irresistible, I went to her. I can remember to this day the sensation of that embrace, and to this day I cannot describe it. The sweet warm envelope of her perfume was like hot chocolate, like cotton candy, like summer skies with striped balloons floating high. Her arms, slender yet soft, the crinkle of silky fabric, a sound that I would forever more associate with the simple peace of being safe; the sigh of her breath, warm and faintly redolent of exotic spices, across my cheek. And yet those were externalities. The whole of her embrace, the thing I cannot describe, was like being infused with scent, like tasting warmth, like hearing star song. I know now what it was, this purely human reaction to a close encounter with one of their kind; the sensory overload, the electric gasp, the flood of wonder. But I was a child, and all I felt was the dizzying rush of adoration.

She lifted me to her hip and took me out of that room, past the gawking women who were gathered outside, the clip-clip-clip of her staccato heels growing faster, their rhythm almost ebullient as she carried me up the stairs. I fastened my arms tight about her neck, my eyes big and excited to see the places I hadn't seen before, the fountains that cascaded from the open mouths of golden wolves, the trees that grew indoors, the gold leaf that sparkled on the arched beams overhead.

We entered at last a large room with furniture done in blue silk and big curved windows looking out over the sparkle of the Grand Canal. There was a woman there, long and lean and dressed in purple, with impossibly white skin and a coil of orange hair cascading over one shoulder. She lounged on one of the sofas with one slim leg tucked beneath her, smoking a cigarette and dangling a martini glass from two fingers. But it was the man, even I could sense, the princess had come here to see.

He leaned one hip upon the corner of a massive carved desk, his own glass held between long slender fingers, laughing at something the woman had said. He was tall and thin, his dark hair swept back from a high forehead, his nose sharp, his dark eyes heavy lidded. He wore a double breasted suit with a thin stripe, and a shirt with stiff cuffs that were fastened by heavy gold cufflinks in the shape of wolves' heads. I remember those cufflinks fascinated me.

"Geof," exclaimed the princess as she burst into the room. She had a soft husky voice that sounded as though it were perpetually discovering a secret she was bursting to tell. "Look what I have found!"

He turned from the laughter he shared with the other woman, and I remember the tenderness that came over his face, the quiet leap of joy that softened his eyes when he saw his wife. Yes, even at five, I noticed that.

The eyes became lit with amusement as they traveled to me. "Why, my darling, I can't imagine. What is it you have found?"

And the woman on the sofa said in a bored, exasperated tone, "Oh, really Ilsa, not another one of your strays!"

The princess shot her an annoyed look, and her tone was cool as she replied, "I really can't think what you mean."

"Honestly, Ilsa!" The orange haired woman drew hard on the cigarette. "Is there a homeless, abandoned or disadvantaged human in all of Europe that you haven't employed? You have one girl whose only job is to change the light bulbs and light the candles for parties!"

That interested me. I thought I would very much like to be the person whose only job was to light the candles at parties.

But the princess ignored her. "He can't be much older than Lara," said the princess, setting me on my feet, "and look how sweet. Not a bit shy."

The woman with the orange hair took another leisurely draw on her cigarette. The smoke came out of her mouth in puffs as she remarked, "He can't even speak."

Of course she would think that. It had been well drilled into me by Nanny that I should never speak to any member of the household outside our apartment unless first spoken to.

The prince looked at me curiously, and even the princess seemed a little uncertain. "Of course he can speak," she said. "I'm sure he's very bright."

"Well, young man?" prompted the prince, regarding me still with an indulgent half smile to please his wife. "Do you speak?"

I replied in a clear, brave voice, "I speak English and Italian, and I can do all of my letters but I can only write words in Italian. Nanny is teaching me French but she says I am not very good."

The prince chuckled and the princess beamed at me, and placed her hands on my shoulders and gave them a little squeeze. The orange-haired woman made an exasperated sound. "There now, you see," declared the princess, pleased. "He will be

17

a perfect playmate for Lara. They can take their lessons together and when we go to the islands this summer she will have someone to splash in the water with."

"Get her a puppy," advised the orange haired woman, rising as she stubbed out her cigarette and glanced at her watch. "I must fly. Aldolpho said if I was late for another appointment he would never dress me again, as if he dared." And then her smile grew kind as she approached the princess, embraced her lightly and kissed her cheek. "Darling," she said gently, "you simply cannot save them all."

And when she was gone the princess reached down and took my hand and held it softly captured in both of hers and she said to her husband, smiling, "And so, Geof? Shall we save just this one?"

He took a sip of his drink and regarded her in a way that suggested he was pretending to think about it. "You do know," he told her, "that there are institutions for this sort of thing."

She made an impatient, dismissing sound in her throat.

The prince looked me over as he sipped again from his glass. "It's really quite unorthodox." And then a kind of merriment came into his eyes as he added, "What do you imagine our esteemed pack leader would think of such a thing?"

The princess replied soberly, "Oh, I'm sure he would quite disapprove." But when I sneaked a quick upward glance at her, her eyes were dancing. "And what a pity, too, since I know how desperately you yearn to please him."

The prince worked his mouth in a way I was to learn indicated that he was struggling to hide a smile, but not struggling very hard. "Oh, I don't know," he said, his tone musing. "I think Alexander might be amused. In fact, he might even applaud our efforts. And what a great feather in my cap that would be."

"Oh, Geof, stop teasing. Your humor is going to bring us all to ruin one day. And you're upsetting the child."

Actually, I wasn't in the least upset, but because I was by now devoted to the princess, I tried to look a little distraught.

The prince saw my effort and smiled. "Well, now we certainly can't have that." He set aside his glass and came over to me. He clasped his hands behind his back and bent down so as to address me directly. "Decide then, young ..."

He glanced at his wife questioningly, and she supplied, "Emory."

"Young Emory," he repeated solemnly, as though committing my name to memory. "So, little man, will you come and live among us, and be one of us?"

I could tell this was a serious matter, and so I thought about it. I said, "Could I swim in the big pool?"

The prince replied, "I shouldn't be a bit surprised."

"Then," I decided gravely, "I think I would like it very much."

The prince's dark eyes were dancing with laughter but he made his face seem suitably somber as he nodded. "I believe you have made a wise decision, young Emory. Welcome to our family."

He extended his hand to me and I shook it just like I had seen the grown men do, with a firm grip. And then the princess, laughing, threw herself into her husband's arms and kissed him on the mouth, and turned to me and scooped me up and kissed me too. "Oh, we are going to be so very happy together!" she declared. "So very happy!"

19

And so there you have it. I owe the man I am today to a preternatural creature with a sense of humor and the mate who knew he would deny her nothing. This was not the first time their kind had intervened in the lives of humans, nor would it be the last. I think it's fair to say, however, that every time they have done so, history has been changed, and not always for the better.

This time was to be no exception.

CHAPTER THREE

The Present

Rolfe watched him with amused brown eyes. Emory sipped his Armagnac, still holding the glass with both hands. The sensation was returning to his fingers, but his wrists were weak, and when he tried to straighten his fingers, the entire hand shook convulsively. The blood blisters had darkened, but had not spread.

Rolfe said, "You are as captivating a raconteur as I imagined you would be. I've read your books, you know."

Emory said, "I'm flattered. Tell me, which did you like better — *A Social History of Communal Man* or *The Origin and Development of Language Centers in Primates*?"

Rolfe smiled. "I found them both quite fascinating, actually.

But I was referring to the book, *Dawn to Dusk: A Tale of Two Species*. Gripping stuff, really. Of course, parts of it are a bit over-written, but one can almost overlook that for the sake of content."

Only members of the pack had access to the digital copy of that book, and there were, to Emory's knowledge, only three bound copies in existence. One was displayed in the museum library of Castle Devoncroix, one was under lock and key in Venice, and the last, so he was given to believe, was secured in the vaults of the Vatican.

He watched as Rolfe rose and circled the table to the bookshelf on the opposite wall. He removed one of the green leather volumes and Emory saw the familiar crescent moon logo stamped in gold. "This part, in particular, is one of my favorites."

He opened the book and read aloud Emory's own words.

"In a time now long forgotten, when the earth was new and the stars so bright they cast shadows upon the plains, in a time of crisp white snow and glistening glaciers, of wet, fetid springs and lightning-cracked summers, the earth was their playground. They raced the moonlit prairies, they hunted the fertile valleys, they ate until their bellies were heavy and they slept the deep and dreamless sleep of those who have absolutely nothing to fear. They were the perfect predator, evolved not only to survive, but to thrive in the world of brutality, chaos and upheaval from which they had sprung. Their senses were sharp, their brains were large, their muscles strong, their synapses fast. They were the penultimate example of an adaptive species.

"Their most distinctive adaptive quality, of course, was the ability to change their form at will to meet the challenges of their surroundings. They were quadrupeds, with thick harsh coats of fur to protect them from the arctic winds and tropic sun, with teeth designed to tear and claws designed to rip; muscles that could propel them effortlessly over chasms and hearts that would pump steadily and strongly as legs ran for days without stopping. And they were bipeds, with hands and feet that could climb tall trees or scale sharp cliffs; with long, supple fingers and opposable thumbs that could hold a tool or build a fire, with vocal cords that could produce spoken language. Their prey was any species that could not outrun or out think them. They were at the top of the food chain.

"Eons passed, climates shifted, the earth heaved and shuddered and settled itself again. During this time, so the legend goes, our magnificent dual-formed heroes ruled the earth. And who was to stop them? The jungle cats who fled from them, the canids who crept in at night to scavenge their leavings, the filthy, cave-dwelling humans with their underdeveloped prefrontal cortex and a lifespan of less than twenty years? Prey.

"As is inevitable when the necessities of survival are abundant and leisure is plentiful, creatures of imagination begin to yearn for that which will endure beyond them, and a civilization is born. In the vast underground caves of the frozen north, in the equatorial jungles, upon volcanic islands now long since submerged, they began to build, exploiting the possibilities of their bipedal form to the fullest. And so with their nimble fingers they drew patterns in the earth and fashioned tools, with their two legs they walked upright and reached for things they could not see. They fired pottery and carved stones; they harnessed the power of roaring water and blazing sun. They discovered pleasure in harmonic sounds and complementary colors and symmetrical shapes. They built shelters and gathering places, they wove textiles and cultivated gardens.

23

"By the height of the Greek civilization, the symbiosis between human beings and the species we'll call, for the time being, lupinotuum was well established. Art, architecture, sculpture, poetry, theater, the diatonic scale—only the truly naive would believe they sprang into being with nothing more than the beneficence of a sunny island and a strong fleet of trading ships. Our dual-formed predators—often called gods by historians of this era—had long since mastered and forgotten the skills that form the cornerstone of what is now called the birthplace of modern civilization. They brought these gifts to the human race much in the way a pet owner will indulge his beloved companion, for something much more interesting than Greek civilization had developed over the anonymous centuries: vanity. Species lupinotuum, with its supercharged senses, its enhanced brain and lightning-fast synapses, had fallen in love with its own reflection in the water, and that reflection was the human race."

He caressed the page with his finger in the way a true sensualist might luxuriate in the touch of silk, and the expression upon his face was that of a connoisseur who was in the throes of deep appreciation. "Words," he murmured. "I do love them." He closed the volume and returned it to the shelf with great care.

Emory set the glass on the table and noted with interest that it took a moment to command his fingers to release it. Yet his response time was improving from the last attempt he had made. He said, "Odd. All my life I wanted to see Castle Devoncroix. But I never expected to come here like this."

Rolfe said, with only the slightest touch of impatience, "You are growing tiresome on that subject. What difference does it make where you are when you have very little hope of ever leaving?"

After a slow moment, Emory inclined his head in agreement. "Point taken."

Rolfe straightened his cuffs in two curt gestures and returned to his seat, his expression now only pleasantly curious. "So tell me, these creatures of yours, these ... what is it you call them?"

"Lupinotuum," supplied Emory politely. "It's from Latin. It means 'part man, part wolf.'"

He nodded. "So you would have us believe that they roam the world quite freely, and have done so for centuries."

Emory played the game. He had nothing to lose. Nothing at all. "Evidence suggests they are at least as old a species as Homo sapiens. I think they may be older."

Rolfe laid a finger aside his lips, tapping thoughtfully. "And they walk about among humans unimpeded and undiscovered, even in today's world of sophisticated information technology — the Internet, spy satellites — and no one has ever learned of their existence but you?"

Emory laughed softly. He couldn't help it. "First of all, they control the Internet. They invented satellite technology. They could take down the entire human communications network with one keystroke if they wanted to. And I didn't say no one has ever known about them but me. Human history is filled with references to them — the wolf gods of the Mayas and the Egyptians, the myths of Greece and Rome. I know for a fact that other humans have lived within their households, and have known them for who they are. But I think I may be the only human who has studied them, and written their history down."

"Which of course is what makes you of such great interest to me," agreed Rolfe. "I want to hear the story from the source. How long were you with them?"

25

Emory glanced down at his nearly empty glass. "All my life," he said softly.

Rolfe reached across the table to refill Emory's glass, and after a moment Emory began to speak again.

CHAPTER FOUR

V enice in the nineteen seventies was rife with their species. I think there were at that time more of them than of humans, but that might simply be my perception.   Geof and Ilsa Fasburg were, for appearances' sake, virtually indistinguishable from any of the numerous wealthy Europeans who made Venice their home in the seventies.   They were attractive, elegantly groomed and exquisitely mannered. They played tennis and squash and swam laps in the Olympic-sized pool whenever the notion struck them; in the winter they skied the Alps and in the summer they cruised the Mediterranean in their yacht. In the evenings they donned their couture attire, complete with evening gloves and fur-lined cloaks, and went to the opera, or the theater, or to an Embassy party or the home of a friend for dinner. They looked to be in their late thirties, early forties at most. They were, in fact, over ninety years old.

I mention this here for two reasons. The first is to remark on the strength and longevity of their species. The average lifespan is around one hundred fifty years. They are resistant to most of the diseases that threaten humans, and their recuperative powers, in the case of injury, are noticeably superior to those of humans. Their ability to heal from sudden trauma is greatly dependent on the ability to Change, but the very act of changing from one form to the other, while it floods the body with healing hormones, uses up enormous amounts of energy. So it is not a foolproof system.

Of course that nonsense about silver bullets is just that: nonsense. They are living creatures, and they can be mortally wounded just like any other living being. They die of accidents, injury, or simple old age. But because of their generally robust health, they reproduce well into their later years.

And that is the second reason I mention the Fasburgs' age. They had four children, widely varied in age, scattered across the globe. The oldest, Freda, was in her sixties, a research scientist of some renown and, as I later learned, a close companion of the oldest Devoncroix offspring. The youngest was five years old, the delight of her parents' waning reproductive years. Her name was Lara, and she was the reason for my good fortune.

On that first day, the day I came to live with them, the princess led me by the hand to the nursery, a long, sun-washed room with shelves of books and colorful games and a little girl in a pink-flowered dress earnestly occupied with modeling clay at a work table in its center. A tall man all dressed in black, who I would later come to know as Teacher, watched her from behind a big carved desk across the room. He stood as the princess entered, and so did the little girl.

"Mama, Mama!" she cried happily, holding up a very precise rendering of a bird she had fashioned from clay. "Look what I made!"

"How fine it is, my precious," exclaimed the princess, beaming as she held both my shoulders, pushing me a little in front of her. "Now come see what I have brought you. His name is Emory, and he is going to be your new friend."

Lara was dark haired and green eyed, like her mother, with porcelain skin, a deceptively cherubic face, and an impish bent for mischief. She came around the table and stood before me, sizing me up curiously, seeming to sniff the air as she turned her head this way and that, regarding me. Then, without any warning whatsoever, she lunged at me and bit me hard on the cheek.

I howled in pain and immediately bit her back, catching her just under the eyebrow and pinching hard enough to draw blood. Her scream pierced my ears and I stumbled back with blood and tears streaming down my face and the frankly not-very-satisfying taste of her blood in my mouth. The princess drew back her arm quite calmly and cuffed Lara across the face, hard enough to send her tumbling backward across the schoolroom floor.

This in itself was enough to make me gasp and stare, since I had never before seen a child struck in that way. But then the most astonishing thing happened. The little girl hit the floor with a kind of shimmer of light, a little explosion no more dramatic than the dark/bright blink of an eye, and then there was no longer a little girl at all but a small black-furred wolf cub with green eyes, all tangled up in a child's pink dress and underwear. My tears dried up. I forgot all about my bleeding, throbbing face. It was all I could do to keep from laughing out loud in delight. I

29

stared in open-mouthed wonder and absolute approval.

Even at that age, the power of their Change can enrapture a human. The little cub huddled in the corner, regarding the princess with mewling sounds and big, reproachful eyes, and the princess stepped forward and scooped her up, disentangling her from the clothing almost absently as she embraced her and stroked her fur. I wanted to stroke the fur too, but was transfixed.

"Really, madame." The man in black was wiping the blood from my face with a cloth, his grip tight and a little painful on my chin. "I wish you had consulted me first. There could have been a serious accident. "

"Don't be absurd, Artemis, they are children," replied the princess. "Besides, how else is she going to learn about humans? The world is filled with them you know." Her eyes had a merry twinkle to them, and she nuzzled the little wolf's neck. The cub licked the princess's face, and then began to pant happily.

The man in black smeared a green goo on my wound but I struggled away; not because it was unpleasant, but because he was blocking my view of the little wolf, who now began to squirm in the princess's arms until she set her on her feet.

"Very well, belissima," said the princess. "Enough."

And with a little *pouf* of light and a smell like vanilla and roses, where once there was a furry wolf cub there was now a naked little girl with tangled black curls. I gasped in wonder.

"Lara," said the princess sternly, "what do we know about humans?"

The girl child stuck her finger in her mouth and mumbled, "They are not to be eaten."

"Or?"

"Bitten," acknowledged the girl, gazing at me.

30

The princess nodded approvingly and held out the little girl's underpants, which she obligingly stepped into. "And what else do we know?" she prompted.

The little girl smiled easily, revealing a sunny disposition that was not so much different from my own, and a missing front tooth. "To be mindful of our clothes," she replied. She held up her arms and her mother draped the pink dress over them.

"Correct," said the princess. "Monsieur Baptiste spent hours and hours sewing your pretty little frock, and he would be heartbroken to see how carelessly you've treated it. We must be respectful of our possessions, yes?" She turned the child around and deftly tied the sash into a big bow at the waist. "There, now. Go and apologize to your friend Emory."

I was aware of the smell of the green goo, and of the man in black standing over us with arms crossed and a scowl on his face. But mostly I was aware of Lara. The place where I had bitten her was nothing more than a pink scar bisecting her eyebrow now, and her eyes were wary and unsure.

"That," I said on a breath, "was super. Can you show me how to do it?"

Lara grinned at me, and from the relief that flooded her face, her shoulders, her whole body, I suddenly knew that she had been far more afraid of me than I ever had been of her. "Don't be silly. You're a human. But I can teach you how to run fast and swim underwater."

I was intrigued. "In the big pool?"

She nodded solemnly.

"Lara," prompted her mother.

"I'm sorry I bit you." She flashed me another one of her quick ebullient grins, and she shot out her finger to lightly brush

31

the still-weeping wound on my face. "But now you have my mark. You are my friend forever."

Not to be outdone, I touched the faint pink scar on her eyebrow. "You have my mark too."

And we grinned at each other.

"There now Artemis," said the princess, smiling contentedly as she gave us each a brief, affectionate stroke on the head. "Didn't I tell you all would be well?"

The dour-faced teacher made a grunting sound in his throat, but didn't reply.

This incident should of course go to dispel whatever Hollywood-like misconceptions might still linger about humans being turned into werewolves by their bites. I laughed the first time I saw a movie—I must have been ten or twelve—that was based on that premise. And then, to be truthful, I think I was a little wistful. How fine it would be if such a thing were possible. How unfair that it was not.

As I grew to adulthood, the bite mark faded, but I still bear the small crescent-shaped scar of Lara's teeth on my cheekbone. Lara's scar could no doubt easily be disguised with makeup if she chose, but she never does. Whenever I see her, I always look carefully. And my mark is always there.

Excerpt from **DAWN TO DUSK: A TALE OF TWO SPECIES** by *Emory Hilliford, PhD:*

The culture of the lupinotuum is rich with legends, for theirs is greatly an oral tradition. Though they pride themselves on keeping accurate pack records of births, deaths, and matings, and though the epistolary tradition is one that is honored among them, much of their history and their myths—for so often the two are intertwined—are recorded for the first time in this volume. For other historical references, I am indebted to various artists, chanteuse, poets and historians of their own race (see Appendix 1). The following rendition of the tale of Romulus and Remus was taken from an account by the lupinotuum historian Matise Devoncroix, about whom very little biographical information is available.

The reader may be surprised at how often human myths have intersected with lupinotuum history. You may be sure that whenever there is a tale involving humans interacting with wolves, their race was certainly involved. Take, for example, the legends of Tu Kueh, Zoroaster, Siegfried the hero, Romulus and Remus—all great men who were purported to be suckled by wolves. And what manner of creature might suckle at the breast of a wolf but arise to walk as a human except one of their kind? Pay attention to the details, and you see their race recorded between the lines of every human history book.

The legend of Romulus and Remus is the one to which we turn our attention now, for they are credited in both cultures with having changed civilization. Long before the birth of Rome, of course, the lupinotuum had ruled the temples of Greece and the palaces of Egypt, amused themselves in the wilderness of China and the jungles of India, and they had grown to enjoy the art and the order of what is today known as civilized society. Rome, and all it implied, was a space out of time, waiting to happen.

Twins are not a common occurrence among their kind, and Romulus and Remus, as it happened, were born to a powerful merchant family who became delayed in the hills of Italy too long to return to their clan in time for the birth. When word got out, their clan travelled to them, bringing gifts and praise to honor the wonder of the twins and the splendor of their parents. They came with fine silks and gold-painted caravans to convey their treasures, and the poor human shepherds who inhabited those Etruscan fields must have been quite struck dumb by the sight of so much luxury, so many wonders.

The weather was amenable, the herds were plentiful, the land arable, and the clan began to build their homes upon the seven hills. They brought with them all the best of the civilization they had built in Greece—elaborate plumbing, irrigation and waste-disposal systems, their love of art and architecture, a taste for luxury and a knack or commerce. Of course the humans who surrounded them called them gods. Of course they worshipped and adored them. How could they not?

And it is only a fact of nature to return adoration when one is adored.

For centuries this magnificent civilization grew and thrived, spreading out from the seven hills to tame all the world. This was, by all accounts, their finest moment, and perhaps the finest thing about it was the humans they brought into the fold to live among them. They taught their humans to read and write and to build and to think and to create, in many cases, almost as well as they did. They dressed up their human performers and amused themselves with song and drama. They wallowed in their own success. They loved too deeply, sang too loudly, played too long. They indulged themselves, they indulged their humans, and they forgot they were supposed to be gods. And thus the magnificence that was Rome began to crumble.

So much blame has been cast, so much speculation has been put forth as to how, indeed, it all could have been lost in such a short time. Did they grow lazy, drunken, disinterested? Perhaps. Vain and careless, convinced of their own infallibility? No doubt. But this above all must be remembered: the gods did not abandon their city. They did not set fire to their own holdings, they did not pull down the marble edifices or cast asunder the columns of their own palaces. They merely watched, in helpless disbelief, as the humans they adored destroyed everything they had built for them, and eventually cast out the gods from their own paradise.

The last great civilization of the old world fell to ruin not because its creators hunted humans, warred with humans, or hated them, but because they loved humans, far too well. It is a lesson they have never completely forgotten.

Or forgiven.

CHAPTER FIVE

I grew to be an odd boy, which is hardly surprising under the circumstances, I suppose. Because intellect was so highly valued in their society, mine was cultivated by simple default, and learning came easily to me. I was a prodigy by human standards, some might even say a genius. But among their kind I was merely amusing; passably bright for a human. Yet in living among them I think sometimes I forgot I was, in fact, human, and I developed a brash confidence, a thirst for adventure, and a sublime conviction of my own infallibility that was sheer werewolf.

What is more surprising is that Lara, who was by nature what I could never be, had none of my courage or, if the truth be told, reckless bravado. She seemed to have been born a happy introvert who, only with the encouragement of someone like me, could achieve even a fraction of her potential. She depended on me. I depended on her. Life was simple for us then.

It took Lara and me no time at all to discover that the window in my room opened onto a roof that gave way to a lower roof that was a mere springing step away from a wall we could scramble down to the street below. We used to sneak out of the house at night when we thought no one knew and stalk the streets of Venice, hunting rats, she in wolf form and I in dark clothing and bare feet, the better with which to grip the slick stones and vertical walls. From Lara I learned to be silent and swift, to melt in and out of shadows like a wolf on the prowl and to balance on a narrow ledge as though I had four feet instead of two. From me, Lara learned to be fearless. The two of us, together, were utterly reckless, completely unstoppable, and as foolish as any two children ever had been.

We never guessed that Teacher, whose sworn duty it was to protect his charge, was never more than a hundred feet away. The night we learned the truth was a milestone in my education, in more ways than one.

Venice is filled with blind alleys, bridges that cross and cross again and lead nowhere, narrow streets that wander forever in circles, and mists so thick they can swallow a child — or a young wolf — whole in an instant. At three in the morning, there is black water below and black shapes beyond, and very little else. It's a world of sound and scent, not of sight. It's their world, not mine. I knew this, and I was jealous. Jealous, and determined to prove my worth.

If we had thought about it for even a minute we would have realized that in a city like Venice, one ten-year-old wolfling would not have been the only one on the prowl in the dark dead hours of the morning. The need to run in wolf form is a physical necessity for them, and in most of the major cities of the world there are green spaces designated for just such a purpose. In Venice there are rooftops and bridges, wholly unsatisfactory for the most part, which was why house parties in the country were such a popular form of entertainment. But nature would not be long restrained, and it was inevitable that we would eventually meet up with one of their kind who had the same idea we did.

Lara scented them first, a group of three adolescents just beyond the bridge we were about to cross, and she stiffened and crouched low, her fur bristling. I knew her body language well enough by now almost to read her mind, and I dropped down low beside her on the wet cobblestones, listening for what had frightened her. I heard the drip of mist from an overhanging eave, the slap of water below, and, eventually, the soft snuffling and breathy growls of animals in the dark.

Lara turned carefully to melt away back toward the direction from which we had come, but I held up a hand to stay her, and I crept forward. I don't know why. I was curious. I was stupid. I was a boy.

The young males had chased down and killed a small dog, and they were arguing playfully over the remains. Muzzles bloody, fur damp with the misty night, they postured and posed, tossing the carcass around, snapping and lunging and retreating and advancing; werewolves at play. They caught my scent before I even crested the rise of the bridge and abandoned their game at once, turning, crouching low as Lara had done, searching the blackness with narrow yellow eyes.

They couldn't see me if I stayed to the shadows, I was certain of it. I was also certain—for some absurd reason I cannot justify to this day—that if I charged them they would scatter. I was wrong on both counts.

As though orchestrated by an unseen hand, they spread out in a semi circle, approaching me. I lunged up out of my crouch with a mighty roar, waving my arms and leaping toward them. In a sudden flash of perception, I imagined I could see malicious laughter in their eyes as they charged me, two of them dashing wide to circle behind me while the third crouched low with teeth bared. I turned and ran.

I could not outrun them; I knew that much. But I had no other plan. I sensed, rather than saw, the brush of black fur as Lara raced past me and I heard the scrabble of claws on the wet stones behind me. My heart was thundering and my legs were pumping and my breath was screeching in my ears. I saw the shape of a building, its entrance half-illuminated by a shadowed street light, and as I ran toward it I saw it was a church. Churches were always open. I screamed, "Lara!" with the last of my breath and sprinted toward it. That was when the three hot-breathed wolves streaked past me, and I realized they were no longer chasing me, but Lara.

I made it to the steps of the church and screamed again, "Lara!" I could not see her. I scrambled up the steps and onto the portico and that was when I saw her break through the mist, running toward me. One of the young males, a wiry looking brown-furred creature, was close enough behind her that I could see the gleam of his yellow eyes. I grabbed the heavy door and pushed it open. "Come on!" I cried. "Hurry!"

Lara reached the bottom of the steps, and stopped.

I was on the inside of the door, now, ready to push it closed the moment she was inside. "Hurry!" I shouted again. But she didn't move.

The brown one was close on her now, and from the left another one came, flowing out of the mist like a demon. I screamed at her, "Are you crazy? Get inside!" And when she just stood there, frozen, I left the protection of the half-closed door and started running toward her, to drag her inside by the fur if I had to.

It was probably this that galvanized her into action, because with one frantic, desperate glance over her shoulder she bounded up the steps, pushed off with her back feet, and leapt toward me. I saw what she was going to do just in time to fling my arm across my face to protect my eyes and to swing out of the arc of her Change so that only my shoulder and the back of my neck caught its heat. She fell against me in a tangle of arms and legs, and we scrambled inside, gasping, and slammed the big door shut behind us.

There were candles flickering in the narthex, and the whole place smelled like beeswax and musty incense. The luminosity of stained glass caught the gleam of candles here and there with a spooky effect. We leaned our backs against the door, chests heaving, hands braced against the carved wood as though we might at any moment be called upon to hold the door closed with our brute strength. Then Lara gasped, "They won't ... follow us in here."

I shot a skeptical look at her. "They can try."

She shook her head, swallowing once, regaining her breath. "We're not allowed."

Cautiously I opened the door just a crack, and peered out. She was right. The three of them had stopped at the bottom of the steps and were pacing angrily, muttering and snarling to themselves. But they made no move to ascend the steps toward us. I closed the door softly again.

"We can't enter a church in our natural form," Lara explained, shivering a little in her bare skin.

I stared at her. "Why not?"

She drew breath for an answer, and closed her mouth, looking faintly puzzled. "I don't know."

"Will you, like, burst into flames or something?"

"I don't think so." But she didn't sound all that sure. "It's more like ... bad manners."

I knew enough about their strict regard for manners and protocol not to take such an edict lightly. I had read stories in which loup garoux had willingly sacrificed their own lives before committing a breach of etiquette, so great was their dedication to, and their regard for, the tenets of civilization. Still, the whole thing was beginning to sound suspicious to me, particularly with three angry werewolves pacing the stones outside, and I demanded, "But it's not bad manners to enter a church naked?"

She shrugged.

I pulled my sweatshirt over my head and tossed it to her. Now I was cold, my skin prickling in the damp interior of the church.

"You should have left them alone," she accused, tugging on the sweatshirt. "Now what are we going to do?"

I opened the door a crack, peered through and closed it again. They were still there. I closed the door and tried to remember what I had learned about the architecture of cathedrals. Was there a back door? All I could remember was that the concept of the flying buttress was designed by a werewolf called Helios in a place called Byzantium in AD 320. We only had an hour or two before dawn and if we were caught missing ... I'd almost rather

41

face the angry werewolves. Lara, having changed so precipitously into human form, would be unable to change back for as much as an hour, and until then I was responsible for keeping her safe. My mind raced, my eyes scanned. I caught Lara's hand.

"Run," I told her abruptly. "Run as fast as you can."

Without giving her a chance to question or to lag, I burst through the church door at a dead-out charge, propelling Lara with me. The portico was about fifty feet wide, and the small pack below easily outdistanced us as we raced across it, knowing that when we came to the rail we would have no choice but to climb over and drop to the ground—and into their eager, waiting maws. But as we approached the railing I shouted at Lara, "Jump!" and held on to her hand as tightly as I knew how.

She sprang into the air and so did I, although her leaps were so magically strong there was very little effort required on my part. It was as close to flying as I have ever felt. Our feet struck the rail with just enough momentum to push off again and we soared over the narrow walkway below, screaming with terror and exhilaration all the way down.

We hit the black water of the canal feet first and with enough force to sink straight down. There was a heart-stopping moment in the cold darkness when I lost Lara's hand, but then I broke through the surface and there she was, looking shocked and scared but then laughing to see me, and I grabbed on to her and laughed too with the sheer thrill of it all.

But our delight was short lived. The three werewolves paced the wall of the canal above us, angrier now than before. As we watched, one of them crouched and prepared to dive in. Too shocked to turn and swim, paralyzed with dread, we caught a sudden silent flash of movement, a single, impatient snarl, and a fourth wolf-form streaked around the corner of the church. He was long and black and efficient in movement; he snatched the brown one by the scruff of the neck and threw him against the side of the building. He turned on the other two in a fury of bared teeth and flying saliva and they rolled and tumbled and screamed for nothing more than five or six seconds, while Lara and I watched with dirty canal water lapping into our open, astonished mouths. Then there was silence, and the three adolescent wolves ran away.

Huge grins spread over our faces and we gripped each other in celebratory joy, hardly able to believe our good fortune. Then the long black wolf turned and looked at us with cold and steady eyes, and our grins faded.

It was Teacher.

On Tuesdays and Thursdays, while Lara practiced ballet, I had fencing lessons. The princess had learned from one of her human friends that fencing was the sort of thing well-bred young human children were taught at an early age, and she thought it would be amusing to bring in Monsieur to instruct me twice a week. We had our lessons in the third floor ballroom, a vast empty space with shiny wood floors and tall arched windows lining either side, which were open on this bright spring day to the sounds and smells from the streets below.

The prince strode in as I was preparing an elegant thrust and snatched my foil out of my hand as one might catch a fly in mid-air. "Good day, Master Emory," he greeted me, and bowed slightly to Monsieur. "*Bonjour, Monsieur Forcat. Allez-vous, s'il vous plait."*

It's always been fascinating to me that the loup garoux, who have no need for language in their natural form, have such a quick ear for it that they effortlessly learn to speak any human language upon hearing it only once or twice. Lara was fluent in seventeen languages, including Chinese, before I mastered French.

Monsieur saluted him with his upraised foil, bowed, and departed the room. I reluctantly removed my mask from my sweaty face, and made myself stand tall. I knew I was in trouble, as any sensible boy would.

The prince regarded the foil that was in his hands thoughtfully for a moment. "I've never understood the foolishness that requires you humans to put such faith in your weapons." He took the foil and snapped it effortlessly in two over his knee. The discarded pieces clattered upon the floor. "Only a coward relies upon steel and iron to fight his battles for him," he said.

And then, in an abrupt change of demeanor, he declared airily, "I have come, Master Emory, to seek your counsel."

I was wise enough to say nothing, but to watch him closely.

"What would you do," he inquired, with every appearance of sincerity behind those dark, earnest eyes, "if you were the father of a young daughter who had been bullied and terrorized by three young rogues twice her size?"

I remember an enormous wash of relief. It was about them, not me. I said without hesitation and with a great deal of force, because I had been terrorized, too, "I would have them arrested, and put them in prison without delay."

He nodded thoughtfully, tapping his index finger across his

lips, regarding me. "Sadly, we have no facilities for incarceration. Our means of justice are much more direct."

When I looked confused, he explained "Life or death."

"Then," I offered immediately, "I would kill them."

Perhaps a slight amusement twitched at his lips. "I see."

I wondered if I had said something wrong.

He said, "Shall I tell you why murder among my species is so rare as to be almost extinct? There is a peculiar physio-chemical reaction that occurs at the moment of a violent death, in which the thoughts, memories, passions, fears and joys – in essence, the entire soul – of the dying werewolf flows into the mind of his killer. In order to kill another, you must be willing to live the rest of your life with him inside your mind, as part of you. Very few of us are willing to accept those consequences for a moment of rage or revenge, so we do not kill each other. The same thing happens, oddly enough," he added casually, "during the mating bond, which is why, although we may have sex with many, we love only one. I believe quite the opposite is true among your people."

I nodded absently, far more fascinated with violent death than with sex. I was a child. That would change.

I thought about it for a moment, and inquired, "But if you can't put them in prison and you can't kill them, how do you punish criminals?"

He smiled. "There are, of course, exceptions to the death penalty."

And before I saw him move, without a flicker of a lash to give me warning, I was flying through the air and out the open window, dangling by my wrist alone three stories above Venice. There was a moment, approximately a heartbeat, when I did not believe it, when I simply did not react. And then I saw the people below me like dolls on the street, and the sunlight glinting off the water, and two levels of window boxes, tumbling with flowers, on the buildings surrounding me, and I felt my body sway, unsupported in the void. I couldn't swallow, or make a sound. My testicles shrank into my body. How I managed to avoid soiling myself I'll never know. I was a mass of sheer, quaking terror.

The prince gazed down upon me, dispassionate. "We have a vastly different moral code, young Emory," he explained to me. "You will do well to remember that."

My nails dug into his wrist. I felt myself slipping.

"If I were human, for example," he went on, "I would open my hand, and let you drop. I would watch your bones splatter onto the pavement below and feel what? Perhaps less than a twinge of regret. I would take my chances with your courts and my own capricious conscience and be done with it. However ..."

With a single effortless haul, he lofted me over the windowsill and back into the room. I staggered when my feet met the floor, and he released me.

"Fortunately for you, I am not human," he said. He took out a handkerchief to wipe his hand of my sweat, and glanced at me in passing. "And as a matter of interest, did you know that one of the few remaining crimes for which death is sanctioned among our kind is the intentional harm of a human?" A shrug. "I've always found it fascinating that we value your lives so much more than you do."

He was close to me suddenly, his dark eyes like a volcanic fire that consumed everything in its path — my will, my thoughts, my courage, my self. "Listen to me, little man," he said lowly.

"You will never be stronger than we are. You will never be faster. You will never be smarter. You can't outrun, out swim, out jump, out fight or out think us. Your only chance, if you are to survive among us, is to earn our respect."

His finger darted out suddenly and tapped my forehead. His touch was like a bullet to my brain. "This," he told me, "is your weapon. Learn to use it."

One might think, after such a terrifying display from one who had previously shown me only kindness, my trust would have been shattered forever, my affection for him dissolved. The opposite was true. Because there was no rancor in his actions, no vindictiveness or anger, I understood that this lesson was as much a sign of his love for me as were his kisses, his patient supervision of my studies, his carelessly expensive gifts. They are harsh teachers, the lupinotuum, but fair. It is far kinder to strike a child once for biting a human than to condemn her to a life of the desperate savagery and ostracization that results from a lack of inhibition. Was the prince's lesson a cruel one? No doubt. But it was one I never forgot.

He stood, and added casually, "Cleverly done, by the way, running into the church. How did you know they wouldn't follow you?"

I swallowed hard. "I didn't, sir. Not until Lara told me."

He seemed surprised. "Then you have luck as well as cunning on your side. An unbeatable combination, most would say."

My fencing whites were drenched with sweat and my hair was plastered to my eyes and my guts were swimming with residual fear, but those few, approving words from him were all it took to make the world right again. I struggled mightily to keep my voice steady and was desperately proud when I succeeded. "I would never let anyone harm Lara, sir."

He smiled at me. "I know you wouldn't."

"Sir ..."

He had turned to go, and now looked back patiently. "A question?"

I hesitated, and then blurted, "Why wouldn't they come inside the church? What would happen if they did?"

If he was at all surprised that this, of all the questions I might have asked, was the one I had chosen, he did not show it. He was thoughtful for a moment. "It is a matter of respect, I think," he decided. "Long ago a human priest did us a great kindness, so the legend goes, and we honor his symbols as a way of remembering. To do less would be to negate our history." And as he saw me draw breath for another question, he lifted a finger in amused remonstrance. "A perfect subject," he suggested, "for you to research on your own. Do let me know if you find anything of substance."

Monsieur Forcat did not return, and the next day I began research on a book it would take twenty-five years to write.

Excerpt from *DAWN TO DUSK: A TALE OF TWO SPECIES by Emory Hilliford, PhD:*

The year was 1342. It was a time before reason, a time of great intellect and terrible superstition, a time of desperate poverty and expansive wealth; of petty wars fought with stone projectiles and boiling oil, of rampant disease and squalor. It was a time when humans—who had once conversed with the likes of Plato and Aristotle, who had lived like gods in the palaces of Rome—shared shelter with the oxen and fought dogs for scraps of meat. They suffered the punishments of a God they could not see; only one in a hundred could read or write his own language, and they believed with absolute certainty that werewolves walked among them.

In this, of course, they were right.

In France, the Devoncroix took over the lush wine country of the Loire, and from their magnificent palais in the heart of the valley they ruled the pack. The humans there regarded them with reverence and awe, and called them les loups garoux. In the villages that surrounded the grand chateaux of les loups garoux, humans continued to die of filth and disease and ignorance, and were ignored as long as they didn't lie too long in the street, or were killed outright if they became too much of an annoyance. It was here that the most legendary of all the pack leaders came into power, the loup garou who is credited with saving the human race. Her name was Eudora Devoncroix, and she is known, among her species, as the Mother of Civilization.

Despite the accomplishments of the ruling family, centuries of primitive living had taken its toll on the numbers of the pack, just as it had with the human population. Moreover, there had been a recent alarming increase in the infant mortality rate, leading some of the best scientists of the day to suspect a viral pandemic in the making, most likely caused by exposure to humans. Mass killings of humans were recommended by radicals, and in some cases they were carried out. But infants of the lupinotuum continued to die of the mysterious disfiguring condition they called the Scourge, in which newborns left their mothers' wombs as half-formed humans, half-formed wolves. Unable to breathe through half-formed lungs, unable to digest nourishment through half-formed intestines, suffering the agonies of a hundred malformed bones and muscles, they died horrific and heart-wrenching deaths unless—as was most often the case—a family member stepped in at the moment of birth and performed the ultimate act of mercy. The experts of the day predicted that, should the infant mortality rate continue to rise at its current rate, their entire species would be extinct within two generations.

And everyone looked to their young, unmated queen to stop it.

It was imperative that Eudora find a mate and produce as many healthy offspring as possible, both for the morale and the survival of the pack. But her selection of mates among a declining population was limited, for the deadly birth defect had begun to surface in even the smallest and most remote clans. And the best-kept secret in the pack was the fact that the highest incidence of the Scourge occurred within the Devoncroix line, which eliminated the possibility of her mating with one of her own clan, as was customary.

In the midst of the crisis of the pack's survival and her concern about the human threat, outrageous rumors reached Eudora regarding the family of loup garoux called Fasburg, who had, it was said, set themselves up in the North as humans in the midst of humans, mocking everything that was lupinotuum. Reluctantly, with far more weighty matters burdening her young shoulders, the queen turned her entourage toward the Black Forest, and her attention to the Fasburg problem.

The Fasburgs were a clever, if dissolute clan, who in many ways represented all the worst of what Rome at its peak had brought to the world—and who, in other ways, were a perfect example of the pragmatism that is essentially loup garou. Two centuries earlier, they had come to realize that even the bounty of the Black Forest could not feed a clan of werewolves in their natural form indefinitely. They grew tired of living in caves and of killing humans before they themselves were killed by them. Far better, they reasoned, to use humans to create an easier life for themselves.

And so they did. They employed humans to build a stone castle and to fortify it with a wall impenetrable to invaders. In return for their labor, the humans were given sections of land and taught how to farm it, and they were allowed to keep enough of what they harvested to make their cattle fat and their children strong. If more land was needed to support their ever-growing dynasty, the Fasburgs sent their humans out with swords and armor plating to claim it. When other humans swarmed down to challenge the castle, the Fasburgs took all the village inside the walls of their fortress and fed them from their stores and kept them safe. They conversed with humans, sheltered, fed and protected them; they even gave humans weapons and trained them in acts of war. Perhaps most outrageous of all, they paid for what they might so easily have taken from humans. They had humans in their homes and dined in human form at the same table with them, and none of the humans with whom they so blatantly mingled ever guessed their true nature. And, as a final insult to the pack and all it stood for, they took for themselves the titles of human royalty: Prince Eric of Fasburg, his sisters the princesses, an alarming number of royal dukes and duchesses and counts and countesses. The Fasburgs thrived; the humans thrived. Life was abundant and that, according to their reasoning, was all that mattered.

But of course their reasoning was, according to pack law, completely untenable and only this side of treasonous.

Before the arrival of Queen Eudora, Eric Fasburg had lived his life as a careless bon vivant who venerated neither werewolf nor human, and who prided himself on the fact that no living thing escaped his mockery. He and his family had lived an isolated existence in the north that depended greatly on their own resourcefulness; they had neither asked nor taken any assistance from the pack in all those years. Consequently,

51

the Fasburgs in general and Eric in particular tended to regard the remainder of the pack and its leaders as a frivolous, inferior and largely superfluous bunch, worthy of mockery and little else.

Legend has it that he prepared a surprise welcome banquet for the Queen that included, as its centerpiece, a human head, fashioned in the rictus of its death throes, from marzipan. She was unamused. In retaliation, she called the pack into a spontaneous Change, and—legend has it—Eric Fasburg was captured in the throes of her chemistry.

It is true that the Change can occasionally enrapture and emotionally enslave a werewolf of the opposite sex, but evidence suggests that this is more of an excuse than an explanation for unexpected passion. This much is known about Eudora Devoncroix: she was fierce, she was brilliant, she was compassionate. She was an artist who is credited with introducing three-dimensional realism into oil painting, and a poet whose songs are still sung today among the lupinotuum. She was also, as evidenced by her portraits, quite beautiful. There was much to fascinate a werewolf of Eric Fasburg's tastes. It is entirely possible that he simply fell in love with her. And love, among the loup garoux as well as humans, needs no further justification.

There is a common misconception that the lupinotuum, as supremely intellectual beings, choose their mates in a logical fashion for the betterment of the pack and the strengthening of the line. No doubt logic does play a role, particularly among the ruling class. But among the loup garoux there is no such thing as a political marriage, for without passion, there is no reproduction, and without reproduction, there is no marriage. The writings of Eric Fasburg make his passion for Eudora the queen very clear. As much as he fought his emotions, he was obsessed. He was ensnared. He adored her.

As for the passions of Eudora the Queen, much less is known.

What is known is the fact that, when he proposed his suit to her, Eudora's willingness to consider it was based on far more than her obligation to the pack. The attraction she felt for him was based upon anything but logic. Two more disparate personalities could not have been found, and there is very little explanation for the sudden reversal of Eudora's position regarding Eric Fasburg except, perhaps, the inexplicable chemistry of a love attraction.

It should be noted that the Fasburg line showed no evidence of the killing sickness that was decimating the pack, and certainly this must have played a part in Eudora's decision. An infusion of their blood into the gene pool could save their race, and no rational leader would have overlooked that factor. So what might have seemed on the surface an outrageous proposal from Eric Fasburg was, in fact, accepted, and the queen agreed to take Eric Fasburg as her mate. She left the Black Forest for the Valley of the Loire to prepare the mating festivals, with Eric and his household to follow at a later date, as was customary.

It was during this period that some of the most passionate love songs in the culture of the lupinotuum were written, and they are accredited to Eudora Devoncroix. Yet it is difficult, if not impossible, to determine whether the songs were written to her fiancé or to another: the human who loved her and who, it is possible to suppose, she gave a portion of her heart as well. Between them, they would change the course of history for both their races.

CHAPTER SIX

The Present

Rolfe leaned back in his chair, fingers templed at his chin, black eyes unfathomable. "I was interested, as I read your book, by the personal fascination you appear to have with the stories from the middle ages that surround Queen Eudora."

"It was a pivotal point in history."

"No doubt. But there have been others equally as important." He smiled. "I think you are a romantic, Professor."

"I only wrote what I discovered."

He changed the subject abruptly. "Now, the Fasburgs, were they the only ones of their species you came to know?"

"No. I encountered many members of the pack over the years. Some have dealt with me kinder than others." Emory shrugged. "Just like humans."

"Tell me more about the pack. Is there but one pack, or many?"

"Alexander Devoncroix is credited with uniting the pack for the first time since the fall of Rome into a worldwide empire at the beginning of the twentieth century."

"Ah, the famous Devoncroix again."

Emory fixed his eyes upon his glass, and kept his voice neutral. "Before that time there were sects and family clans and tribes who would bond together for a generation or two, then begin quarrelling among themselves and disband. A few of them rose to prominence over the centuries—if you've read my books you know this—the builders, the inventors, the artists and scientists that most of history has recorded as human. But as a race they never had any real power because they were so scattered. The Devoncroix united the clans into a world-wide corporation, and they came to dominate the global marketplace, as well as the arts and sciences, in less than a hundred years."

"It is logical, I suppose," agreed Rolfe absently. "If a species possessed superior intellect, sensory ability and longevity, and if all members were united behind a common cause and well motivated by greed, it would not take long to become the dominate species on the planet. But a financial empire. A corporation. It all sounds terribly civilized to me."

"They are an ancient race. They grew weary of savagery long ago."

He smiled faintly, and all too knowingly, it seemed to Emory. "Did they indeed?" And then, briskly, "How many of them are there?"

"I don't know. A million, three million, five. The queen of the pack knows all the names and family lines. I'm not sure anyone else does."

"I see. And assuming I accept your claims as fact, I am curious. Why would they be so careless with their secrets as to share them with a human boy? Why risk exposure in such an unnecessary way? And if others before you have known them as intimately as you, how can their society have existed undiscovered for so long?"

Emory shook his head slowly, smiling. "I think you're missing the point."

"Pray." Rolfe turned a casual hand, palm out. "Enlighten me."

Emory was silent for a moment as pictures unrolled inside his head and concepts so deeply embedded into his consciousness that they had never been expressed before formed themselves into thoughts, and finally into words. "Once," he said at length, "in college, I got very drunk and spilled out my entire long tale of werewolves in Venice upon the pillow of the girl with whom I was infatuated at the time. She was enchanted, hanging on every word I spoke. And she broke up with me the next day. Do you know what she said to me? 'You're just too deep, Emory. Just too tortured and deep.'

"Another time I noticed that the corporate recruiter with whom my lab partner was interviewing for a job was a lupinotuum, and because I was going through an angry, rebellious phase, or perhaps just to see what would happen, I told him so. He laughed. When I pressed the point he became annoyed, and told me to get some help. We were never very close after that."

He shrugged. "So you see their secrets are not as much at risk as one might think. And even if they were — and here is the real key — *they don't care*. It's not simply that they have nothing to fear from exposure. It goes deeper than that. The truth is, I think, that there is a part of them that will never be complete until we know them, fully and completely, for what they are, and worship them once again, as we did during the Golden Age of Greece and Rome."

He reached for the glass, managed to close his hands around it, and lift it to his lips. He drained the contents. His voice was flat. "But that's just what I think."

Rolfe was silent for a moment. "Well, my friend," he said at last, "an interesting theory to say the least. But I deal in facts, not theory. And I am most interested in how you came to be the person you are today — the one upon whom all history pivoted, for a single moment, for better or worse. Will he choose rightly, or wrongly? If he goes right, the human race will be saved. If he goes left ... alas, a tragic loss. So tell me that story, if you please. How did you come to make such a gruesome mistake?"

"It wasn't a mistake," Emory said sharply. He added, "And I am not your friend."

"Ah, but you will be," Rolfe assured him, "before our time together is done. You will be my friend, or you will be dead." The cool, humorless smile did not touch his eyes. "Perhaps you will be both. Only time will tell, eh? In the meantime, we did have an agreement. Tell me your story. "

Emory was silent, arranging his thoughts. "I can't tell you my story without telling you theirs," he decided after a moment. "The Devoncroix."

His smile was mild and humorless. "Somehow I suspected as much."

"Most of what I knew about them as a child I learned from

57

history books. They were legendary, of course, since the time of Silas of Gaul, when they began to rebuild the world that had crumbled during the fall of Rome. They ruled the pack virtually unchallenged for over six hundred years."

"According to their history."

Emory was quiet for a time, lost in his own thoughts. "Oddly enough, my story began to intersect with theirs before I even met them. In 1980, the entire pack was invited to attend the ascension ceremony of Nicholas Devoncroix, heir designee, who was only thirteen at the time. He was a genius of sorts. Most of his contemporaries were sixteen to eighteen before gaining their ascension."

"Ascension?"

"It's a ceremony that marks the completion of their primary education and declares their status and their function in the pack. They are introduced to the pack by name for the first time and for the first time they take Eudora's vow. After that they are considered adults."

"And I presume you witnessed this momentous event, as you have done so many others."

"No. I was furious to be left behind, but there was no question of taking a human to Castle Devoncroix." A faint smile, remembering. "But Lara and I had no secrets. I saw it all through her eyes and ears, and the eyes and ears of children are everywhere and seldom noticed. It was only many years later that I began to put together the story she told me of that magnificent week at Castle Devoncroix with the events that later tormented us. And I realized that was where it had all begun. At Castle Devoncroix."

CHAPTER SEVEN

Castle Devoncroix
1980

Deep in the heart of the Alaskan wilderness, buried so thoroughly within the natural edifice of the Rocky Mountain range that it was almost indistinguishable from the mountain itself, the spires and chimneys of the ancient structure grew skyward as though they had been created to do so. There were no roads, nor any need for them. There were no concrete parking structures, since the area was inaccessible by automobile. There were no lighted runways, no golf cart paths, no bridle trails. From the air it would be virtually impossible to recognize the vast sweep of rugged forest and jutting mountaintops as a destination unless one knew exactly what to look for. But as one grew closer, a landing pad emerged, and beyond it flashes of a rolling green meadow barely visible through the veil of towering evergreens. Castle Devoncroix. And for everyone who came here, it was home.

The helicopter dipped below the cloud cover into a blinding sunburst of green tree canopy and blue lakes and then, suddenly captured by a wind shear, shot upward into gray oblivion again. The loup garou pilot, casually accustomed to the caprices of nature that protected the destination below, banked, circled, bided his time, and rode the next downdraft to the landing pad. The massive machine hovered for a moment, fighting the whims of nature with its blades, lost a few dozen feet, won another dozen, and settled its mass firmly upon the stone surface at last, blades whirring in a steadily slowing whooshing rhythm.

As soon as the pilot cut the engine, an opening appeared in the wall that flanked the landing pad and two liveried stewards emerged, their sensitive ears shielded by headphones to protect them from the noise of the slicing blades and their hands clad in the traditional white gloves that would protect the guests of the castle from the scent of those who served them. They moved quickly across the carpeted walkway to greet the new arrivals and to escort them to their quarters in the vast complex. The scene had been repeated dozens of times over the past forty-eight hours, sometimes as often as once every five minutes.

The door of the helicopter opened and a ramp began to lower automatically from it. The prince descended first, wrapped in a cashmere coat and stylish white muffler, his dark hair tossed by the wind and his nostrils flaring as he took in the scents that assailed them: pine forests and crisp bright glaciers, the musky hot blood of herd beasts; the intoxicating taste of ancient earth and brittle stone and werewolf, of secrets long dead and secrets not yet discovered; of *home*. One could not come to Castle Devoncroix, no matter what one's place of origin or family affiliation, without feeling a sense of profound connection, as though the very rocks themselves were wrapping themselves around you in welcome. He drew deeply of the air, and let it fill him with power.

The princess was next, and his leather gloved hand came out to assist her automatically. Her eyes were protected by dark glasses against the brilliance of the sun, and her aristocratic profile half-shaded by a wide-brimmed black hat that was trimmed with the same silver fox fur that adorned the collar of her coat. Lara clung to her other hand, looking small and awe struck in a blue velvet coat and matching beret. The wind kept whipping long strands of her hair across her eyes, obscuring her vision, until she caught her hair with one hand and held it tight against her shoulder, not wanting to miss a detail of the moment.

One of the stewards collected the luggage from the cargo hold, and the other fell into place behind the family, keeping a stiff and sentry-like pace as they followed the plush carpet back to the door. As soon as the heavy steel door closed behind them, he bowed deeply and said in French, which was the language of protocol at Castle Devoncroix, "Family Fasburg, it is my very great pleasure to welcome you, on behalf of our pack leaders and all of their family, to Castle Devoncroix on this most illustrious occasion. You will find an agenda of activities in your suite, along with a light meal and certain other items of comfort which we hope will make your stay more enjoyable. Also ..." He took a breath here, signifying the importance of his next statement. "Madame and Monsieur Devoncroix request the pleasure of your company at a private dinner in their quarters this evening."

As he spoke, he gestured toward a bank of smoked-glass elevators set into the stone wall, each of them octagonal shaped and lit from within by a bronze light. The prince and princess exchanged an amused glance as they stepped into the elevator. "Can we bear the honor?" murmured the prince in Italian, and the princess replied to the steward in French, "Kindly inform Madame Devoncroix that we await her pleasure, of course."

"You do too much to endear yourself, my love," said the prince in a bored tone.

The princess replied tartly, "*My* manners have never been found wanting. And," she added sternly to Lara, who had begun to absently chew her gloved thumbnail, "neither have my daughter's."

Lara quickly folded her hands in front of her and tried to look as bored as her papa, although inside she was bursting with excitement.

The glass bullet of the elevator shot downward through the stone tunnel, slowed to a gentle bouncing stop, and then took a horizontal course down a maze of corridors until it delivered them to their rooms.

Five thousand years ago, perhaps ten, a long-forgotten race of werewolves had made their home on the then-verdant plains of the Alaska wilderness, feasting on the abundant game, running the wild mountain ranges, luxuriating in the crystal lakes and mineral-rich hot springs. They dug into the mountainside for shelter, building rudimentary sleeping caves and cooking rooms, giving birth and nursing their young secure from the elements within the rock walls. As they evolved, so did their shelter, expanding outward and downward in an elaborate labyrinth of chambers, deep water wells, light tunnels and air shafts. They harnessed the power of nature for heat and light, they built complex indoor waterfalls, pools and gardens. Artisans carved detailed portraits and story panels into the rock walls, floors were polished smooth and set with rubies, sapphires and emeralds as large as goose eggs. Entire rooms were lined with that soft, abundantly plentiful metal that would later be known as gold. Bathing pools were fashioned of onyx and amethyst, and coffered ceilings were lined with hammered silver. There were amphitheaters and observatories, playing fields and reservoirs. The structure was clearly the work of an advanced culture with abundant leisure who took pride in their legacy, and its creation spanned several centuries. Then abruptly, some time before recorded history, the compound was abandoned, and no trace of the race who built it was ever found.

The complex had been rediscovered at the beginning of the twentieth century during an expedition that Alexander and Elise Devoncroix, the newly anointed leaders of the pack, made to Alaska. It was named, appropriately enough, Castle Devoncroix. Within a decade the pack headquarters was moved from the grand palais in Lyon, France, to the fortified underground compound in Alaska.

Seventy-five years later, modern day engineers were still marveling over the elegant simplicity of the architecture, and trying to decipher the subtleties of the geothermal energy system that supplied the entire complex with an apparently endless source of power. It was widely speculated that much of the structure, and perhaps many of its most advanced secrets, were yet to be uncovered. Already the compound encompassed an area of over two square miles, and could, if need be, shelter the entire pack in an emergency. On state occasions and during festivals and specials events, like this one, it regularly hosted thousands of guests.

Prince Fasburg pointed out all of this to his daughter in properly stentorian tones as they were escorted down the tall wide corridor and through the double doors of their suite, even though she had of course studied the history of Castle Devoncroix since she had first learned to read. No amount of reading or lecturing could have prepared her for the reality of actually being there, however. The room to which they were escorted smelled of sandalwood and beeswax, crisp cotton sheets, down pillows, well-turned books, dark chocolate, and flowers, a multitude of flowers. It was a richly appointed suite, with high arched ceilings timbered with heavy scarred beams and paneled in gold leaf. The walls were upholstered in beautifully embroidered tapestries, some of them centuries old. There were two fireplaces, one at each end of the room, and each gave off the merry glow of dancing flames. There were bouquets of white roses on the tables that flanked the large sofa, and in the center of the room, arranged on a marble topped table that was easily large enough to have commanded the lobby of any one of Prince Fasburg's international hotels, was a staggering arrangement of delphiniums, hollyhocks, hyacinths and roses whose collective aroma filled the suite with a heady perfume.

Beside the flowers was a bottle of the finest Devoncroix cabernet sauvignon, crystal glasses and a covered tray beneath which Lara smelled smoked salmon, roast venison, an array of cheeses and soft white bread with melting butter.

There was also a small silver plate containing a dozen perfectly formed chocolates, each in the shape of a different flower and infused with the essence of that flower — orange blossom, lavender, narcissus, rose. Though Lara's mouth watered with the smell of so much lovely chocolate, it would be poor manners indeed to beg for a treat. She waited until the princess selected a tulip, tasted it, gave an appreciative nod of her head and then, with a smile, offered a chocolate rose to Lara.

The prince shrugged out of his coat and gloves and tossed them aside. "A bit over the top, don't you think, my dear?"

That made the princess laugh, and she choose another chocolate and offered it to her spouse with her teeth. He accepted the gift with a small sound of approval and licked the lingering chocolate from her lips.

Lara nibbled politely on her chocolate rose and tried hard to pretend that being in this incredible place was just another ordinary day in her life. She was well accustomed to luxury and certainly, at age nine, old enough to behave in as sanguine a fashion as her parents might wish. Still, it was all she could do to restrain herself from running from room to room, eyes big, exclaiming like a child. It was more than the gold-plated ceilings or exotic candies or the bath that appeared to be carved from a single piece of marble. More than the high feather beds and stained glass chandeliers. The place itself was magical; the smell of it, the taste of it, the simple fact of it.

There was a window. They were four stories underground, yet the view was of a garden flooded with yellow sunshine. A riot of mandevilla, bougainvillea and hibiscus tumbled down rock walls on three sides toward an emerald lawn that framed the centerpiece — a gilded fountain formed of four giant wolves standing upright, their backs toward each other, their massive heads thrown back in joy, their upraised forelimbs ending in human-formed hands that caught the water as it splashed from above. Guests of the castle strolled the courtyard or lounged about the fountain, some of them nude, some of them clad in gauzy garments that flowed around their slender, elegant figures, some of them in wolf form. Even though the thick glass and fabric-clad stone walls were designed to protect sensitive werewolf ears from intrusive sounds, Lara could hear their laughter, and smell their contentment. Instinctively, and without meaning to at all, Lara pressed her fingers to the glass, and she felt herself smiling back.

That was when she noticed the young, athletic blond wolf leaping from the base of the fountain to the peak of a climbing rock some thirty feet away. He did it effortlessly, without scrabbling for purchase as another his age might have done, and he landed on the pads of his paws without extending his claws, as light as air. He sat in perfect posture, his tail curled around his feet, as though preening himself. Across the distance, over the heads of the people below, through the silence of the glass, his crystal blue eyes met Lara's, and she knew instinctively that she had locked gazes with the heir designee. The chocolate was forgotten in her hand, and she stared at him. For the first time in her life Lara knew envy: to be him, to be bathed in such power; to live in such a place, to belong here. She looked at him for a long time, and even when her mother called her away from the window, she did not want to look away.

For a girl who had never been away from the company of her family, the splendor of Castle Devoncroix during a major celebration was more than a little overwhelming. Lara was not

shy, but she had been raised in an environment that was greatly humancentric, her lupinotuum playmates had been carefully chosen and mostly were members of her own extended family. She found the exposure to such a vast and varied quantity of her own kind both bizarre and exotic ... and a little unsettling. These werewolves had a strange wild smell to them, and their eyes were fierce even in laughter, even in pleasure. They were wanton and ambitious and they smelled too much of blood. They thrilled her and they frightened her, and after less than a day in their presence she felt out of place and self-conscious, yearning for home but strangely, inexplicably titillated by their presence, wondering what it would be like to be one of them and feeling guilty for even wondering.

On their first evening, while the prince and princess dined with the Devoncroix, a Night Run for the children would be led by Nicholas Devoncroix himself. A Night Run with the heir designee should properly be considered the highlight of a young werewolf's life. Here a youth would prove his ambition, his bravery, his skill, and very possibly begin to build a relationship with the heir designee that could insure his future. No one said that out loud, of course. Out loud they said what an exciting opportunity it was to run the wilds of Castle Devoncroix beneath the moon without adult supervision, and how generous it was of the heir designee to lead them, and how this would be an experience they would never forget, though they lived to be two hundred.

Lara did not see the appeal.

The children's welcome tea, however, was fabulous. Lara wore her white frock with white stockings and black patent shoes and her shiny black hair pulled back in a perfect pink velvet bow, and she was without a doubt the most perfectly attired young lady there. Later she had her portrait painted in that outfit and it became quite famous; hundreds of thousands of greeting cards were sold to humans over the next few decades featuring her likeness.

There was a musical pageant performed to honor the heir designee, and afterwards Nicholas Devoncroix, in black trousers and an open-necked flowing white shirt, came out and took a bow. His blonde hair fell like a curtain over his face when he bowed. The curve of his calf was exquisite. The crowd went wild. Lara thought he looked like a character from one of those black and white movies her father kept in his film library.

Afterwards, she filled her plate with sweets — sugared tangerines and almond cookies and buttery scones and chocolate dipped strawberries and pastries filled with hazelnut cream and a feathery white cake piled with icing — and enjoyed every morsel. Nicholas Devoncroix moved through the crowd, greeting each and every child, from the three-year-old who was barely able to maintain his human form, to the sixteen-year-olds who struggled to make themselves appear smaller in his sight. These were his people, and this was his noblesse oblige. His mother's eyes, of course, never left him. And he conducted himself in a manner that would make her proud.

When Lara turned, dabbing the last of the frosting from her lips with a heavy linen napkin, she found herself looking directly into the ice blue eyes of the heir designee. Her heart began to pound, upsetting her digestion.

He said, "Hello. I saw you through the window."

Lara's hair began to crackle with static electricity. She tried to smooth it down, but when she moved her hand away the top layer of it stood away from her shoulders, still crackling, in a most annoying fashion. She said, trying to ignore the phenomenon, "I saw you too."

His eyes narrowed. "You're the Fasburg girl, aren't you?"

She straightened her shoulders. "I am Lara Fasburg. Who are you?"

He laughed. When he laughed, he did not seem so intimidating. But all too soon the laughter was over, and his eyes were sharp again. He said, staring at her, "What the devil happened to your face?"

Self-consciously, her hand flew to her face, wondering if she had food there. She used her napkin. Nothing.

Nicholas turned his head and commanded imperiously, "Mother!"

Elise Devoncroix took her time moving through the groups of children to reach her son. She stopped to speak to several young ones, and secured a drink for another. She was the Queen of the Pack, and answered no one's bidding.

She was a beautiful woman with silver blonde hair that flowed to her waist and the famous Devoncroix blue eyes. She wore an aqua blue caftan shot through with silver, and a single diamond, thirty carats or more, at her neck. She smiled at Lara.

"Hello, my dear. Are you having a good time?"

Lara had no chance to respond. Nicholas demanded, "Mother, look at her face. What is that?"

By this time more than a few of the attendants were staring, and Lara had spread her fingers over most of her face. Her cheeks were flaming. She had no idea what was wrong with her face. She wanted to sink through the floor.

Elise Devoncroix bent close and gently moved Lara's hand

away. "Oh, dear," she murmured. Gently she touched the scar that bisected Lara's eyebrow. "It's a bite mark."

Nicholas said, "Can't you do anything about it?"

Elise straightened up, a look of pity in her eyes. "I'm afraid not. It's a human bite. The bacteria in their mouths prevent healing. There's nothing I can do."

Nicholas stared at Lara. "How did such a thing happen?"

His mother touched his arm, aware of the silence that had filled the room, and the eyes that had turned toward them. "Perhaps now is not the best time," she said quietly. "The story is complex."

Nicholas looked at her, then at Lara. He frowned. "Pity," he said. "It quite ruins her looks." And then he moved on.

It was a casual encounter, and doubtless not meant to wound. But Lara would never forget it. And neither, unfortunately, would any of the other members of the young pack before whom she had been singled out that day. In a very real way, with a single careless comment, Nicholas Devoncroix shaped the woman Lara would grow up to be, and the choices she would inevitably make that would define his future as well. Though he could not have known it, he sealed his fate that day, and the fate of the pack, twenty years before anyone guessed that both were already in danger.

In their culture, there was no room for weakness, or even the appearance of such. In their human forms they displayed such niceties as tolerance, graciousness and sympathy, much in the same way humans had learned political correctness, but at their core they were still the fierce and savage race that had ruled the African plain and the snow-drenched tundra with nothing but a ruthless determination to survive.

Lara, even as a child, enjoyed none of that savagery. She surrendered to her wolf form only as necessary for the exercise that Teacher insisted would keep her muscles strong, and sometimes to amuse Emory, but in her opinion everything that was interesting to do was done in human form. She might have enjoyed the Night Run under ordinary circumstances; after Nicholas had made a spectacle of her at the tea she knew what would happen to her. Nonetheless, she joined the others for the Night Run but stood far at the back of the pack, trying to stay out of notice. For a time she thought she might succeed. The others were so excited about the coming adventure, and so puffed up with their new sense of self importance, that they could barely focus on anything until Nicholas Devoncroix strode through the crowd, quelling the most exuberant youngsters with a look, and sprang lightly to the top of the calling rock.

The moon was low in the sky and the air was blue with its reflected light. The calling rock had been chosen not only for its high visibility but for its location on the northern side of the compound where a steady breeze always blew. The wind buffeted Nicholas's white changing robe and combed back his long hair as he turned to face his young pack, infusing the moment with all the drama it deserved. In twenty years, he would be facing the pack who ruled the world. In twenty years, they would remember this moment. Even Lara, standing far at the back and doing her best to make herself small, felt the thrill of excitement that charged the crowd.

Nicholas discarded his garment and the wind carried it away like a great white bird as he raised his arms, tossed back his head, and lifted his voice in a single long high note of ululation that incited the primal center of the brains of every werewolf who heard it. The glow of his Change was yellow white and the electric current it sent through the crowd was vital, immediate and irresistible. Lara felt it in her skin, in the static swirling charge of her hair, in the tingling of her throat and her teeth and her toes, and she could no more resist the magnetic pull of her nature than could anyone else. The glory of the change—that sweet electric instant when light and dark, sound and color, breath and wind are one, when one's essence is neither wolf nor human but sparks of pure thought, pure wonder, the simple rapture of it—was the only thing Lara would care to remember about that night. That, and perhaps the moment that Nicholas stood for the first time upon the calling rock with the wind streaming through his hair and tossing about his robe, and he raised his arms to the pack.

The energy of a hundred young werewolves only seconds after the change was wild and uncontrolled. They reveled in their new and powerful forms. They tested their muscles, they snapped their teeth, they chased each other and knocked each other to the ground. Lara was quickly trampled in the melee. She tried to run but someone caught her tail. Another tore a patch of hair from her flank. Another grabbed her neck. Strong hind feet battered her face, sharp teeth pierced her forearm. Another set of teeth tore at her ear. Lara had never fought in wolf form, and was not very skilled at it. She fended them off as best she could but it seemed the entire pack wanted a shot at her, charging, nipping, chasing her down. She yelped in pain and showed her throat in surrender, but still they jeered at her, feinting and charging, nipping and snapping, enjoying the game.

Nicholas watched with cool blue eyes until he grew bored,

but he would not intervene for anything less than the spurt of arterial blood. Eventually he turned to run, and the pack, of course, flowed after him. Lara, bruised and whimpering, bleeding from a dozen tiny wounds, turned and limped away.

CHAPTER EIGHT

T o be invited to dine in the private quarters of the leaders of the pack was no small thing. Behind those luxuriously appointed, sound-proof walls fortunes had been made, governments had fallen, assassinations plotted. It was well known throughout the pack that the Devoncroix and the Fasburgs had been financial and personal rivals for centuries; it was in fact rumored – although not widely believed – that the only person in the pack whose personal fortune could approach that of Alexander Devoncroix was Geof Fasburg. Otherwise he would never have had the temerity to conduct himself as carelessly as he did, flaunting about the ridiculous title of "prince" and virtually making his own rules when it came to both his business and his social affairs. It was therefore unsurprising that of all the dignitaries and potentates in attendance on the occasion of the heir designee's

74

Ascension Festival, the Fasburgs should be singled out for attention. Firstly, it was honorable. A wise leader will always give credit where credit is due. Secondly, it was practical. Alexander Devoncroix knew the value of keeping one's friends close, and one's enemies closer.

There was of course no question of the Fasburgs accepting the invitation. This was, in essence, why they had crossed an ocean for the occasion.

The princess wore a silk caftan of peacock blue embroidered with colorful tropical birds in glittering jewel-toned threads around the wide sleeves and hem. The prince wore a loose changing robe in gradients of pewter, silver and white. Because the changing of forms within the boundaries of castle Devoncroix was such a casual, almost wanton thing, the fashions of the outside world were quickly discarded for more practical one-piece garments, or, when appropriate, no garments at all. And it would be very bad form indeed to accept an invitation to dine with the leaders of the pack in their private quarters attired as a human.

They were welcomed graciously, the ritual amenities were exchanged, and a cocktail of oxblood wine fortified with brandy was consumed. They stood on the stone walled balcony outside the Devoncroix suite at dusk with a strong cold wind tossing about the hundred thousand complex scents that was the pure green wilderness, and they watched the puffs of light and tasted the sweet electric smoke that was the Change of a hundred young werewolves. The horizon was lit with peach and aqua and gold and electric blue and rose and purple; a hundred colors, a hundred scents, the future of the pack painted on the sky. In some places in the world, humans still worshipped the mystical

75

glow of those lights.

They turned out of the wind and into the warmth of the pack leaders' living quarters, a vast and elegant room with gold-leaf walls and a high-domed ceiling frescoed in the manner of the old palais in Lyon. The carpets were hand woven and depicted magnificent scenes of the pack's glorious past: the Gathering of 1202, in which clans from across the globe filled the Plain of Salisbury, the union of Caan and Ansal, parents of the modern pack, the birth of Romulus and Remus, the first reading of Eudora's Vow. The furniture was silk brocade, and muraled panels decorated the walls.

Their hosts, the two strongest werewolves in the pack, filled the room with a charge of electric energy that actually raised the indoor temperature a couple of degrees and, to sensitive werewolf ears, hummed like music in the air. As is customary with long time mates, they had grown to resemble each other over the years; their movements and their thoughts in easy synchronization. Elise, tall and svelte, had ivory skin and silver blonde hair that rippled past her hips, braided this night with a long silver thread. Her eyes, like her mate's, were glacier blue. Alexander was lean muscled and sharp featured, broad of chest and quick of gaze. His rich platinum hair swept back from a high forehead and fell like silk around his shoulders. When he moved around a room, the very air through which he passed seemed to crackle.

Alexander served the prince's favorite Armagnac, and Elise complimented the princess on her daughter, as was proper. The prince admired the young heir, and congratulations were offered regarding his early Ascension. They ate cheese and grapes and pretended to be friends.

Later they would run, and there would be no pretense.

They dined at a table set with heavy silver and beeswax candles, and damask napkins embroidered in gold with the Devoncroix crest. There was cold salmon and cream sauce, followed by crystal bowls filled with a delicate broth trimmed with caviar. There were haunches of meat seared crisp on the outside, wild and bloody on the inside, and steaming bread mounded with soft cheese and ripe fruit. The Devoncroix wine was rich with the taste of plums and wild honey and the black earth of the Loire.

Alexander said, "I heard you've taken in a human boy."

The princess smiled and sipped her wine. The goblet was silver, which kept the wine at the perfect temperature, and lined with fine crystal, to preserve the taste. "I have always enjoyed human charities."

Elise returned a similar smile and a regal nod of her head. "How surprised they would all be if they knew how much of their civilization they owe to you and your family, my dear."

The prince agreed, "Our dedication to the betterment of the human population has a long and honored tradition. But of course you know that." His tone was mild, and not a flicker of expression crossed his face. Nor did any change of demeanor register upon the face of the queen, or her spouse.

"How long do you intend to keep him?" inquired Alexander.

"I hadn't given the matter any thought."

"I should be careful if I were you." The queen used her knife to cut the bloody meat, and took a portion between her small white teeth. "Humans can be quiet unpredictable, and treacherous when one least expects it."

The prince nodded to her politely. "So I have heard. Mine is quite bright."

Alexander seemed surprised. "So you intend to educate him? To what purpose, may I ask—aside from your own amusement, of course?"

The prince took up his own goblet, regarding the pack leader pleasantly. "It has been done for less worthy reasons, if memory serves. The young human girl you used to squire about Paris in your youth—what a scandal that was. She was educated to the point of being allowed into the very heart of the palais, if I recall."

The temperature of the room remained unchanged, the air infused with nothing more than congeniality and dark wine, and in the brief silence not even the pulse of a heartbeat altered. The queen of the pack took a sip of her wine, touched the heavy napkin to her lips, and replied, "We were exceedingly fond of the child. Her death was a tragedy."

"Of course it was," murmured the prince. "My apologies for bringing up unpleasant memories."

"She was also treacherous," added the queen with no emotion whatsoever. "It is their nature. I advise you again to have a care."

"Perhaps I shall have better luck," the prince said, "having taken mine in from such a young age. At any rate, it will be an interesting experiment."

"It will indeed." Alexander's gaze was easy, almost disinterested, upon the other man. "And what about your lovely daughter? You aren't concerned he will defile her?"

The prince replied simply, "I'll snap his neck and drop him into the Canal first."

"The sexual impulses of young human males are notoriously difficult to control," Elise pointed out.

The prince smiled. "I've often observed the same of young males of our species."

There was light laughter, and Elise moved the topic toward the activities that were planned for the remainder of the week. A rich cake was brought in, wrapped in dark chocolate and glazed with spun sugar, followed by a collection of pastries stuffed with sweet cream and cherries. They drank dark port and strolled through the corridors of the private sections of the castle, ending at last in the Grand Gallery, where the greatest art treasures of the pack—indeed the world—were stored.

There were sculptures by Michelangelo unknown to the common world, and treatises by Galileo that had never been seen by the public eye. Floating inside a vacuum-sealed glass case was a fairly sophisticated drawing of a lupinotuum in Change on a parchment believed to be over thirteen thousand years old. It was illuminated by a narrow-bandwidth light that allowed only the most harmless rays to penetrate, and it had never been exposed to human breath. There were archetypical drawings of inventions dating back two thousand years, blueprints of ancient coliseums and temple cities, displays of carvings and artifacts from the Ancient Ones that had been discovered when Castle Devoncroix was first opened, and that were so old they defied even the most sophisticated dating technology of their race.

Alexander said, "How are you finding your first visit to Alaska, Geof?"

"A bit cold for my taste. However ..." the prince stopped before a magnificent floor-to ceiling-painting. "I do envy you your art collection."

The painting was legendary among their kind. For generations pack leaders had protected it, preserved it, fought for it. It was considered the most valuable possession the pack owned, and was well over five thousand years old. It depicted the mating of a wild eyed, savage-mouthed human woman and a yellow-eyed wolf against a backdrop of cascading history — human wars and wolf-formed corpses, humans torn asunder in the jaws of wolves, wolves at rest in verdant meadows, humans struggling to survive in filthy cities, The sky was filled with the ghostly images of creatures half human, half wolf, so cleverly depicted among the clouds that their features seemed to change from human to wolf even as one looked at them, and like gods of old they serenely regarded the scene below. The painting was called *The Conception,* and was traditionally believed to be symbolic of the origin of their species.

Their spouses strolled onward toward another gallery, talking quietly, while the two men stood solemnly and respectfully before the painting. "Remarkable," said the prince at last. "One cannot help but feel small in its presence."

Alexander said, "I am always struck by the savagery in the eyes of the human, and the seduction of her smile."

"An accurate depiction of the nature of the species, I should say."

The silence between them was like a breath half drawn.

The prince said, still gazing at the painting, "How odd it would be if this painting were proven to be, after all this thousands of years, more than a symbolic rendering of our origins. If it were, instead, a simple statement of fact."

"Hardly the first time the possibility has been the subject of a philosophical debate. It is of course, physically impossible. Wolf and human cannot mate. And even if they could, their DNA is too disparate to produce offspring."

The prince gave a careless lift of his shoulders. "Today, perhaps. Who can say what conditions existed a millennia ago?"

Alexander's tone was perfectly neutral. "You may be right. But it is not a question that will be answered tonight." He gestured toward the adjacent corridor. "Shall we join our mates?"

Geof did not move, and his gaze remained fixed upon the painting. "What very great fools we make of ourselves," he observed softly, "when we try to contain the uncontainable." He turned and met Alexander's gaze calmly. "I know your secret. I can't imagine how you ever thought I would not."

The temperature in the room dropped a degree, but nothing in Alexander Devoncroix's voice, or in his eyes, was altered. "I have imagined nothing. The détente you and I have formed has always been a matter of consent, not coercion."

The prince inclined his head in acknowledgement. "Well said. A fitting thing, I think, that we should share this secret. If you consider it, there has been a Devoncroix and there has been a Fasburg at every great crossroads in history. What we face today is no different."

Alexander replied, with eyes like stone, "I stand ready to play my role. Are you?"

Prince Fasburg turned back to contemplate the painting, his hands clasped loosely behind his back, his head slightly upturned to better examine the nuances of the artwork. "I can't help but speculate how the pack would react if they knew how far from grace their leader has fallen—far enough, in fact, to corrupt and endanger our entire race. We are a people united by arrogance and an unshakeable belief in our own superiority. The Devoncroix regime has built an empire by exploiting those characteristics. How quickly, I wonder, would it unravel should its foundation prove to be unsound?"

Alexander said, "Fortunately, this is a debate that need not concern us now."

Prince Fasburg looked at him, his eyes cold. "The mighty Devoncroix have committed a crime against nature and the pack. You are destined to fall."

Alexander's met him with an expression as hard as ice-carved rock. "If I fall, the pack falls with me. Is that what you want?"

"If it were," replied the prince, "we would not be standing here discussing the matter."

"I will protect my people," Alexander said, lowly.

And the prince answered, in a tone that was mild but steady, "You must know that there is only one who will fight more fiercely for the welfare of this pack than you, and it is I."

Alexander met his gaze. The air was charged yet static, shimmering and hard, as though encased in ice. Alexander said, "There is a marvelous hot spring, not two hours run from here. Let us collect our spouses, and take to the night. I find I'm quite in the mood to run."

The prince did not flinch, and his smile was cool. "Excellent," he replied. "So am I."

No one knows the details of a private run of the pack leader; no one can guess what may or may not have occurred. The prince never spoke of it, nor did his mate. But there was blood on his garment when it was discarded the next morning.

One might speculate the same was true of the garment of the leader of the pack.

CHAPTER NINE

The Present

Rolfe's expression was thoughtful. "So Fasburg knew, even then."

Emory said, "I later came to realize that there was very little the prince did not know." He glanced around the room. "I would like to use the lavatory."

Rolfe gave an apologetic tilt of his head. "Of course. I'm afraid I've been inconsiderate. There's a small door there, beside the bookshelf."

Emory stood. "You're not worried I'll try to escape?"

Rolfe spread his hands congenially. "Where would you go?"

A light came on automatically when Emory opened the door to the small bathroom. It was tiled in green glass with a blue wave pattern on one wall. The vessel sink looked to be carved from a single piece of lapis. The toilet and the bidet were onyx. The mirror was highly burnished copper. The faucet was a single gooseneck fountain with motion-sensitive controls. The exposed pipes were all of one piece. When Emory tried to open the back of the toilet he found that it, too, was solid.

He urinated, and the bowl was pink with blood. Afterwards, he was lightheaded and had to lean against the cold blue tiles until he pinpricks of perspiration evaporated from his forehead.

The flushing mechanism was automatic, and a stream of jewel blue liquid soap was dispensed via a motion sensor, as was the gush of warm air from the wall that dried his hands. There was no window, no closet, no cabinet, nothing removable or breakable and nothing that could be fashioned into a weapon. He was not surprised.

When he returned a platter of food had been arranged in the middle of the table—bunches of grapes and rounds of cheese, thick sliced white bread, juicy slabs of rare roast beef. Surrounding it were bowls of ripe black olives, pears, apples and figs. Rolfe was working a corkscrew into a bottle of wine with the distinctive gold Devoncroix label.

"Say what you will of them," he observed as the cork slid free, "they were masters at the art of making wine." He passed the cork beneath his nose and took in the scent, closing his eyes appreciatively.

Emory sat down. Rolfe poured a small measure of wine into a tasting glass and passed it to him. "It should breathe," Emory said.

"No doubt." Rolfe took a pear from the bowl and tossed it lightly across to the table to Emory. Emory caught it one-handed.

"Since you have the knife, do you mind peeling the fruit?"

Emory said nothing.

"Cleverly done, by the way," Rolfe observed, "but if you try anything like that again I'm afraid I'll have to break your arm, which would be inconvenient for you and a great deal of trouble for me. So try to be sensible, will you?"

Without taking his eyes off Rolfe, Emory slid the fruit knife he had stolen from the platter out of his sleeve. He sliced the pear in half and spun the knife across the table to Rolfe. He offered Rolfe half of the pear with an open hand.

"You were right," he said, "I'm not much of an assassin."

Rolfe took the fruit and bit into it, watching him with a mildly curious expression. "But that was not your intention, was it?"

"In the current circumstances," replied Emory, "you will understand if I prefer to choose the time and method of my own demise."

Rolfe nodded. "And you will understand that I cannot allow that. However, I may reconsider once you have finished your tale."

"And now I am Scheherazade."

That seemed to amuse him. "More or less. By the way ..." He reached inside his jacket and took out a smart phone. "This might interest you." He tapped a few keys and slid the phone across the table to Emory. "The American government has begun to crumble. Washington is under military rule, public services in New York and Chicago have been suspended, no flights are landing from anywhere outside the country. Riots and mayhem everywhere. It's really quite terrifying."

Emory barely glanced at the video scrolling across the screen of the phone. "I am a British citizen residing in Canada with dual citizenship in Italy. It doesn't concern me."

He shrugged. "Only in as much as its cause can be traced, directly or indirectly, back to you." He nodded toward the phone and added, "There's no need for you to trouble yourself trying to take that from me, in case you were wondering. Feel free to dial anyone you like, or use the Internet. I want to be a good host."

"Thank you." Emory stretched out his fingers, which were once again seized by tremors. "Perhaps later."

Rolfe gave a small shrug and allowed the phone to remain on the table. He reached for a cluster of grapes, and popped one into his mouth. "You should have killed him," he said. There was no expression whatsoever. He took another grape. "Why couldn't you simply do as you were told?"

"That," replied Emory, "was never an option."

Rolfe looked at him, chewing thoughtfully. "You are a puzzle."

Emory said, "I know you aren't with the CIA or Interpol. Do you work for the World Security Organization? What is your authority?"

Rolfe simply smiled. "I need no authority." He gestured gracefully with one hand toward the platter of food. "May I serve you something?"

Emory glanced over the contents of the platter. "Meat," he said, "and cheese."

"Excellent choice." Rolfe used the fruit knife to slice the wheel of cheese, and to transfer it with a portion of meat to a small plate. "Protein will restore your neural function." He passed the plate to Emory. "Eat," he invited. "Enjoy. And when you are ready, I pray you continue. These Devoncroix. They fascinate me. Aside from their wine ...." He lifted the bottle in a small salute. "They seem to be a most remarkable and unpredictable people. Tell me what you know. Did you eventually meet them?"

Emory tore the meat with his fingers, wrapped it around a piece of cheese, and put it into his mouth. He held out his glass for wine. Rolfe filled it.

"I did," he said at length. His eyes were steady on those of the other man. "I did eventually meet them."

CHAPTER TEN

I was thirteen before I came to know the Devoncroix as anything other than names in a history book. They crossed the prow of my life and, as it always is with them, left everything profoundly changed. In many ways this was for the better. In most, it was not.

Despite my burgeoning adolescence, I was at this point still young enough, and protected enough, to believe that — all my education to the contrary — our idyllic existence in Venice was a normal way of life and, because it was normal, secure and unthreatened. I knew who they were, of course. But until what I like to call The Summer of The Devoncroix, I didn't really *know* them.

During the late nineteenth and early twentieth century, when Elise and Alexander Devoncroix began to organize the pack into what was to become the most powerful consortium of financial, scientific, commercial and natural resources the world has ever known, the Fasburgs were the only clan who maintained independence. Because their small principality was the source of almost unlimited wealth in the form of uranium, coal and — perhaps most importantly — a certain rare mineral essential to the proper functioning of what we now know as orbiting communications satellites, they had little motivation to join the global pack initiative, and the Devoncroix had every reason to want them to. It took decades for an agreement to be reached, but in the end the Fasburgs ceded political control of Auchenstein to the humans — under, one assumes, the discreet guidance of the Devoncroix — and entered into a financial agreement with the pack whose terms were hugely favorable to the Fasburgs. Resentments over the finer terms of the agreement, though never resolved to the complete satisfaction of either party, remained disguised by the veneer of polite civility. The Fasburgs still, for the most part, lived outside the pack, far more comfortable in the society of humans than in that of their own kind. The Devoncroix, for all practical purposes, ignored them. But now and again, perhaps to keep up appearances, perhaps simply to assert their authority, the leaders of the pack would make a grand gesture in which the Fasburgs were expected not only to participate but to welcome. Such was the case in 1983, when the leaders of the pack decided to favor the Fasburgs with a long and festive visit at their summer home.

The Fasburgs owned a small island in the Aegean called Tyche, and each summer the entire clan would reunite there for several weeks or a month at a time — aunts, uncles, grandchildren, cousins. Free from the restraints of schedules and instructors,

Lara and I ran as wild as little goats all over the white cliffs and fragrant fields, exploring brilliant blue pool caves, splashing in the surf, building castles from seashells. Sometimes Lara would join in the night games with her cousins, but not very often, which was disappointing because I liked to watch the young wolves running and tumbling and picking playful fights with one another along the beach. I liked to watch and pretend I was one of them, and later advise Lara how she might play better next time, or outwit her bigger cousin Marcel, or run faster than Ursa. Not surprisingly, she didn't find it nearly as much fun listening to my critiques as I did formulating them.

Often the prince and princess would entertain their human friends or business associates on Tyche, and we would dine in the big open air pavilion with the sea breeze billowing white curtains and tossing about the flames of torches while the sun set in brilliant colors over the Aegean. The adults would drink ouzo and smoke Turkish cigarettes and laugh and dance far into the night. Sometimes they swam naked in the moonlit turquoise ocean, and made love on the beach. It was all very abandoned and thrilling , but civilized. I never realized just how civilized our uninhibited little island of Tyche was, until suddenly it was not.

Of course the prince resented the Devoncroix's proposed visit from the moment it was announced, but there was never a question of refusing. To deny hospitality, no matter how great the provocation, was simply not an option in their culture — not to mention the fact that, in this case, it would have been impolitic. It was implicitly understood that there was, of course, an ulterior motive in this visit, but if the prince and princess knew what it was they did not share the information with us.

They arrived on a bright blue Aegean morning in a magnificent forty-foot, mahogany-prowed yacht that flew the blue and gold flag of the family crest—"bloody arrogance," muttered the prince when he saw it—and whose hold was loaded with enough wine, caviar, Kobe beef, French cheese, and Mediterranean seafood to sustain a small nation for the summer. We all came down to the beach to greet them—the prince and princess, the aunts and uncles and cousins, and the small army of servants and support personnel that were required to properly entertain dignitaries of such import. Although we had been told the exact time and place to assemble, I had insisted that Lara and I be there two hours early, so that we could watch them approach.

I had never seen anything so marvelous in my life as that yacht, emerging out of the blue horizon like a gift from the gods and growing bigger, shinier and more impressive with every moment. Brass glinted and sparked. The hull glowed whiter than the Greek sun, and I was mesmerized by the brilliant gold half moon crest painted on the side. These were the leaders of the pack. I had read about them in history books. They were responsible for shaping the world we knew today. They did not have to work very hard to impress me.

"Papa doesn't like them," Lara said, holding on to my hand as the great boat lowered its anchor and a veritable fleet of small tenders was dispatched across the water to greet it.

"I know," I said, and added importantly, "it's all because they want the Fasburg's money."

Lara replied darkly, her gaze fixed on the yacht, "Not all." I wanted to question this, but then she wound her arm around mine and snuggled in closer, as though for protection. "I don't like them either."

I reminded her that the unhappy events of the Night Run at Castle Devoncroix had been a long time ago, and all involved had been children. That was no reason to hold a grudge against the entire family.

She looked unhappy and ill at ease. "It's not just that," she said. "Can't you smell it? They're so ... intense. So *loup garou*."

I laughed and tugged at her hair where it tumbled over her shoulders. "So are you, silly."

I suppose, in looking back, that her unhappiness must have increased at that, but I was far too occupied with the activities on the yacht to notice. I bitterly regretted the fact that Prinze-Papa had assured me binoculars would not be appropriate for the occasion, and had confiscated mine the minute he saw them.

As the dignitaries boarded the first tender I gently unwound Lara's arm from mine and stepped away. "You should go stand with your cousins," I told her.

She stared at me. "Why?"

"Because it's not respectful to be here with me when they arrive." I had been doing a good deal of reading on the subject of pack protocol since I learned we were to be hosts to such illustrious guests. "They're the leaders of the pack and I'm—"

"A member of our family." The princess came up behind us and placed a hand upon each of our heads. I twisted around to look at her and she smiled at me complacently. Her hair was upswept into a Grecian knot, and she was wearing a gauzy sea green caftan that highlighted her nipples and the contours of her waist, and turned her eyes to emeralds. Without shifting her gaze or her expression, she stretched out her fingers and the prince came into them, dapper in sailing whites and a sea blue silk ascot.

They leaned into each other, arms around their waists, free hands embracing Lara and me in a perfect portrait. I swelled with pride and contentment.

But I privately thought the prince should have taken the tender to the yacht to greet the pack leader. It was protocol, after all.

The first tender was boarded and the second loaded with the priority luggage of its occupants, and my mouth dropped open as the small boats grew close enough for me to recognize some of the occupants. I nudged Lara hard in the ribs. "Look, it's —"

She gave me a quelling look. "I know who it is."

I snapped my mouth shut and tried hard not to show my lack of sophistication again. The werewolf who had caught my eye was a rock star of gargantuan proportions; I had been collecting his recordings for years without knowing he was one of them. Next to him was a face I recognized from the BBC, and a movie star who had won three Academy Awards. Over the course of the next few days I would meet captains of industry and technology, world-famous athletes, an opera star, a Nobel prize winner, a statesman whose photograph had been on the cover of *Time* magazine only the month before. Lupinotuum, all. As I have said, until that point I don't think I truly understood who they were, these grand, outrageous creatures among whom I had lived so complacently, nor how far and wide their influence was spread.

And none of them would impress me quite so much as Nicholas Devoncroix.

As we watched the tenders approach the beach, a tall blond youth on board the yacht shed his clothes and dived overboard. The prince stifled an exasperated sound that was half laugh, half groan.

"Behold," he said, "the heir designee to the pack."

Unlike the human monarchy, the reins of power in loup garou culture pass to the youngest in the line of descent, which prevents the occasional embarrassing incidence of the old ruler outliving his heir, and always ensures strong and vigorous leadership. Nicholas was the last of the progeny of Elise and Alexander Devoncroix, and although he had not been officially named, everyone knew he was being groomed to take over the pack. If he proved himself worthy, he would be ceremonially anointed at age thirty, and would co-rule the pack until his father either stepped aside in his favor, or died.

But on that day, when the Devoncroix first anchored their yacht off the coast of Tyche, he was just a sixteen-year-old show-off, and I have to admit I was fascinated as I watched him plow through the water, clearly intending to outrace the passenger motorboat to shore. A cheer rose up from the crowd on the beach, urging him on. I was hard put not to add my voice to it as the wake created by the youth began to outdistance that of the motor boat. Even the driver of the boat, throttling up the engine, could not help but spare a grin of encouragement as the sleek blond head, diving in and out of the water like a dolphin, began to pull steadily ahead of him. By the time he reached the shallow green-gold water of shore, a good ten meters ahead of the boat, the crowd on the beach was roaring approval, and I could hardly contain my own grin.

He stood and shook out his long light hair like a dog, then smoothed back the water from his face with his hands, wading toward us with the effortless stride of a god of old. One of the most distinguishing characteristics of the loup garou is that they do not develop body or facial hair, although the hair on their heads grows at an extraordinarily rapid rate and, if they choose to wear it short, must be barbered every day. You'll notice that most of the nudes painted by Renaissance masters have no body hair, and often are graced with long, flowing curls. I don't know whether the models were werewolf. But I know the artists were.

Nicholas Devoncroix put me in mind of one of those Renaissance paintings as he approached the beach, lithe, lean and perfectly formed. He came first to our party, as was only proper, and the tender that bore his parents to shore was just docking when he bowed to the prince.

"Sir," he said. "The compliments of my father, the leader of the pack."

I could hear the dour amusement in the prince's voice as he replied, "You might have saved yourself a swim, young Nicholas, and allowed your father to present his own compliments."

The sky blue eyes of Nicholas Devoncroix twinkled in the sunlight, but his face remained properly sober. "That would not have been nearly so interesting, sir."

The prince replied ruefully, "I suppose not. Kindly make yourself known to my mate ..." Nicholas bowed again. "And my daughter Lara ..." A slight nod in her direction. "And Emory Hilliford, a human."

He looked at me, and, because I was thirteen, my eyes went, inevitably and uncontrollably, to his genitalia — which was, as I recall, somewhat impressive. He noticed, and grinned, and clapped me on the shoulder. "Never mind, little human," he said, "yours will grow."

My face flamed and I was speechless, and he bowed again to the prince and princess and sauntered off down the beach,

95

toward the tender that was just tying off on shore. Lara said, quite clearly, twining her hand about mine, "Forget him, Emory. He is a prick."

The laugh that burst from my throat was pure astonishment, because I hadn't expected that from her, and even though she should have been reprimanded for her rudeness, the prince's mouth was twitching too, and even the princess jerked her gaze away and compressed her lips, as though trying to hide her own mirth. But my amusement died when Nicholas glanced back over his shoulder, laughing too, and winked at me, sharing in our private joke that was no longer private, or funny.

I don't know whether what I felt for him then was admiration or resentment. Over the years the two became so entangled in my head I'm not sure I ever could tell them apart. And even today, when I think of him, the image that so often comes to mind is of that day, and his careless laughter, and the way Lara clung to my hand as we watched him walk away.

Alexander Devoncroix was the most striking creature I had ever seen. He was tall and straight shouldered, with hair that was already brilliantly silver when I first met him and eyes so blue that looking at them was startling; they made you blink, and forget what you were going to say; they made you never want to look away and they made you afraid to look again. When he entered a room the air around him seem to hum with potential. His wife Elise, whom they called the queen, was of the same elegant, regal build, with a cascade of hair that, when loosed, tumbled below her hips and sparkled and glinted like diamonds on snow. I thought no one could ever be more beautiful than my princess. It felt like a betrayal even to look at Elise Devoncroix.

She was wearing a big sun hat and dark glasses to shield her pale eyes from the sun, and a sarong-type dress in a colorful print with sandals that were beaded in turquoise and diamond chips. When the boat failed to make the last few feet to shore, and before her son could reach her to assist her, she simply removed the expensive shoes, caught up her skirt, and waded onto the beach. It was difficult not to like her after that.

"What a paradise you have here, Ilsa!" she declared warmly, both hands extended. "How generous of you to share it."

"How generous of you to come." The two women embraced in the customary style, holding shoulders, touching cheeks together on one side, and then the other. There are scent glands, very subtle, behind the earlobe, that traditionally emit an odor when one lies—which is what is meant when a werewolf says he can smell a lie. The cheek-to-cheek greeting is a gesture of sincerity, like the handshake is among humans.

Because it was the queen, the females of the family were greeted first, and I had to push Lara forward when it was her turn. There were fifteen female members of the Fasburg clan present on the beach and by the time they were done the pack leader had arrived, and Nicholas Devoncroix had found some clothes and dried his hair, and the ritual began all over again. It was all very complex, in terms of who greeted whom at what time and with what words and gestures, and I wondered how they kept up with it all. But this was what Lara studied while I practiced Tae Kwon Do, I supposed, and I was glad, because I wanted her to explain it all to me.

By the time they were all assembled there, all the Devoncroix and all the Fasburgs, the kinetic power on the beach was so thick it practically shimmered, and I could feel it crawling in my flesh, tickling my lungs when I drew in the air, fighting with my pulse like the shadow of a panic attack. I had never known that kind of sensation before. I had never known the Devoncroix.

It was one thing of course for the prince to make a casual introduction of me to the impudent Nicholas Devoncroix when he appeared so informally upon our shores, but I did not expect to be acknowledged by the pack leader—nor did I want to be. I stayed far back from the proceedings—close enough not to miss a detail, of course, but hiding myself among the servants and workmen until I saw Alexander Devoncroix lean his head toward the prince and say something, then the prince turned and searched the crowd with his eyes until he found me. He beckoned me with a lift of his hand, and I came forward, heart pounding.

I hesitated when I reached the prince, but he placed his hand firmly upon my shoulder and drew me forward. Those around us—the queen, some of the older Devoncroix offspring, even the princess, who seemed to enjoying her duties as hostess far more than the prince was enjoying his as host—grew quiet, watching curiously. The prince said, simply, "Emory Hilliford, a human. Emory, this is Alexander Devoncroix, about whom you may have heard." I could hear the amusement in his voice and he added, "Emory is quite an admirer of yours, I believe, Alexander."

The great man with his silver hair and gleaming blue eyes turned his gaze on me. "Is that so, young man?"

Immediately I lowered my eyes. It would, frankly, have been difficult to do otherwise. "I have read about you in the history books, sir. It is an honor."

"Nicely mannered," observed Alexander Devoncroix.

"Of course," replied the prince.

"You take a risk," added Alexander, his tone still casual, "bringing your human along on a holiday such as this."

And the prince replied, equally as at ease, "But he is my human."

I was aware in the brief pulse of silence that ensued of a contest of some sort taking place between the two males, and then, when I chanced a quick glance upward, I saw the pack leader smile. It seemed a cold thing. "Well then. You'll be certain to keep him safe, won't you?"

He looked at me then, his eyes twinkling, and I thought my heart might stop. "You, young human, will make an effort to find me when I'm not otherwise occupied, and tell me what you have read about me in history books, eh?"

I managed to nod, and to sputter, "I will, sir. Thank you, sir."

And then he turned away to make some comment to his spouse, and the prince was chuckling as he gave me an affectionate shove on the back of the neck. "You are far too easily impressed, little man. Away with you, now, and find something with which to occupy yourself until the Great Ones deign to notice you again."

The Devoncroix brought gifts of all description for their hosts, their hosts' servants, and their hosts' children—which included, to my astonishment and delight, a prototype 3-D video game which took the rest of the summer for me to master, but with which Lara was bored within a week. I was, however, most fascinated by the barge that drew up behind the yacht, and began to disgorge a small herd of goats and sheep which, once shepherded down the high-walled ramp onto the rocky beach, were simply allowed to disperse at will all over the island.

"*Eh bien*, my friend," declared Alexander Devoncroix, clapping the prince on the shoulder in a gesture of familiarity even I could see was false, "we will feast on hunt night!"

"What is hunt night?" I asked Lara. "What are all those animals going to do?"

By now the formalities were dispensed with, and everyone intermingled happily on the beach, or explored the island, or settled themselves in the great marble villa on the hill. Lara and I had found a perch on a rocky overhang a little removed from the action, but close enough that I was certain not to miss anything important.

"Poop all over the island," she replied. I could tell she was put out with me but I didn't know why.

"Are they really going to hunt them?" I insisted, wide eyed as I watched the herd flow this way and that through the rocks and gorse. "For real?"

She was frowning over a delicate gold chain, beautifully worked in delicate roses of white and pink gold, that Elise Devoncroix had given her. "They are brutes," she said. "Why did they have to come here? Why couldn't we just have our pleasant holiday like we always do?"

I said impatiently, "Because we can have a pleasant holiday any time. How often do you get to meet the leaders of the entire pack? This is an adventure, Lara! You'll tell your grandchildren about it!"

She gave me a look of disdain. "You are such a sycophant."

"It's better than being an idiot," I shot back, and we stood there for a moment, glaring at each other.

Then, because I was far too excited about what the rest of the adventure might hold to fight with her, I said, "Look, it's going to be fun, you'll see. Just give it a chance, all right?" Then, nodding at the necklace she worried in her hand, I said, "That's pretty. Do you want me to fasten it for you?"

Her eyes flashed suddenly and she balled up the necklace and threw it at me. "No," she said, and stalked off.

I called after her, but she didn't look back, and I didn't try very hard to get her attention. I was far too intent upon everything that was going on around me to worry much about Lara. But I did remember to pick up the necklace, and give it back to her when I saw her later. She didn't even thank me.

I could not get enough of the visitors. Where they were, I was, watching them, listening to them, observing them, absorbing every nuance and subtlety about them, sometimes even interacting with them, although always in the most superficial way. Nothing was forbidden to me, no place was off limits, yet it was understood that my freedom was provisionary. I might wander among them as long as I did not make a pest of myself and observed protocol. But if I trespassed, I would not only bring humiliation to the prince and princess, I would very likely be sent home. So I was careful to stay out of the way and draw no attention to myself. And I became very good at stalking.

Of course, even I knew better than to attempt to stalk the leader of the pack.

I came upon him accidentally one purple twilight as I was making my way back to the villa after an afternoon of watching a group of females in wolf form dive for fish from the low cliffs on the south end of the island. He swam alone in human form, cutting in and out of the water with long, leisurely strokes, a thing of beauty to see. I sank quickly into the shadows before he noticed me, then scrambled off the pebbly beach and over the rocks to take the longer route home. I had not gone twenty steps along the steep path that wound toward the villa when I saw him standing there a few dozen meters before me. I had no idea how he had gotten there before me. But he was waiting for me. I approached slowly, my tongue dry in my throat.

He had combed back his wet hair and had donned slacks and leather shoes and an open gauze shirt. He was as strong and fit as the prince, for they were about the same age, but there were hard edges about the pack leader that made him seem somehow even stronger, sharp-muscled and poised. And he had eyes that could cut steel.

He said easily, as I reached him, "We can hear you, you know. No matter how silent you make your feet, we can hear your heart beat from half a mile away, and hear your breath even when you hold it, and the fluids that flow through your body. Still," he conceded, "you do well, for a human."

I swallowed—something else he could hear—but said nothing.

"You may one day learn to disguise your heartbeat," he went on, turning as I reached him to continue along the path, "but there is nothing that can be done about the smell. It's quite distinctive, and lingers long after you've gone. So you see you'll never be completely invisible to us."

I cleared my throat. "I wasn't trying to be invisible, sir. I was trying not to intrude."

"You were spying," he corrected, without accusation.

I knew the futility of lying. "I was trying to," I admitted miserably, and to my surprise, the great werewolf chuckled.

"An admirable effort," he said, "if misplaced."

We climbed higher, my legs stretching to keep up with his long and effortless stride. He said, "So what is it that you make of us, Emory Hilliford, the human, now that you have found time to study us? Have you learned anything you did not already know?"

I could not begin to put my thoughts into words. I admitted, "I already knew a lot."

"Ah yes, your history books." He seemed amused. "Tell me what you've read of me from them, then."

This was the moment I had been waiting for. I cast a quick eager glance at him. "I read that you and your mate Elise are the parents of modern commerce. That you have brought more wealth into the pack since the beginning of this century than all the other leaders who have gone before you. That you traveled to Alaska and discovered Castle Devoncroix, which was built thousands of years ago by a race of loup garoux that died out long ago, and you moved the pack headquarters there from France. And started the gold rush in the Americas. And bought up all the oil. And invented the airplane. And ..." I had to paused for a breath. "Singlehandedly rounded up and destroyed the Brotherhood of the Dark Moon, when no one in a thousand years had been able to do it. You brought civilization to all the world."

Again that amused look. "There is no such thing as the Brotherhood of the Dark Moon, my boy, never has been. It was a myth about a group of wild loup garoux who plotted to bring down the pack so that they could be free to devour humans and wreak havoc upon the earth. Mothers used to tell it to transgressing children to keep them in line. I think your teacher

103

may have been having a joke on you."

I was disappointed, and confused, and I wanted to point out to him that I had not discovered the Brotherhood in one of Teacher's assigned books, but in the private papers of the prince's library. But when he looked at me, his gaze steady and even and completely neutral, I was certain I saw a challenge there, daring me to speak. And because I knew I had to say something, or be the fool, I blurted, "Prinze-Papa says that history is written by the victors."

He was silent for so long that I thought I would have been better after all to be a silent fool, and my heart started to pulse under his slow, dissecting gaze. Then he murmured, without removing his eyes from me, "Your prince was right, young man, on many counts."

The villa was in view, misty in the twilight with lamp lights and torch lights spilling all around, and I could hear the music and the laughter that drifted across the wide dark lawns.

"You are a very rare and fortunate human," said Alexander Devoncroix. "Respect your good fortune and continue your studies and who knows?" He smiled then, and winked at me merrily. "One day you may come to work for me."

He descended the path toward the villa, chuckling softly to himself, and I hung back until he went inside, which was protocol. Then I made my way to the house alone.

This is what I know about the loup garou. They are brilliant, far-seeing, manipulative. They do not think in terms of years, but of centuries. I honestly don't believe that, all those years ago, Alexander Devoncroix could have known what his plans for me would be.

But I do think he had a plan.

Renegade

CHAPTER ELEVEN

Until I knew the Devoncroix, I had no concept of the wild beauty of their kind, a barely controlled savagery tempered by absolute elegance. I watched them at night, when I was supposed to be sleeping, their naked human forms and their sleek, diamond-eyed wolf forms running together and tumbling together on the brilliantly moonlit beach, sparks from their bonfires shooting skyward, wolf voices and human-formed song mixing with the whisper of the Aegean into the most exquisite music I have ever heard, music that wound its way deep into my soul and seemed to pull a part of me, the most essential part, outward toward it.

They were completely uninhibited, carelessly confident in who they were, in what they were, and when they were around

105

all the rules changed. They wandered about in wolf form in bright daylight. The Fasburgs never did that, even in the seclusion of Tyche. They Changed at will, sending the flashing pulse of their Passion across the wake of anyone who happened by, seeming to taunt the unsuspecting into joining their unrestrained celebration of themselves, of their mastery. The entire island was charged, it seemed, with a different electrical signature than it had been before. Rocks hummed and waters sang. Nothing was static. The very air we breathed seemed to be poised to burst into flame at any moment, all because they were there.

The adults were indulgent of me, occasionally amused, mostly oblivious. The adolescents were cautious at first, then curious, sniffing about me warily and posturing when I came upon them in wolf form. I think they were intrigued that I wasn't afraid of them—all except Nicholas of course, who never lost an opportunity to be condescending or mocking toward me, directing his young pack members to be certain to take advantage of the opportunity to fully investigate the rarest of all species, the civilized human. Lara was right. He was a prick.

But aside from Nicholas, the Devoncroix fascinated and thrilled me. They were the epitome of hedonism, careless in their unrestrained pursuit of pleasure. My upbringing was a far reach from the comparatively modest environment of a normal human child; the loup garoux were as casual about sex as they were about other functions of the body, which is only natural when one can melt between two physical forms at will. I was not easily shocked. But never before had I known the sheer beauty of werewolves in their natural, joyful state, the absolute conviction with which they devoted themselves to the pursuit of pleasure. I saw them in their sex games, their pearlescent white limbs entwined about one another beneath the brilliant wash of the moon, their tongues and hands caressing, their careless joyful laughter, their playful chases and wanton surrender, and the mere watching could transport me to a state of sexual rapture. Watching them, I knew from whence the Greeks had gotten their stories of gods at play.

Until the summer that the Devoncroix invaded our soft and civilized and oh-so-human world, I knew nothing of the passion that governs their race, which is to say, I knew nothing of them at all. Theirs is an existence ruled by intensity, by mastery, by a fierce and joyful adoration of all that it means to be werewolf, so that even the Change—that rapture of transfiguration in which they metamorphose from one form into the other—is called *the Passion*. It's about raw and unfettered emotion; about desire, pain, celebration; it's about truth. Until you understand that you will never know these creatures. Never.

And yet, from the moment of their arrival, I was aware of Lara retreating into herself, rarely appearing at public events and never joining in the games, hiding herself in the alcoves and grottos of the villa when everyone else was running on the beach, taking her meals alone, disappearing to her room. I missed her, and I was pissed with her, because nothing was as much fun without her, and I wanted her with me for this, the most important time of discovery in my life.

I found her one sunrise when the sky was pink and the water was misty gray, swimming alone in a tidal pool on the far side of the island that we had discovered years ago and liked to think was our secret. It was not, of course. Since the Devoncroix had come, nothing was secret anymore.

107

She was wearing a yellow bikini, and because she was dressed I knew she had walked here in human form, which was oddly typical of her. It was a long way from the villa, and in wolf form she could have covered the distance in minutes. It would have taken her over an hour to walk.

She was long and lean, with slim hips and barely budding breasts, and her lazily floating form, which was clearly visible beneath the clear water, was flattered by the swimsuit. I stripped off my tee shirt and sandals and waded in to join her. Since I had developed pubic hair, I was no longer entirely comfortable being naked around her, so I wore the tennis shorts in which I had started out.

When I was chest deep beside her, she flipped over on her back, floating effortlessly with her dark hair spread out like a halo around her. She said nothing. Her eyes said everything.

I put my arms around her. "What's wrong?"

She looped her arms around my neck and sank into me, her face on my shoulder. "Everything," she said softly, clinging to me.

We allowed ourselves to float deeper, wound around each other in silence while the water lapped around our ears and the sun pushed a golden sliver above the horizon. Suddenly she tightened her arms around my neck and tilted her face back to look at me, and there was a kind of desperate ferocity in her eyes as she demanded, "Will you run away with me?"

I stared at her. "What?"

"Now, today, quickly before they find out. Before they make me—"

"Before they make you what?" She started to kick away from me and I reached back and caught her hands, holding them

108

around my neck. "What are they going to make you do? What are you afraid of?"

She looked at me, her eyes wet. "The hunt is tonight," she said.

"I know." I felt a rush of adrenaline, just thinking about it. "It's your first one, right? You're so lucky. You've got to remember every detail, and — "

She broke away from me suddenly and struck off furiously. When I caught up with her she was crying.

"What?" I demanded, grabbing her shoulders. "What's wrong with you?"

She struggled with me childishly for a minute, thrashing in the water, but I wouldn't let her go, and then she cried, "I hate you! You're just like them and I hate them! I hate them and I hate you and I hate ...." She wrenched away from me and slapped the water hard, sending sprays into the air between us. "*This*. Being this! Being what I am." And, as I stared at her in astonishment, she suddenly flung herself back into my arms, holding on tight, and whispered fiercely, "Oh Emory, I'm so afraid. I can't do this. You've got to help me. You've got to."

I held her while the gentle waves lapped against us and the water turned golden. I patted her hair and let her cry and told her everything was going to be all right. And my head was reeling. I suppose that, knowing how traumatic her first pack run among the Devoncroix had been, I should have been more empathetic. And to a certain extent I was, or I tried to be. But I also understood, and think she did too, that this was a rite of passage for her, and — perhaps more importantly — a test of power for her parents. No one would force her to go, but she was well past the age of consent, and was expected to take her place among the pack. The prince would be disappointed, and the princess would be embarrassed, if she did not.

I said, "Lara, listen, it's fine, it's going to be fine. It's just like hunting rats in Venice, nothing to be afraid of there, eh?" She looked up at me and I gave her an encouraging smile. "I'll be close by, and keep an eye on you, I promise. You don't have to do anything, no one is judging you, you just have to be there. Just go with them. Be who you are."

"I don't *want* to be who I am," she said, her eyes anguished. "Why did I have to be born this way? Why can't I just be like you?"

And now I was truly astonished because all I had ever wanted in my whole life was to be like her.

I said, "I'll be close by."

She pressed herself close to me, her bare skin against my bare skin, her mouth open on my neck, her breath hot. "Let's have sex together, Emory," she whispered. Her leg snaked between mine beneath the water, coiling around my ankle. "Let's do that, please. Then we'll have our special secret that I can remember forever. You want to. I know you do."

Of course I did. I was already hard against her thigh and my heart was pounding so hard even I could hear it. The loup garoux can smell desire on a human just as they can smell everything else, and mine was coming off me in thick, choking waves. Of course I wanted to. There is only one reason a thirteen-year-old boy will ever turn down an offer of sex with a girl: because he is afraid.

Nonetheless, when she wound her arms around my neck and opened her mouth against mine, I took her tongue inside my mouth as though it were a feast I had been waiting all my life to

110

devour. I grasped her buttocks beneath the water and lifted her up and she twined her legs around my waist with nothing separating us but a brief expanse of space and a scrap or two of clothing, and I let myself drown in the fantasy of heat and flesh and sheer, impossible wanting.

I had grown up in a household in which sexuality was unaccompanied by shame or angst, where it was openly discussed and expected to be enjoyed, and where there were few, if any, taboos. There are, however, protocols. Having sex outside one's own species was a breach of a primary one.

The loup garoux mate only in wolf form, and only as a result of the grand passion that is the fullest possible celebration of what they are. There is no such thing as adultery in their culture, nor rape, nor divorce. At the moment of mating the entire essence of one flows into the other – the emotions, thoughts, memories – and becomes so intermingled that they never are separate again. There are no secrets between a mated pair. There is no loneliness, jealousy, misunderstanding. They are, mentally and spiritually, as one. The mating bond is so strong between them that when one spouse dies, the other usually follows within a matter of minutes. Theirs is the kind of passion that I think we humans will never know, and perhaps that's why we are so helpless beneath their allure. We ache to have what they have, to know what they know, to feel what they feel. And we, for them, are mere playthings.

When they have sex in human form it is completely unrelated to mating, or even to affection. It's playful, casual, unrestricted, and generally holds less social significance than the act of running together. Of course, to pretend that loup garoux have not, upon occasion, had sex with humans would be naïve in the extreme. I had discovered in the prince's library entire volumes of erotic poetry dedicated to just that topic. There are dirty jokes and pornographic films centered around the subject. But it is not the kind of thing Prince Fasburg would accept from his daughter and his adopted son in the presence of the highest-ranking members of the pack. For they would know. If we did this thing, of course they would know. They would smell it on our skin, hear it in our whispers, see it our eyes. And we would all be shamed.

I wrenched my mouth away from hers, staggering with the effort and almost falling in the water. "You are cruel," I gasped. I put my hands on her knees and pushed hard to disentangle her from me. How easy it would have been instead to slip my fingers beneath the tiny yellow bikini bottom. Instead, I pushed her away so forcefully that she flailed backwards and almost went under. I caught her and hauled her upright just before she inhaled a mouthful of water. She stared at me in astonishment, water lapping at her chin.

"What are you talking about?" she demanded. "You want to, you know you do! Why—"

"You're using me, that's why!" I shot back at her. "Because if we had sex your parents would be mad at you—at us—everyone would be mad and no one would want you on the hunt. That's what you think, isn't it?"

Still, she didn't seem to get it. "Is that so bad? Why is that bad? Emory ..." She pushed closer to me, finding the shelf on which I stood, so that the water now came only to the top of her breasts. Small breasts, firm and athletic. I wondered what they tasted like.

She caught my hand, and looked helplessly into my eyes, but she did not try to force herself against me, as she had done before.

She looked hurt, and confused, and she said, "Don't you love me even a little?"

All the breath left my lungs in one long slow sigh. I stroked her wet face, tangling one finger in her hair. Every part of my adolescent body ached for her. I said, in a voice made husky with hormones, "I love you a lot. I love you more than anything. And I'm going to take care of you tonight, don't worry. You're going to be fine. I'll be there, I'll be close, nothing's going to happen to you. Don't be afraid. I'll always take care of you. But you've got to do this, Lara. You've got to."

No doubt she had known from the beginning that she had never really had a choice. I will never forget the look of sorrow and resignation in her eyes as she said, "I'm not like the others, Emory. They know that, they can sense it. I can change my form, but I can't change inside. I don't have the soul of the wolf inside me. I never will."

I refused to believe her, which is perhaps the greatest hurt I inflicted on her that day. She tried to tell me who she was, and by refusing to listen I robbed her of what she knew to be true. In so many ways I would spend the rest of my life trying to make that up to her.

But right then, all I knew to do was to hold her tight and repeat, "You can do this, you're as good as any of them. I'll be there."

I felt the fight seep out of her as she slowly, sadly, and with a great sense of defeat, laid her head against my shoulder. The fingers that entwined with mine felt small and fragile.

"Do you promise?" A small reluctant hope crept into her voice. "You won't let me out of your sight?"

"I promise," I told her, and felt a great sense of relief as I

113

encircled her with my arms, patting her shoulder. "I promise."

I thought the prince and princess would be proud of me. I thought I had done the right thing.

But that was before I witnessed the hunt.

I will abbreviate my telling of this because the memories are, as with so many pivotal life events, too powerful, too complex for language. If I had the words of a hundred thousand men I couldn't make you understand what it was like on that night, to be me, to be within the heart of it, to know what I knew and feel what I felt. So I will use instead a few simple words to tell what I observed.

It was the night of the new moon, and they gathered under the white-columned open air pavilion that overlooked the sea. Never has there been so dark a night. The torches were not lit. Even the stars were under cover. The only things that moved were the shapes of their gossamer garments, stirred by the wind as they stood in silence, waiting for the leader of the pack to raise the call.

No one had to tell me to stay inside. Yet the prince did happen upon me in the late afternoon, and he said to me with dark and fevered eyes, "This is not a night for humans, little man." Yet he said it absently, almost in passing, so that it seemed more of a suggestion than a command. Of course had he given me a direct order, my dilemma would have obvious. Perhaps he knew already I would not be able to resist the temptation of this, the grandest and most basic ritual of all their kind and he did not want to put me in a position to disobey. Perhaps he really didn't care. Already he had begun to change, in manner and in purpose, as had the princess. Charged from every direction by the electrical anticipation of their own kind, they grew wilder, more sharp-sensed, more alert and reactive with every moment that passed. The entire island seemed to be throbbing with the pent up energy of the pack. I could feel it in my throat, and the prickling hairs on my arms, and the faint aching at the back of my sinuses, as though I was breathing air that was too thin. The prince was right. This was not a night for humans.

When I touched Lara she was trembling. "Stay at the back," I whispered to her. "Stay where I can see you. I love to watch you run." I knew that telling her that would make her want to show off for me, and make her remember I was there. Besides, it was true, and that of course is the essence of it all: I loved what she was more than she did. I wanted her to do this not for her sake but for mine.

And even then, she would do anything for me.

She flashed a look on me that was a fierce wondrous mixture of savagery and joy, gratitude and dread, and then she slipped away from me, as helpless as any of them to resist the pull of the pack.

All of the lights in the house had been extinguished, to better prepare their eyes for the hunt. I slipped away under the cover of darkness to position myself among the rocks overlooking the pavilion. No one noticed me. They wouldn't have cared if they had.

I did not think there had ever been a human who witnessed a pack ritual like this, involving a mass change. I was thrilled to my core with the anticipation of it. Nothing could have kept me from this night—not the prince, not my own good sense, not the pack leader himself. I crouched atop the rock overhang and let my eyes adjust to the darkness. I thought I could make out Lara

115

near the back of the crowd with the other adolescents, looking small and frail in her thin white changing robe with her long dark hair lifting and drifting around her with the crackle of static electricity. I remember the rustle among them, the heightening of excitement as the leaders of the pack strode forth among them in gowns of royal blue and stood on a dais with their arms uplifted and their heads thrown back. I recall when their garments fell away. There was a rush and a roar inside my head, the feeling of my guts being turned inside out, a thundering wave of percussive light, and that's all I knew until I was lying face-down in a pool of my own vomit, shaken, disoriented, terrified, and too weak to even stand.

I could sense them all around me, flowing in and out of the shadows, I could hear the scratch of their claws on the rocks and feel the heat of their breath; it was like being trapped in the midst of a stampede. I covered my head with my arms and rolled aside, hiding as best I could inside a thorny bush. I saw the flash of eyes in the dark. I saw teeth.

In wolf form they are enormous. No mass is loss in the change, so that if he is six feet tall and weighs 180 pounds, he will be six feet long and massive in wolf form. Their paws are the size of human hands, tipped with razor-like claws. Even in human form, they are, pound for pound, five times stronger than a man. In wolf form, their muzzles can snap small tree trunks. The earth thunders when they fly across it. The leaves on the trees rush upward in their wake, grasses bend, small creatures huddle quaking in the shadows, paralyzed with fear. Small creatures like human boys. Did they know I was there? Of course they did. But tonight I was not their prey. They did not even slow down.

The pack dispersed around me, racing across the cliffs and

into the night, and all I wanted to do was crawl back to the villa, lock all the doors and windows, and find a closet in the furthest corner of the house in which to secure myself. No, I wanted to leave this place, I wanted to run from the island as fast as I was able, to swim if I must, to safety. But then I remembered Lara, and my promise to her. Covered with scratches and smelling of vomit and shivering from head to toe, I stumbled to my feet and into the thick of it, searching for her.

This is the power and the horror of the hunt: the screams of terror and howls of victory, blood sprayed across the rocks, entrails spilling, bones cracking. This was my dark eyed prince, with jowls dripping blood, my elegant princess, her muzzle buried in a steaming carcass. It was wild, fierce madness that was almost incomprehensible in its intensity, and yet so elemental and extreme that I instantly understood it, even as I shuddered with fear in watching it. Pacts were made, characters were tested, souls were bared and alliances destroyed through the hunt. Life and death decisions were faced. Missteps made here were never forgiven. A month from now, a year, even a decade hence, two pairs of eyes would meet across a conference table and recognize each other from this night, and the fate of an industry, a nation, or a people would be determined on the basis of what had occurred on this bloody battlefield. I think I understood that, even as a boy. And I think that knowledge, as much as the savagery of the hunt itself, was what terrified me most. Their alienness. Their complete and utter otherness. Their life, their culture, their world was all I knew. Yet I would never be a part of it. I would never even, with my small and primitive human brain, fully comprehend it. And I would never belong.

The terrible irony I was too young to understand was that neither would Lara. And that we would both spend the rest of our lives desperately trying to make ourselves into something we could not be.

I did my best to stick to familiar paths, to stay out of the fray, but I wandered in the dark and the savagery was everywhere. They hunted in packs of two or three, racing across the night and exploding out of the dark with guttural sounds of greed and triumph. Blood would spray and a ragged bleat of heart-stopping terror would sear the air and what was living would live no more. They ripped out hearts and lungs, and turned on each other with snarls and snapping teeth and rolled and tore at each other with a viciousness that sometimes brought blood, and then they would separate and form another pack, and it would all start over again. I scrambled from one such scene to the other, staying as far away as I could, desperately trying not to run because I was afraid that if I did I might become prey. I couldn't find Lara. I was gasping, desperate, furious. Why couldn't I find her? I had told her to stay at the back where I could watch her. Where was she? But I hadn't known it would be like this. I hadn't known.

I thought I saw a shadow, smaller than the others, a flash of green eyes, dash across the trail below me and I wanted to shout because it might have been her, but I didn't dare. I started down the rocky incline, half sliding, half scrambling on my heels and hands, and then my foot caught something slippery and went out from under me. My shoes plowed a bloody path into the eviscerated carcass of a goat; my hands, grasping for purchase, caught nothing but entrails, still warm from the kill. When I leapt to my feet, gagging and frantically trying to wipe my hands on my shorts, my feet were squishy inside the blood-soaked sneakers. I turned then and ran, my breath like sobs in my throat, half-blinded by tears of fury and shame and disgust and cowardice, for home.

That was when I found her. She had been trampled in the melee, caught in a squabble, or had simply fallen from one of the island's many rocky precipices; no one ever knew for sure. She was unconscious and helpless in her human form, entangled in brush at the bottom of a broken trail a few hundred feet ahead of me. She was bleeding from an ugly gash on her flank, and a young blond wolf stood over her, powerful paws planted astride her, his voice raised in a victory ululation.

What I did then was born of fury and instinct, not heroism. This was my Lara, they had done this to her; I was responsible, and it was enough; I could bear no more. With a great cry of rage and anguish I rushed down the hill and I flung myself on her, striking out at the wolf with my shoulder and forearm with enough blind force to knock him aside. I smelled the air turn to fire but my eyes were buried in Lara's hair as I gathered her to me, her cool damp skin sending shivers through my soul. When next I looked it was Nicholas Devoncroix crouched beside me on his haunches in naked human form with his long golden hair streaming around him and his blue eyes crackling in the dark and his teeth, still shiny with streaks of blood, bared at me. I said in a low choked voice that shook with repressed fury and blazing determination, "Get out of my way." I picked up my poor broken little Lara, hardly feeling her weight as I crushed her to my chest, and staggered to my feet. *"Get out of my way."*

I don't know whether he did or not. The pack was streaming in and I held her close, looking neither right or left as I pushed forward, a lurching Odysseus in my Motley Crue tee shirt and blood drenched Nikes, fueled by outrage and bitter, bitter betrayal. I carried her through the press of hot furred bodies and the yellow-sulfur flash of Change and the smell of blood and dead flesh and scalding breath and I didn't look at them, I didn't blink. I held on tight to Lara even though she was heavy and I stumbled; even when the princess knelt before me and opened her arms I shoved past her blindly and I kept on walking until I carried Lara safely home.

So they tell the story in the pack to this day of how I faced down Nicholas Devoncroix and proved my courage and my honor on hunt night. And even though I was only a scared thirteen-year-old boy consumed with guilt for what I had made Lara do, the pack loves a hero and I could not shake my reputation. I won't begin to speculate how many doors have been opened for me throughout my life because of that night so many years ago.

Because what happens in the hunt is never forgotten.

They took her away from me, the princess and the female nurses, and I went to my quarters and stood under a scalding shower until my skin turned red, until the hand-milled soap formed a puddle of foam that reached to my ankles, until I had no more tears to cry. When I came out they all were there, milling about in their civilian clothes in the upstairs lounge and all along the terraces downstairs, drinking martinis and nibbling cheese cubes on a stick and laughing and talking among themselves as though nothing at all had happened, as though they were human. I hated them.

I wound my way past them, looking neither right nor left,

and if their gazes followed me or their conversations paused I did not notice. I opened Lara's door without knocking, as though I belonged there. And, in my mind I did.

She was fully recovered, of course, and sat up in bed in a pretty rose-sprigged nightdress with lace around the neck and her hair all combed out and gleaming on the pillow around her. There were dishes of ice cream and chocolate and sweet cakes stuffed with fruit and whipped cheese, and the princess was trying to tempt Lara to eat more, and even more, because a loup garou, after the expenditure of energy that's required to heal an injury like hers, requires enormous amounts of calorie-laden carbohydrates to replenish her reserves. Lara saw me, and smiled, but it was a slow, sad thing that clutched at my heart.

The princess got up and kissed my cheek. I stiffened when she touched me; I couldn't help it. If she noticed, she said nothing. The prince, who sat at the foot of his daughter's bed, squeezed her blanket-covered calf when I approached and moved away, giving us privacy. I did not look at him.

"Hello," I said to Lara, standing awkwardly beside her bed.

She said, "I'm not dying, you know." And she patted the place beside her on the bed. She was trying hard to act normal, but her lips were pale, and there was something in her eyes ... or not in her eyes. Something that made my chest cramp, that stabbed an ice pick through my stomach, and made me wonder what had happened to her out there. That made me wonder, with a horrible and roiling dread, what I had done.

I sat down. "You scared the shit out of me," I said roughly.

She fumbled for my hand and grasped it tightly. Her eyes were dark with things unsaid. It was a big room and the prince and princess were far on the other side of it, but they might have

121

been hovering over us, so intently were we aware of their presence. "I'm glad you're okay," I added.

She said softly, "Thank you for taking care of me." There was numbness in her eyes.

My throat convulsed in on itself in a single painful knot, choking me. "My God, Lara," I whispered raggedly. "What did they do to you? What did they *do*?"

She simply turned her face away. She couldn't even meet my eyes.

And then I couldn't stand it. I dropped down close to her, my fingers tangled in her hair, my face only inches from hers, and I whispered, "Lara, I'm so sorry. You don't have to tell me, it's okay. I'm sorry for what it was, whatever it was, that happened to you, I'm sorry you got hurt. I'm sorry I wasn't there. I'm sorry I didn't ..." And because I knew they could hear us, they would always hear us, I finished simply on the softest of breaths, "I'm sorry I didn't ... do what you asked me to, this morning."

She looked confused. "But you did. You watched over me, you ..." And then she understood, and her features softened. That horrible emptiness was still in her eyes. "It's all right now, though, isn't it? You were right, I had to do it, and now it's done, and it's all right. I wasn't very good at it though, was I?" she added tiredly. "I knew I wouldn't be."

I wanted to tell her that I didn't know how she had done or had not done because I was too busy stumbling about in the dark, reeking of my own vomit, sliding into the carcasses of dead beasts, and weeping like a child in terror and frustration. But just then I caught sight of Nicholas Devoncroix just outside the door, and I told her, "I thought you were great." I kissed her boldly on the forehead. "The best of them all. Truly. I'll see you in the morning, okay?"

She nodded, drowsy with exhaustion and stress and sugar and the effort of pretending to me that everything was all right when in fact it was not, and it never would be again. I started toward the door, my eyes on Nicholas Devoncroix, rage thumping in my ears.

The prince was beside me suddenly and silently. "Before you do that," he said quietly, "you should know that it was Nicholas who first found her. He was summoning the pack for help when you came along."

And now I couldn't even hate him. My rage was dark and impotent and completely irrational, because if I could not blame the Devoncroix for what had happened to Lara, who was I to blame? Myself? If I could not hate them for this vicious twisted nightmare of the people I once had called my own, who was I to hate?

The prince reached out a hand to touch my arm but I jerked away. He did not react. "Perhaps you are familiar with a saying," he said. "'If you would be our friend, first know what it is to be our enemy.'"

We looked at each other for a moment, my gaze turbulent and confused, his serene, even distant. Then he turned and went through the glass doors that led to the terrace. In a moment I followed him into the night.

I thought I could smell death on the air.

He took out a cigarette and lit it. Tobacco is used as a pleasure drug among them, its effects much like the ones cannabis has on humans. The prince rarely smoked. I wondered now if it was a ritual for him peculiar to the hunt.

He said, inhaling thoughtfully, "Did it occur to you to

123

wonder why I allowed you to come with us this summer?"

I watched the plume of smoke disperse into a mist and drift over the terrace and into the garden. I said, tightly, and the words surprised even me, "I think it was a test, sir."

His face was in shadow, and difficult to read, but I thought I saw the quirk of an eyebrow. "You are as clever as ever." He drew again on the cigarette, enjoyed it, released the smoke. "It was also an essential step in your education. You do understand that, do you not?"

I said nothing.

"We are, all of us, shades of dark and light," he said. "Your kind, and mine. We choose each day, most of us, to live a careful balance between the extremes. Until you know the depth of your darkness, you cannot know the light. And you cannot choose. It is as simple as that." And then, oddly, I thought I saw him smile as he lifted the cigarette to his lips again. "We are not the only beasts in the jungle, little man," he said. "We are not even the most dangerous."

He smoked a time in silence, his gaze beyond me, on the figures behind the glass doors inside the room. Then he looked back at me, his eyes dark and somber. "Tonight, young Emory," he said, "you are no longer a child. You will leave this place with more knowledge than any human of your time, if that is what you choose, and no one will stop you. We will find you a safe human school, and see that all your needs are met, and you will grow secure and strong among your own kind and, eventually, you may look back upon your time with us as nothing more than a vague oddity, hardly worth remembering." He paused, and let the significance of what he was offering sink in. I simply stared at him.

"But if you stay," he went on, "you do so knowing full well what we are, and what you are, and you will bear the responsibility for that knowledge for the rest of your life. Do you understand that?"

I looked at the beautiful elegant creatures inside the house, with their long upturned necks and sly smiles and their tailored trousers and martini glasses and throaty laughter, and I hated them, and I loved with them with a fierce passionate awe I cannot, even to this day, put into words. To leave them, to be banned from their world, to forget about them ... I could no more imagine it than I could imagine ripping off my own arm and walking away with nothing but a bloody stump. I looked at Lara, now almost asleep on her pillow, and the princess, with the smile of a mother's love on her face, sitting beside her, stoking her hair. To leave her? To leave them? It wasn't a choice. It wasn't even a possibility.

I didn't answer the prince. Not then, not ever. I stood for a moment in silence, and then I turned and went back inside the house. I walked over to the bed and looked down at Lara, the crescent shadows of lashes on her cheeks, the gleam of tumbled hair, the smooth familiar features. I said to the princess, quietly and without removing my eyes from Lara, "I'll sit with her."

There was a moment's hesitation, and then she rose, and left the room. I sat down beside Lara and sought her hand, and held it throughout the night.

Here is the truth about these creatures, the thing I had always known but until that moment, until I had to choose, had never understood: they steal your soul.

They steal your soul.

125

CHAPTER TWELVE

The Present

Rolfe stopped him with a lift of his finger and a small moue of distaste mixed, in a manner that was not altogether convincing, with concern. Emory touched a spot of moisture on his upper lip and felt the slick texture of blood. Rolfe passed him a folded handkerchief.

"How uncouth of me." Emory blotted the blood from his nostrils, folding and refolding the fine lawn cloth. Surreptitiously, he examined the handkerchief for a monogram, but found none. "That, unfortunately, is what you get for dining with humans."

Rolfe smiled, feigning sympathy. It was another one of those smiles that never reached his eyes. "You came in with a small brain bleed," he said. "It sealed itself spontaneously, and doesn't appear to have affected any vital functions. Amazing," he mused, "how little surface of the brain is actually used by humans. You might have had a half dozen strokes this past year without even noticing."

"Reassuring," said Emory. The nosebleed seemed to have stopped as suddenly as it had begun, and he folded the handkerchief into quarters and offered it back to Rolfe. Rolfe held up both hands, palms out, in protest. Emory smiled briefly and tucked the blood stained cloth into his pocket.

Rolfe was thoughtful for a moment. "Clarify something for me, if you will. On this Aegean holiday, you never overheard the prince and the Devoncroix discussing their secret? Surely this is why the pack leader came, and why Fasburg allowed it—so that they might share information."

Emory hesitated. "I did. Once. It made no sense at the time. I overheard many conversations. The pack leader was trying to buy one of the prince's properties. The prince was a harsh negotiator. The pack was invested in one of the prince's films. There were disputes. It is the way with them. They don't consider a victory genuine unless it is fought for or stolen."

"The point?" prompted Rolfe.

Emory said, "They guarded their words carefully around other loup garoux, because they knew how easily they could be heard. But around me, a mere human, it was often as though they forgot I existed. The prince and the pack leader had drinks one evening in the pavilion overlooking the sea. I was coming up from the beach, and hid in the rocks because, as I told you, I was terrified of breaking protocol and being sent home. I could hear their voices clearly. The prince said, 'You may recall that once we discussed a mythological creature. I wonder if you have had any further insights on the matter.' And the pack leader said, very shortly, 'No.'

"And then the prince said, 'You are not the only one searching for him, you know. It would be most unfortunate indeed should the subject of our discussion fall into the wrong hands.' And the pack leader said, 'I know.' That's all I heard."

"You're sure?" Rolfe's voice was sharp.

"I am."

"You should have told me before."

Emory shrugged. "My memory is not what it once was."

Rolfe scowled. "I am disappointed in you, Professor. I counted upon you for accuracy. I dislike a story told out of sequence."

Emory said, "I'm sorry." He took up his wine glass, glanced at it, noted it was empty. He met Rolfe's eyes. In another moment, Rolfe's features relaxed. He lifted the bottle and refilled Emory's glass.

"On the other hand," he said lightly, "you do have a flair for a dramatic tale. So I pray, continue at your pace and in your own style. When was it, exactly, that you decided to betray your own race? Not to mention, of course, the exquisite Lara, whom you professed to love."

Emory gazed at him steadily for a long moment. He sipped the wine. He said quietly, "You cannot imagine how much I loved her."

Rolfe said nothing. He simply waited.

And after another very long time, picked up his story.

*Excerpt from **DAWN TO DUSK: A TALE OF TWO SPECIES** by Emory Hilliford, PhD:*

Here is the story of Eudora the queen and the human who loved her:

His name was Louis Phillipe Montclaire. He was a priest of human affairs, a student of science and arcane knowledge, a keeper of secrets. He was also a privileged member of a highly clandestine organization which , since the tragedy of Rome, had striven to restore the balance of power between humankind and werewolves. No one, not even the members themselves, knew how many of them there were, nor how many might be human and how many werewolf. The humans among them wore a small brand in the shape of a cross on the backs of their necks, easily hidden under their hair or beneath a high collar.

Through the centuries they had quietly manipulated events that might improve the lot of humankind and restore to them what was lost when the loup garoux deserted them: a trade route that would not otherwise have been discovered for centuries might find its way conveniently into human hands, for example, or an obscure herb with particular efficacy on a certain human disease, or a crucial bit of engineering that would allow their ships to cross greater distances or their buildings to stand taller. But the ways in which they interfered in the course of history were always minor ones, gentle corrections to the course from which human and werewolfkind had strayed. The game they played was a delicate one, a constant juggling of the balance of power, and none of them could afford to lose sight of the consequences that could be wrought by a single misstep.

Bound by a covenant of silence and the inviolable belief that Nature, in balance, was their strongest ally, they risked the wrath of the pack, the superstitious terror of humans, and even their own lives to do what must be done. They called themselves the Brotherhood of the Dark Moon, and they were such an anathema to the pack that their very existence was barely acknowledged; the penalty for belonging, should one be discovered, was death.

Louis Phillipe kept his church at the bottom of the hill that was overlooked by a grand palais in the Valley of the Loire, conducting his affairs among the humans of the village and never overstepping his bounds. But he knew full well who, and what, the residents of the palais were. He listened with a thrill and yearning to the sounds of their wolf song at night, he watched them pass in their elegant human forms by day. He studied them from afar and adored them in silence.

And then one day Eudora Devoncroix, queen of all the pack, was returning from a journey north when her carriage broke a wheel not far from the doorstep of the church, and slipped into the ditch. The priest Louis Phillipe came to assist, as of course he would. But his human strength was not up to the task. He slipped in the mud, became trapped under the weight of the vehicle, and was gravely injured.

The queen's advisors suggested that the sensible thing to do, and perhaps even the kindest, would have been to end his suffering with a quick snap of his neck, and toss his body into the ditch to be disposed of by his own kind. But the leader of the pack, who no doubt was still pondering the strange customs of her fiancé toward humans, or perhaps even wanting to explore his theories for herself, gave another order. She commanded that the broken human should be taken back to the palais, where he could benefit from the healing skills of her own court.

The human priest mended quickly under the ministrations of the lupinotuum; their advanced medicines and healing techniques speeding the recovery process beyond anything that was known to his people. And in return, Eudora's education on the subject of humans grew by leaps and bounds, and she began to see for herself, and almost against her will, that the Fasburgs' claims about the intelligence of humans might be valid. He showed no fear of her, nor of any of their kind. He could quote Homer in the original Latin. He could play chess. He could speak of matters of philosophy that actually made sense to her. And his questions for her were as numerous as were hers for him; they seemed to hold a mutual fascination for one another. Eudora did not object. It is always flattering to be the object of another's adoration, and almost inevitably, affection is returned.

To change one's life, habits and deeply held convictions in an instant is not an easy thing, and the mere possibility that she might have been wrong about humans—that her father, her mother, their ancestors before them and indeed all the pack might have been wrong—the very notion shook the foundations of her world. Because of Louis Phillipe she began to change everything she had always believed, and to become someone she had never imagined.

And that was why his betrayal, when she discovered it, was so bitter.

Eudora the Queen was naturally aware of the threat posed by the Brotherhood of the Dark Moon—a band of misfits and outcasts dedicated to destroying the pack and all that it valued. They used their wealth, their wit and their influence to wage a secret war on all that was werewolf, rejecting the standards that had kept the race strong and powerful for over five centuries and disguising their true motives under the banner of balance in nature. She had heard rumors that they had even taken certain humans into their numbers, and shared with them secrets few werewolves knew and no human ever should. But she did not believe it until she saw with her own eyes, etched into the smooth flesh of the human's neck, the sign of the Brotherhood of the Dark Moon.

She was wounded to the core. He had used her for a fool and infiltrated the very heart of the pack, the palais itself. He had gained her confidence and caused her to question all she thought was true. She had come to think of him as friend. And now, he would cause her to order his death. And for that, above all else, she could never forgive him. She even went so far as to beg him to recant and betray his fellow brethren, so that she might have an excuse to save his life. He refused.

Louis Phillipe, this quiet scholar, this keeper of secrets, had sworn his fealty to the Brotherhood long before he knew and loved Eudora. And so had Eric Fasburg.

CHAPTER THIRTEEN

I
f the narrative of a man's life is dictated by his choices, I will take you now to the choice that determined the course of the rest of my life, and took away all the rest of my choices. It was the occasion of my twenty-first birthday, which is significant in human culture but not so much noted in the world of the loup garou. Still, I marked the date. I was legally an adult. I could manage my own funds, drink alcohol in adult establishments, vote and sign contracts. The fact that I had been doing all of those things, except, perhaps, voting, for some time now was beside the point. It was important to highlight the traditions of one's own culture.

I had been studying at Oxford University since I was sixteen and now was just completing my master's degree in anthropology. How does a home-schooled orphan, even an

132

exceptionally bright one, gain admittance to Oxford at the age of sixteen? He either has a very wealthy and influential sponsor, or he has a reputation for having faced down Nicholas Devoncroix during a pack hunt. Sometimes he has both.

I devoured my studies in my time at University, as I was expected to do. I had sex with human girls, as I was expected to do. I learned to enjoy the pursuits of ordinary young humans, more or less. And every weekend I traveled home to Venice. No sooner would I drop my bag inside the doorway than I would hear Lara's footsteps clattering in the marble hall and she would fling herself upon me and wrap her legs around my waist and cover my face with kisses and I would laugh and stagger and pretend to fall and kiss her back; I would kiss her back.

Because away from her, I was only half alive.

I loved Lara fiercely, possessively, and with a kind of intensity that I'm not sure it's possible to explain. She was mine, to protect, adore, cherish and care for. She always had been and always would be. She was everything I was and everything I could never be; she was entwined around my consciousness like ivy around a rose, she consumed me. Oh, how sorry I felt for the human girls in whose wanton, sweaty embraces I tried to escape the ache that was the absence of Lara. I never remembered their names. But even days later, Lara could smell them on me. And then the ache was like a black hole.

Because here is the most amazing, the most wondrous, and, inevitably, the most agonizing thing: as much as I adored Lara, she loved me even more.

In my years at the university I came across the names of Devoncroix and of Fasburg; I spent hours in the stacks, reading and researching and marveling at the hands behind the hands that had guided so much of human history. On the weekends I delved into the prince's private library, fascinated by the unexpected twists and turns in the Fasburg family history. I began to unravel the mystery of the human priest who, according to legend, had done them a service once long ago. I knew, long before I reached my majority, that the passion of my life would be research, whether it be in uncovering the secrets of the past or decoding the human genome. Having been raised in such a thick, enticing soup of arcane mystery, I cannot truthfully imagine ever having been lured by any other profession. And though it seemed to me then I was delving into the secrets of the ages, treading ground where none before me had ever gone, I should have known that I was uncovering only as much as the prince wished me to know. As much as any of them wished me to know.

And so when I was twenty-one, and too desperately absorbed in the present to give more than the vaguest of thoughts to the future, Lara crept up silently behind me in the great, mahogany shelved, vaulted-ceilinged library of the palazzo and slipped her hands around my eyes. She leaned in close to my ear, so that her hair tickled the back of my neck, and murmured in a voice that was throaty with laughter, "Today you are a man."

I smiled with the pure pleasure of having her near. I had been home from school for almost a month and was growing comfortable with seeing her again every day, but still her presence never failed to surprise me, and fill me with joy.

I was sitting at a big carved desk that was arranged in an alcove against a painted mural of nymphs at play, the papers I had just taken from the printer spread out before me. The computer stations that were located in several places around the grand room would have been an anachronism had they not been so sleek and compact as to be almost unnoticeable. It was 1991, and the loup garoux were already discarding as obsolete the technology humans would not enjoy for another twenty years.

I caught her wrists and pulled her around and down upon my knee. "And what was I before?"

She pretended to be very serious as she studied me, but her eyes were laughing. "I wish I knew."

How beautiful she was, with those magnificent green eyes and skin like satin and her thick dark hair pulled up atop her head in a playful ponytail that fell to her shoulders. She was wearing a tiny silk shift with big flowers that tied on one shoulder and barely covered the middle of her slender, naked thighs, and I let my hand caress the curve of her hip through the fabric, loving its feel and its familiarity. Loving her warmth and her weight and her shape and her scent; loving everything about her.

I said, "Do you know you might be related to the Devoncroix?"

She looped her arms around my neck, brought her face very close to mine, and said, "Do you know how much I don't care?"

"I'm serious." I reached behind me for one of the papers, teasing her because I knew how much it annoyed her when I became obsessed with my research. "I think your ancestor might have mated with Queen Eudora. I found some old writings of his."

She put the tip of her nose on the tip of my nose. "I," she said distinctly. "Don't. Care. Besides ..." She sprang up, catching my hand, eyes sparkling. "I have a surprise for you in the garden.

Come with me."

I let her tug me along to the courtyard outside the west entrance, with its wisteria covered arbor and weathered wicker furniture. It was a private place, used only by the family, and Lara and I used to love to play there. She made me close my eyes when we reached the door, and I let her lead me, stumbling, across the paving stones. Of course I peeked, but still I laughed out loud in delight when she positioned me before the table she had set up beneath the wisteria, and commanded me to open my eyes.

There was an elaborate cake in the center of the table, decorated with sugar flowers and garlands, tiered with dozens of tiny lit candles—I guessed twenty-one—that had begun to melt and drip wax all over the frosting. We never celebrated birthdays in this way, and I was touched that she had gone to the trouble to research the tradition and do this for me.

"Hurry!" she urged, clapping her hands in pleasure at my surprise. "Blow out the candles and make a wish!"

"All of those? By myself? You'll have to help."

So she leaned in close and we blew out the candles together and we laughed when wax and frosting spattered on the tablecloth. No one loved cake more than Lara, and she lost no time in cutting two slices while I poured the wine. We sat beside the fountain, where water splashed from a marble vessel with musical sounds onto a bed of polished blue glass pebbles below, and we toasted the future.

"So," she demanded, scooping up a large dollop of frosting with her finger and popping it into her mouth, "what did you wish for?"

"Not a thing," I told her. "I have everything I want right

here, right now." And to prove it, I leaned over and offered her a scoop of my frosting from my finger.

"You're lying," she said matter of factly, but accepted the frosting anyway. "You wouldn't waste a twenty-first birthday wish on nothing."

She was right of course. But what I had wished, I couldn't tell her.

"Anyway ..." She slanted me a sly glance. "I know what you wished for."

I set my cake aside and reached for her, smiling. "Do you now?"

She hopped up and whirled away, eyes dancing. "More cake?"

I leaned back and picked up my wine glass, smiling after her. "Wrong."

She cut herself another generous slice. When she returned to me she had her cake plate in one hand and the other hand behind her back. There was a look of glorious secrecy in her eyes. "This is what you wished for," she said, and taking her hand from behind her back, presented me with an envelope.

She watched me open it expectantly, and I was smiling, even through my puzzlement, when I drew out the contents. "Two tickets to Paris?"

"Two tickets to freedom," she corrected.

She put her cake plate on the retaining wall beside mine and sank into my lap. She must have seen something in my eyes because her arms went around me and she put her lips close to my face and there was urgency in her voice as she whispered, "I can't do this any longer, Emory. I have to get away from them. I've waited so long, but you have your silly degree now and you can go anywhere you want, if you don't like Paris, we'll go to New York or Sydney or Hong Kong, I don't care, it doesn't matter, you can teach at a university just as you always said you would and I'll be your wife and give lovely parties for all the humans you want to impress and I won't even mind if you spend your evenings in a dusty library somewhere, let's just go, Emory, oh please, let's just *go*."

She said it like that, all in a breath, and when she finished my head was spinning with her words. I took her face in my hands and tilted it away from mine so that I could see her eyes, and I felt dampness on my fingertips. My heart wrenched in my chest, and stuttered with longing, and at the same time broke in two.

Only in retrospect can I see what quiet courage it took for her to wait so patiently and so hopefully for this moment. While I was happily, feverishly and selfishly immersed in my studies, greedily taking in everything the prince had to offer and thinking of very little beyond my own needs, Lara had been thinking of this day. I would be twenty-one, I would have my degree, we would leave the Palazzo together. She could have left at any time, and every day she waited must have been torment for her. But she had waited for me. She had waited for me because she was Lara and she knew only one way to love: desperately, completely and single-mindedly. She had waited for me because we had been together for so long neither of us could imagine being apart. She had waited for me because she believed in me.

Even now, she could not see how dreadfully misplaced her faith in me was.

"Lara," I said hoarsely, "you know that can't be."

All these years I had never surrendered to the one thing I wanted more than anything in the world. All this time of loving her, of being with her, of knowing how easily and happily she would have given herself to me, I had never had sex with her. I don't mean to make myself sound noble, for I wasn't. Ask any of the girls I so carelessly and callously took in her place how noble I was. I was a bit of an idealist, yes. But my ideals were not for her as much as they were for me.

I don't know what, if anything, I imagined would become of us as adults. I know I never imagined my life without her. But to take her away, to live with her as my lover, to humiliate the prince and princess and incur the scorn of the pack ... that never had been within the realm of possibility.

She whispered feverishly, "It can. It can be. All we have to do is make it so."

"You'll be exiled," I said, desperately trying to make her understand what was at stake. The pack would turn its back on Lara ... and on me. Was it worth it?

She kissed me again, and I knew with all my soul that it was. It was.

"I don't care," she said, her voice low and tight. "It's not my pack. I don't belong with them. I belong with you."

I cupped my hands around her neck, breathing deeply of the fragrance of her skin as I tried to calm my thundering heart, my unsteady breath. I whispered, "Please don't do this. Lara, you know this is madness."

"No," she said. "It's madness to continue this way, pretending this is normal, pretending this is right." She gripped my hands at the back of her neck and held them hard. There was desperation in her eyes. "Let's go tonight, Emory, let's not wait another day, please. If we wait any longer I'm afraid ..." She hesitated, and dropped her eyes.

"What?" I demanded softly. "What are you afraid of?"

She looked at me again. "I'm afraid I'll lose you," she said simply.

Foolishly, I thought she was afraid I'd fall in love with some human girl. "You'll never lose me," I told her firmly. "Not to anyone."

"Tonight, please." Those brilliant, pained, soul-eating eyes flicked back and forth over mine, searching, begging. All I wanted to do was to make the desperation in her eyes go away.

And I remembered then the last time I had seen that look in her eyes. She had begged me to run away with her then, too. She had begged me to save her. And I had refused.

I felt a chill.

I said, "Prinze-Papa is taking me to dinner tonight. I can't refuse; he'll know why."

She stiffened in my arms with such a look of dread that I thought she might have misunderstood what I had said. But before I could clarify she said, "No." Her fingers tightened upon my skin, urgently. "Don't go with him tonight. Not tonight."

"Lara ..." I disentangled my hand from hers to stroke her hair, and because I simply could not bear that look of pleading in her eyes I brought my forehead to touch hers and I whispered, "Meet me then, at the station, at midnight. Don't be sad. I'll take you to Paris. We'll go tonight. I promise." I would like to believe that I had every intention of keeping that promise. But I think I only wanted to take the sadness from her eyes.

A measure of hope crept into her expression. "Come back to me, please," she begged softly. "Don't break my heart, Emory. I don't think I could recover from that."

I enfolded her in my embrace and promised her that I

wouldn't, and she did not smell the lie because at that time I believed with all my heart that I could never hurt her, that I would not even know how.

But some things are so inevitable it almost seems a waste of time to look back upon them, and worry the details, as though in the retelling one might find a different ending. There was only one possible ending. Lara knew that, I think, which was why she was so afraid. And so did the prince. It was no hardship for him to sacrifice the heart of his youngest daughter to the vision he had for me. Their race sees long, and it sees far. He knew what he was doing. He had known it from the moment he knelt before me and looked at me with his laughing eyes and said, *So, little man, will you come and live among us, and be one of us?*

CHAPTER FOURTEEN

I had my first taste of Armagnac that evening in the library with the prince. Outside the large arched window the sun turned the canal blood red. Inside, the wood beams, the ancient books, the fine paintings all were burnished with its rosy glow. The prince lifted his glass to me, smiling his approval as he set aside the papers he had just finished reading.

"And so," he congratulated me, "you have distinguished yourself with this research. I'm not certain anyone in our own race has ever uncovered so much detail regarding the truth of Queen Eudora."

I was enormously pleased. "I'm honored you think so, sir."

"Tell me, then. Is it your opinion that the good queen was enraptured of her human priest? Clearly he was utterly obsessed with her."

"It's difficult to say," I admitted. "It was far easier to uncover data on Montclaire than on the queen." My search for writings and records referencing the medieval priest had taken me into the dusty vaults of Oxford University, the Louvre, and even to the Vatican itself, both in person and via correspondence with other historians who had come across references to him in their own research. The field of medieval history is not so broad a one as might be expected, and eventually all roads cross if one is persistent enough.

"The human clergy of that era was trained to keep records," I explained further, "and they wrote elaborate letters. The loup garoux, however, do not generally keep written correspondence, or records of any kind."

"That's because our history is passed down by tradition," agreed the prince, "which does occasionally allow for exaggeration or misunderstanding. It will be useful to the pack to have your written history — even if it does occasionally reveal things about ourselves we would prefer not to know. Do you think they were lovers, the queen and this human priest?"

I said, "Nothing I've found suggests so. But my story is filled with gaps."

"It would be interesting, though, would it not, to discover that even the great Queen Eudora herself had a carnal lapse with a human?"

I said nothing, and he merely smiled, faintly.

He sipped his brandy, and when he lowered his glass, I tasted mine. I will never forget the sensation of that smooth rich Armagnac on my tongue, liquid gold, and the glow of the setting sun, and the breeze that wafted all the glory of Venice in through the open window to be captured, for just that moment, inside that room. I thought it was a perfect moment.

The prince was watching me, as he often did, with a studious, thoughtful expression on his face. He went on, "Of course you know the tragic end to which the human priest came. It has been ever so when humans have dared to love one of us."

I felt everything in my body quicken with attention. His eyes bored through to my soul.

"I wonder, however, if your studies have uncovered any reference to the suffering endured by the poor queen," he went on, his tone musing. "Very little thought is ever given to the pain she must have endured. She lost her betrothed, she lost her human, but most tragically of all she lost her faith. It was years before she found a mate, you know, and then one must wonder if it was not only from obligation. What a tragic end to a tale of such great passion."

I said, with a very great effort, "It seems to me a tale of destiny, sir."

"Destiny," he told me, "is what we make it. And it seems to me it would have been a much kinder thing had the human kept his place, and never tried to befriend the queen at all." I could see the crimson sunset reflected in his eyes, like bloody water on polished stone. "Because when humans and loup garoux indulge themselves in their passion for one another, it invariably ends badly for all concerned. I think you will agree that history bears this out."

I swallowed hard, but did not flinch from his gaze. I said, "Yes sir."

In a moment he gestured me to be seated, and made himself comfortable in the deep velvet chair across from me. He said, "I have never regretted taking you in, Emory. You've matured into a strong, dedicated young man, accomplished in every pursuit. You are as fine a human specimen as I have ever known, and proof of what is possible for your race, given the right circumstances. I am proud of what you've become."

"I'm glad of it, sir," I said sincerely. He had never spoken to me like that before.

He sipped his brandy, dark eyes watching while red light crept across the room. "But you are still human," he said. "And no human has ever been accepted into the pack."

There was no doubt in my mind that he knew about Lara's conversation with me in the garden. He knew about the tickets to Paris, which I had tucked safely away in my cupboard upstairs, and he knew that his own daughter had turned to me to help her escape his house. And as much as I wanted to drop my eyes in shame, I did not.

I said, keeping my voice strong even though my skin was beginning to prickle with the physical power of his gaze, "I know that, sir."

"Of course you do," he murmured approvingly. "You very likely know more about our history than I do by now. Some day you will no doubt be famous among the pack for your research."

I said, "That would be an honor."

"Because," he went on easily, "while no human has ever been accepted into the pack, there have been one or two, over time, who have done us a service, and earned our respect, and have been accepted *by* the pack. Life for these humans was vastly different than for others."

I knew, suddenly, we were no longer talking about writing history down. We were talking about *history*. My heartbeat speeded, acknowledging my understanding, and he heard it.

He lifted his glass. Red sparks caught in the crystal and shivered across his face. He sipped. "Have you given thought to your future?" he asked companionably, just as any father might ask of his son upon the occasion of his twenty-first birthday. "Do you have plans?"

I said, choosing my words with care, "I would like to continue to study, perhaps to travel, one day to teach the sciences. To live with honor, and to bring honor to you, and to everyone you love."

The faintest smile of approval. He sipped his brandy in silence for awhile, enjoying the dying evening, and so did I.

The crimson cast had faded from the sky; the golden rim upon the clouds had paled. Inside the room the shadows were blue and purple. The sounds of motorboats and laughter and fast Italian voices drifted up from the canal below as the population of Venice sailed off to meet their dinners. Somewhere in the distance a gondolier sang for the tourists. The dying light did harsh things to his face, planning it into sharp angles and sunken shadows. I could not see his eyes, though I thought I saw a glitter there, as hard as a sunspark caught on a blade, as he watched me in long and speculative silence. I could feel my future spinning slowly on the edge of that silence.

When at last he spoke his tone was mild, his expression easy.

"Well then," he said. "I promised you an evening together, and it's time we were on with it. I go tonight to a place few humans of this or any other century have seen, to participate in an ancient ritual few have ever witnessed. It is possible for you to be among those few, if you wish." He must have noted the speeding of my pulse, the catch of my breath. He must have smelled the anticipation that flooded my pores. Because he fixed me with his dark gaze and he added, "Of course, we are likely to be out quite late. Well past midnight."

146

I knew then what he had known since well before we sat down for this conversation — what, in fact, I had known as well. I was going to break Lara's heart. I would do that believing I spared her from a greater pain. I would do it to save her from the tragic ending I always had known was inevitable. I would do it believing I served a nobler purpose. But I would do it nonetheless.

Yet he kept his expression neutral, his tone conversational. "Or we could sit here for a time a longer, and enjoy another glass of brandy, and later take a vaporetto to Al Fontego and have some of Chef's excellent sea bass. I quite have a taste for it tonight myself, but you choose. After all ..." He smiled and raised his nearly empty glass to me. "It is your special night."

And just like that, I chose.

Renegade

Excerpt from DAWN TO DUSK: A TALE OF TWO SPECIES
by Emory Hilliford, PhD:

For Eudora the proof of trust misplaced was her broken heart. The treachery of the priest had only proven what she should never have doubted at all: the Fasburgs, with their simpering, indulgent ways toward humans, were wrong. Humans were a danger to the pack, to all it stood for, and Eric, the mighty prince of Fasburg, must be made to see that. The time for tolerance was over. The human population must be taught a lesson. And so, at the welcoming banquet arranged for her betrothed, Eudora declared that the traitorous human should be sentenced to death, and thrown to the pack at midnight.

But Eric, Prince Fasburg, could not allow a fellow Brother to suffer such a fate. He stole into the castle dungeon and freed the hapless human. Louis Phillipe should have fled the palace grounds, the province, the country, with his life as his treasure, never to look back. But he had learned to love the queen. He had come to know the glory of her kind. And he counted his life a small sacrifice for the knowledge.

Here is the truth about the deadly birth defect that was killing the offspring of the lupinotuum: it was carried in human blood. The reason the Fasburgs had thrived so well was because of their peaceful relationship with humans, and their lack of exposure to their blood. But the rest of the pack were hunters, and killers of humans. And once the disease entered the bloodline of a werewolf, it was there forever.

There was a cure for this disease, a simple remedy that could rid all the pack of its plague. But this cure had a steep price, and was known only to certain members of the Brotherhood of the Dark Moon. Its use was strictly forbidden. On that night, the human Louis Phillipe, who had come to know and love too well a species that

148

was not his own, broke the vow he had made to preserve the balance of nature, and he brought the cure to Eudora the queen.

The rest is the stuff of epic legend. Through the ages the tale was told of the human priest who loved the werewolf queen and who, having been discovered unwarned in her sleeping chamber, was torn to pieces by her guards. How she, the good queen Eudora, arose weeping from his bloodied corpse to vow to the skies that never again would a human being know harm from werewolf hand.

And this much is true. From that day forward there went out a decree: never again should one drop of human blood be spilled at the hand of a werewolf, no longer would humans be hunted or abused, and the penalty for ignoring or disobeying that law would be death, and the shame of all the pack. From that time forward, no werewolf child has reached the age of majority without making that most solemn covenant, Eudora's Vow.

And until this day, none of them has known the truth.

CHAPTER FIFTEEN

We traveled under the shadow of a midnight sky in the prince's private gondola down the Grand Canal to a narrow street that climbed an ancient bridge and wound its way to a tall narrow building with a door carved in worn wolves' heads. No one forced me to pass through that door, or to follow the prince down the steep stone staircase into a room that smelled of dampness and earth and candle wax and ancient secrets locked in stone. We entered a small anteroom lit only by two bare candles on opposite walls. The prince stripped off his clothes, and advised me to do the same. But when he dropped a cowl-hooded robe over his head, he did not pass one to me.

"No unproven human may come before us clothed," he told me. "It will be cold, but you're in no danger of hypothermia. You may leave at any time, and no one will think the less of you. What we offer is a gift, not a threat. Do you understand?"

I said that I did, and already I was shivering as he opened the door that led to another spiral stone staircase. We climbed down and down in the dark, for so long that it seemed the act of descending was a destination unto itself, the dark a tangible, breathing thing. The sound of the prince's bare feet on the stones before me was my only orientation. My hand trailed the wet stone wall for balance until my fingertips were numb. I could feel pressure in my ears and my chest, and I realized we were far below sea level; I could almost hear the weight of the ocean pressing on the walls and I marveled at how old this place must be, at the engineering that had kept it strong, at the unfathomable brilliance of those who had built it.

At last the footsteps stopped, another door opened, and I felt the gust of air that came from the cavernous room beyond. For a moment I was too disoriented, and my eyes were too slow to adjust to even the dim light beyond, to fully understand what I was seeing. Then I heard the prince's voice, loud over the murmurs of others, echoing throughout the room: "This is Emory, a human and a seeker, who is under my protection."

There was silence, and I felt the prince's hand on my bare shoulder, pushing me forward. The room was as big as a public auditorium, and it was filled with dozens of shapes in long cowled robes, like the prince wore. The hoods were up, so that no faces were visible, and when I glanced to my side, I saw that the prince had raised his hood as well. At some point during the hours that followed I became separated from him, and could no longer distinguish him from the others, or know whether or not he had even stayed. The only light came from a brazier in the center of the room, and from torches that were placed around its perimeter every dozen or so feet. The flames glistened off the weeping stone walls, and the air smelled of heat and burning pitch. The prince stepped away from me then, and I stood cold and naked while they passed before me in a ritual manner, each in turn circling me, inspecting me, taking in my scent, assessing me, memorizing me. I never saw a face. I did not know whether they were male or female, if they were strangers to me or acquaintances. But I knew what they were. Who they were.

The assemblage—I did not count how many, because I did not know to do so—completed their first examination of me, and then a pair of strong hands grasped my shoulders and pushed me down, forcing me into a sitting position against the cold stones in a pool of shadow. I folded my legs beneath me, trying to gain my balance, and I felt a warm spray of liquid on my face. I recoiled instinctively, brushing at my face, and there was another spurt of liquid, acrid and hot, and another, in my hair, on my shoulders. The smell was strong, and unmistakable. They were urinating on me. I recoiled and shouted in protest, I tried to shield myself, but the urine splashed in my eyes and my mouth; it drenched my hair and trickled in hot salty paths down my back and chest and pooled in my chest. I tried not to gag. I breathed between my fingers. They were marking me.

I, a twenty-one-year-old human boy, had been brought into the ranks of a fraternity as old as recorded history, so secretive that even the leader of the pack denied its existence. *You may leave at any time*, the prince had said. Yet even though I sat trembling with cold and fear and humiliation, even though the pounding of my heart shook my entire body, even though all the horrors of Dante's hell might be yet ahead of me in this place, nothing could have made me leave. I saw my destiny unfold before me, and I embraced it.

You will want to know the details, the rituals, the secrets of that night. I will not tell them. There was no torture. There were no honeyed drinks laced with hallucinogens, there was no bacchanalia of sexual frenzy, there was no coercion. The prince did well when he chose me, he did well when he raised me, he knew when I was ready. He would not have brought me there otherwise. What I did, I did of my own free and gladly given will.

There was no time. I might have been there hours, or days. At some point, when I was weak with exhaustion and cold and the emotional and mental impact of what I had experienced, the torches were extinguished, one by one. I sat in the center of their circle in absolute blackness and silence for so long that I seemed to float. I lost the sensation of my arms and legs, of the cold and the aching muscles, and became something entirely outside myself. I realized later that this was an effect of sensory deprivation, and so, perhaps was what happened later, but I don't think so. After an eternity of this floating void, I became aware of a soft shushing sound, rhythmic and soothing, like wind through the leaves, like the breath of a sleeping infant, accompanied by the faintest tympani of a soft-skinned drum. It was singular at first, an eerie, lonely sound, but then it grew weightier, as though multiple instruments were playing the same song, and then it became a mighty wave of susurration and a thunder of drums and I realized what I was hearing was their heartbeats, the pulse of their blood, and it seemed something not outside of me but a part of me; it bore me up and into it and I trembled with the sheer ecstasy of being part of them, of knowing such a sensation. The air was suffused with a perfume, no, a dozen perfumes, sweet and bitter, sharp and smooth, rich

153

dark spices and heady chocolate notes. I could taste their scents, they flowed into me, rolled around inside my cells, filled me with euphoria and yearning and wonder, each of them unique, each a part of me. I came as close as it is possible to come to knowing what it was to be one of them; that was their gift to me. No human, having come so near to touching the face of the gods, could remain unchanged.

And so I took the vow of fealty, I smelled the burning of my own flesh as the brand of the cross sank its mark into my neck, because that was what I was born to do, what I had been raised to do, what I had been trained to do. I belonged to them now, and forever more.

But when had I not?

CHAPTER SIXTEEN

I had been underground for almost three days. When I emerged my senses were befuddled, my body was all but broken, and I think had it not been for what happened afterward, I might even have convinced myself the whole had been a dream. The prince took me to a private suite in one of his hotels; I don't recall which one. I remember lying down fully clothed atop a tufted silk counterpane in an ornately decorated room. And then I remember Lara's voice: "Oh, my love, what have they done to you? What have they done?"

The voice came to me as though through a tunnel, and I saw the blur of her face, such concern in her eyes, such anxiety. I wanted to comfort her, to tell her everything was all right, I was fine, all was well. I was too tired. I couldn't lift my arms to hold her, couldn't summon the breath to speak. I could barely keep my eyes open. I felt raindrops on my face. And then I realized they were not raindrops. They were tears.

I dozed and dreamed, dreamed and woke, drifted in and out of fever. I dreamed of countryside flashing by from a train window, of Lara touching my face with a cool cloth, of the leather seats of a luxury car. I dreamed of Lara in a big hat and sunglasses, and Lara spreading over me a wool cape trimmed with foxtails.

When I awoke I was lying on a tufted couch in what appeared to be a hotel lobby — no, it was larger than a hotel lobby, and more sparsely furnished. The great domed ceiling was glass, like a solarium, but the dust and grime on its panels was so thick the sky was barely visible. I pushed aside Lara's cape and sat up slowly.

Lara sat beside me swiftly. "Oh, Emory, you're awake. I was so worried." She pressed a cup of cold liquid into my hand. "Drink this. You haven't eaten or drank anything in days."

I glanced into the cup groggily. It had a greenish tint. "What is it?" My voice was gruff, as though from long disuse. I coughed to clear it.

"Sugar, mostly, and some mint. I don't trust the water here, so I boiled it and made tea."

I took a cautious sip, and then drank more. It was thick and sweet, and the mint cleared my head. I looked around slowly.

I could see our footprints in the layer of dust on the pink marble floor. There were tall Palladian windows all around the room, and a thin light filtered through the vines that covered them, giving the room an eerie underwater feel. The walls were covered in panels of silk moiré that might once have been blue; now it was faded and torn in more than one place, nibbled by mice in the corners.

"What is this place?" I said. "Where are we?"

156

"It's the old palais, just outside Lyons," she told me. "It's been abandoned for almost a century. It was the only place I could think of that we would be safe. Humans are too afraid to come here, and the loup garoux never think of it anymore."

"Palais Devoncroix?" I stared at her. "Eudora's palais?"

She smiled. "I thought you'd like it here."

I stood up. The sudden movement made my head spin, and the burn on the back of my neck throbbed like fire. Instinctively my hand went to the bandage that was hidden beneath the high neck of my sweater, and I winced when I touched it.

Alarm crossed her face and her nostrils flared as she caught the scent of the wound. "You're hurt." She reached for my neck but I caught her fingers.

"It's nothing." I tried to find a smile. "A muscle strain, that's all." I don't know why I lied. I couldn't keep it from her forever. But I was suddenly ashamed, and uneasy.

Lara caressed my arm, her eyes still dark with concern. "You're dehydrated," she said, "and half starved. I brought some food from the village while you were sleeping. Come, let's eat. Time enough to explore later."

She started to move away, but I caught her arm. "Lara, what is this? What have you done? Why are we here?"

"Oh, Emory." Her eyes were soft with compassion, and she lightly touched my cheek. "Did you think I wouldn't try to find you? You are my dearest friend and my truest love. How could I leave you there?"

My head swirled with images of the night. The cold, the darkness, the visions, the rapture, the molten red cross that seared its mark into my flesh. The vow. My voice was hoarse. "How did you find me?"

157

She lowered her gaze, her lashes forming crescent shadows on her pale skin. "I knew you wouldn't meet me at the station," she said quietly. "I overheard what Papa said to you. I know you thought you couldn't defy him, and you were trying to protect me."

My heart clenched at that, and I had to look away in shame, because even after I had broken my promise to her, even after I had hurt and betrayed her she still loved me, and would not abandon me. The depth of her devotion made me feel small, and unworthy. Human. And I could not tell her what I had done.

I said simply, "I will never love anyone the way I love you." Beneath its damp and oozing bandage, the brand on my neck burned fiercely.

"I was angry at first," she said. "You had chosen him over me and I had begged you not to go, I had implored you to love me. I cursed you to your human hell and I wanted to leave you to wallow in the juices of your own mistakes ... But then you didn't come home. I went searching for you, and finally found the hotel where Papa had left you. You were barely alive, barely conscious. I couldn't leave you there." She smiled a little, a tight, uncertain thing. "I told the conductor on the train you were drunk. You slept the whole way. And then I got a car in Paris and drove here."

When she lifted her eyes to me again there was a hardness there, a cool and quiet determination I had never seen before. When I last had seen her, she had been a girl. She was no longer.

She said, "Don't think I don't know who he is, my papa. He offered you a bargain of some kind if you would go away from me, and he made it look like a gift. Don't think I don't know his seduction. But it is a cruel and calculating thing that will one day

158

exact its pound of flesh, and a pint of blood as well. I love you too much to leave you to him."

I touched her hair, cupped her head with both hands. I draped my arms about her neck. I brought my forehead slowly, gently to rest against hers. I breathed, "Oh, my love."

I felt old. I had the taste of a thousand smoky nights on my tongue, the weight of a hundred thousand days in my bones. The innocence in me was gone. From the things I had seen, and done, and promised there was no turning back. Yet when I touched her, when I held her, I felt a thrill of such wonder, such incredible possibility, that it was as though I had been created anew for just this moment.

I wanted to tell her the truth. I wanted to tell her the choice I had made, the vow I had given, the possibilities that I had let slip through my fingers. For a hundred reasons, I could not.

I whispered, "I will never deserve you."

I saw the tendons in her throat tighten as she drew in a breath, and started to speak, but then the breath was released unspoken with the taste of strawberries that fluttered across my lips.

She forced a faint, brave smile and she looked at me with eyes that begged me to say no more. That begged me to allow her to believe in me, for just a little longer.

She said, "I found wine, too. Come, we'll make a picnic."

We ate fresh bread and soft cheese with fruit and wine, and afterwards we explored the great abandoned halls that had been erected as a monument to the most magnificent creatures ever to walk the face of the earth. Those walls bore the scars of the

159

masterpieces that once had hung there, the walkways displayed pedestals that were devoid of sculpture, and the rooms echoed with the absence of the opulence that once had furnished them. But here Eudora the Queen once had walked. Here had sat Elise Devoncroix, and her father before her and his before him. Here had been born the tales of treachery, heroism, brutality and sacrifice that I had only imagined. Here the walls sang with magic.

We could not see it all, of course. It was far too vast, and many of the rooms were not accessible to human forms. But when Lara, with a secret smile that lit up every cell of her being, took my hand and led me through a series of musty corridors that opened into large stone sleeping chamber, my breath caught. I knew where I was.

I said softly, "Is this — can this be — Eudora's bedchamber?"

Lara pressed her cheek briefly against my shoulder. "Mother tells of visiting it when it was a museum room. Of course all the real treasures were moved to Castle Devoncroix and put on display there. They still have her nightdress, stained with the blood of the human, in a big glass case. I guess they couldn't move the bed without dismantling the room, and the other pieces are reproductions. But it feels magical, doesn't it?"

The bed was a wide elevated platform of smooth, highly polished stone that seemed to grow right from the wall that formed its headboard. It looked like nothing so much as a great stone altar. There were tall carved chairs and marble tables, and silver candlesticks grown dark with age. In a human museum, these cast-offs would have been highly guarded and proudly displayed for their age and workmanship; to the Devoncroix, whose coffers were overflowing with treasures more ancient and

160

more rare, they were not worth packing.

I walked around the room in state of suspended wonder, touching a table here, a chairback there, the mammoth beam of the carved oak mantelpiece. I walked to the window and looked through the thick wavy glass to the valley below. Through the tangle of vines and thick forest branches I could see the spire of a small stone church. I managed, "Is that ..."

Lara nodded, looking as proud and happy as a child whose secret gift has been delivered at last and received with all the joy she had anticipated. "That's the church where her carriage broke down, and she met the human priest."

I turned, my breath all but suspended, and walked back to the great bed, and the most incredible wonder of all. All along the wall and upward to the high ceiling a living canopy of roses had formed. The sturdy vines had dug themselves into the stones, and the blossoms they produced were a rich dark pink with a blood red center. The wall was lush with blooms, and a carpet of pink petals was thick upon the stone bed. The entire room was filled with the breath of roses.

"It's called the Eudora rose," Lara said, coming over to me. "Mother tried to grow them in our garden in Venice but they were engineered to grow here, and don't thrive anywhere else. Of course the legend is that they sprang from the blood of the human, but they were actually created by a horticulturist in the eighteen hundreds. Mother said they brought in special soil for the planter boxes at first, but eventually the root system grew all the way through the stones to the hillside below."

I had felt this way once or twice before. When I stood on Hadrian's Wall and looked across the Tiber River, knowing that gods had stood there before me. When I touched the fallen

161

columns of the Parthenon and stepped into the shadow of the Great Pyramid of Giza. *Here lies history. Here lies magic. Here lies the imprint of a thousand powerful souls who have gone before you.*

I had walked into a fairy tale. I had walked into the promise of the future. My heart soared, and everything that I was, or had ever been meant to be, congealed into that moment.

I climbed the steps and stood atop the stone platform, scattering the delicate rustle of rose petals as I moved. I reached to snap off a blossom and turned, holding it out to Lara. She came to stand beside me, and I tucked the rose into her hair. "There aren't any thorns," I noticed.

"That's how you know it's a hybrid." Her eyes filled the whole world. "Nature always makes thorns."

I kissed her then, and her arms wound about my neck and she pressed herself into me and though we had shared a hundred kisses before this one was like the first. This kiss was greedy and hungry and huge and demanding, for if we had been children before we were no longer. Now I belonged to something larger than myself, now I came to her as one who knew too much and had lived too little, and with a wild aching hunger for something that I knew already was lost to me forever.

I tore my mouth away from hers. I breathed, "I have to tell you."

"No, don't tell me." Her eyes were hot and wild, and she thrust her hands beneath my sweater, against my bare chest, caressing my heartbeat. "Don't say anything. I don't want to know. I want you. I want you forever. That's all I ever wanted. Just to be with you. "

I caught her hands, and moved them away. We sank to our knees together on the stone bed with the rose petals drifting down around us, the sound of our breathing echoing in the empty chamber, and I pulled my sweater over my head. I held her eyes as I removed the bandage from my neck and revealed to her the wound there. And I saw the dread that filled her face was nothing more than the proof of a truth she already knew.

She whispered, "No." She looked at the swollen red cross burned into my neck, she looked into my eyes, and the horror that crept into her voice was mixed with pleading, begging me to deny what she already had seen. "What have you done?"

Alarm squeezed through the heart that had beat so wildly with desire only moments ago. I reached for her, but she shrank away. "No, Lara, you don't understand. Listen to me."

She shook her head. "You chose him," she said softly, her eyes dark with disbelief and a bleak and terrible hurt. "I have loved you with all my heart since before I knew how to love, and now I don't know how to stop. But you chose him."

Desperation rose inside me and tried to choke off the words. I wanted to make it right, I was desperate to make it right as I had always done before. But this time words were not enough. I think I knew that from the beginning, but I had to try anyway. "That's not the way it was, Lara. You know I never wanted to hurt you. Prinze-Papa, the others, they offered me a gift, a chance to be one of them, one of *you.* I couldn't walk away. How could I?"

Her fingertip was unsteady as it lightly traced the crescent scar beneath my eye. "What they offer is not a gift," she said. "And the price, when it comes, will be a terrible one." She lifted eyes to me that were dark with despair and brilliant with tears. "Oh, Emory, don't you think I was offered the same gift as you? It is my heritage, isn't it? Just because they call themselves a Brotherhood does not mean there are no females in their ranks.

But I rejected their gift, I rejected it because I could not, would not pay their price!"

The tears spilled over and caught in her voice. "You belong to them now, don't you see that? You belong to them and you can never belong to another. The price is your soul."

"Lara, no." I caught her hands but they balled into fists inside my fingers; I held them even more tightly and the desperation that was winding its steel band around my chest threatened to burst my heart. "Don't you know nothing can take me away from you? Didn't I promise you that?"

"How many more promises will you make me, Emory?" she cried. "How many more times must I believe you?"

She flung my hands away with a gesture that sent me reeling backwards, and the fire that blazed in her eyes dried the tears. She grasped the bodice of her dress and tore it with a sudden savage motion that bared her breasts and her abdomen, and then, with a single slash of her nails, she shredded the remainder of the fabric and let it fall away from her body in tatters. I sucked in my breath as she stood before me on the stone bed, nude and beautiful and ablaze with fury and pain and defiance.

"Do you want to know what it is to be one of us, Emory? Is that what you want?" She caught my hands and pulled me up beside her. Her heat seared my skin, her fingers crushed my own. Her fever was a wild and raging thing that was torn with pain and desperation. "Know me, then." She pressed herself to me, the fever of her torso branding my chest, the pressure of her pelvis burning through my trousers and into my loins. "Know my pain, know my longing, know my love for you! Know the heart that you have broken, know what we could have been and know what you have lost! Be what I am then, love me! Love me!"

164

The small hairs on my arms and legs raised as though with a
sudden wave of polarity, and the air in the room cracked and
flashed with static lightning. Her eyes were wild with the
passion of a great, unspeakable power, and I could not have
pulled my hands away from hers had I tried. Her hair lifted and
lashed about her body as though on a violent wind, and sparks
flew from it. Rose petals scattered and whirled and turned about
her, suspended on their own magnetic charge. I drew in a gasp of
air so thin it shimmered like glass around us. The hot prickling
sensation in my skin was like a thousand crawling ants, and I
cried out her name, I tried to pull away but she held me firm. I
screamed with pain and terror, and my voice was matched with
hers as she tossed back her head, crying out her power, her
longing, her fierce and glorious nature. I felt the great glowing
surge of rapture that formed in my core and spread upward
through my chest and burst from my fingertips, that danced
before my eyes, that swirled through the fibers of my skin and the
nerves of my teeth and the cells of my nails and my hair. It was
intensely sexual, powerful, galvanizing; it was, at its essence, *her*:
Lara in all her wonder, all her devotion, all her glory, pure,
magnificent, essential, Lara. It was a pain so pure it cleaved me in
two; an emptiness so vast it sucked out my soul, a longing and a
thirst and a wild and desperate hope, it was Lara. It was a heart
too broken to beat but too brave to stop, it was a love so pure it
could not conceive of betrayal, it was Lara. My very pores wept
great, bitter tears for what she was, what I could never be; what I
had taken from her.

She filled my eyes with her wild and searing beauty. She was
a thousand shimmering, bursting glowing lights. She was in my
cells, in my lungs, on my tongue, in my brain and the hairs upon

my skin and my fingernails and in my heart, in my heart. I felt her, I saw her, burst into all the colors of ecstasy and it was in my body, too, what she was; it was in my soul. When the great clap of magnetic force threw us apart I saw, just for a moment I saw, the magnificent wolf she had become and I felt her power in my bones; I was, for the briefest moment of sheer splendor and desperate, aching loneliness, what she was. And even when my frail human form could no longer support her immensity and I lost consciousness, my brain was filled with images of powerful legs racing down forest paths, of flashing greenery, of cold streams and brilliant clean air rushing over the tongue ... and of a bleak and bitter sadness that was bigger than the sky, darker than the night, and so hungry that it threatened to consume me alive, because I knew she was saying good-bye.

Though I waited for days, she never returned. When I left the palais, I did so alone.

When the force of Lara's Change separated us, a thin layer of skin was torn from my fingers and palms where our hands were linked. Her brand was on my soul just as plainly as the mark of the cross was burned into my skin.

In the same way a part of my essence, the very particles of my soul, had been torn away from me. Sometimes my hands still stung with the memory of what had been peeled away. And sometimes, I think, her soul still ached for the parts of her that were missing.

And though there were days when she was so much inside of me and so far away from me, that I knew the agony a caged animal must feel just before it chews off its own leg, I never

166

approached her again. I stayed away because I knew that the pain of being with her, and knowing again how deeply I had hurt her, would be worse than the pain of staying apart. I stayed away because I could not hurt her again, and I knew I was destined to do so. I stayed away because I knew that if I asked, she could refuse me nothing. And though it broke my heart anew every day, I was determined not to ask.

Until the day that I did.

CHAPTER SEVENTEEN

The Present

The silence hung over the room like a shadow for a moment. Then Rolfe reached for an apple, sliced out a wedge and bit into it, chewing thoughtfully. "Do you want to know what I think? I think you never loved her half so much as you loved what she was. Lara must have known that on some level. You went with the prince that night because you saw your chance to finally be one of them, and when you did you failed her test. But she had only herself to blame."

Emory said tiredly, "I suppose."

"Still, it was a tragic end to a doomed love story, just as the prince predicted. Wouldn't you agree?"

Emory sipped his drink.

Rolfe glanced at the screen of his phone, which lay on the table between them. A small red light was blinking. He picked it up, touched the screen, and made a mild sound of interest in his throat as he viewed the contents. "The president of the World Bank has been assassinated. A brutal killing, really. It seems the poor thing was eviscerated. They still haven't found most of her internal organs." He shrugged and put the phone away. "Ah well, it was time for a change. Of course, there's likely to be a period of financial chaos, but that will only make it that more effective when the proper party does step in to take control."

Emory leaned back in his chair with his glass cupped against his chest, watching him. "We live in interesting times."

Rolfe spread thick soft cheese onto a slice of bread. "This Camembert is excellent. You really should try some. "

Emory said nothing.

Rolfe regarded him for a moment, chewing. He said, "You know, Professor, I don't believe you that you never had sex with that lovely creature."

"Believe what you wish."

"You have said yourself that their allure is virtually irresistible. And frankly, I have seen the famous Lara Fasburg. Is there any male alive, of any species, who isn't just a little in love with her?"

Emory worked hard to keep his heartbeat steady, his temperature even.

"You can tell me, you know." Rolfe gave a fair approximation of a lascivious grin. "I won't judge."

Emory said, his gaze steady, "I wouldn't care if you did."

In a moment, Rolfe shrugged. "Tell me this then. This mating bond you spoke of, can it exist between humans and the loup garoux?"

"I'm sure I wouldn't know."

Renegade

"Come along, Professor." He looked bored. "You are the foremost authority on these creatures in the world. If you don't know, who would?"

For another moment it appeared Emory would not answer. Then he said, "There may be a bond of sorts. My understanding is that it may be more intense upon the part of the human than the loup garou. It's not a mating bond. They mate only in wolf form."

A faint smile. "Which would seem to be nature's safeguard against the cross breeding of the species."

"Yes."

Rolfe lifted the wine bottle with a questioning look. Emory held out his glass. Rolfe filled it, and sat back. "And so was it worth it, then, this Brotherhood of yours?"

Emory said, "The Brotherhood, as it once was, no longer exists. It has deteriorated into a gang of cutthroats and hooligans."

"A bit harsh, don't you think?"

"They use intimidation and threats to achieve their ends. They kill at will. They have betrayed their vows."

Rolfe gave a small, entirely neutral smile. "What a coincidence. So have you."

He wiped his fingers on a napkin, and gently swirled the wine in his glass. "What became of you, then, after your lovely Lara departed?"

A brief silence, the shadow of a memory. "I returned to Venice briefly, but there was nothing left for me there. For a time I had some notion of finding her, but eventually ..." He lifted his own glass, and sipped, his lashes lowered. "I realized there was no point. The children we had been were gone. There was nothing left to save. And I had nothing to offer her but pain." Absently, he raised his hand to the back of his neck, lightly touching the scar there, and dropped it again. "Lara found the world in which she belonged, and it was the world of humans. My world. And the only world in which I had ever wanted to live was her world. The world of the loup garoux. A fine irony, wouldn't you say?"

"Worthy of O'Henry."

"The humans couldn't resist Lara. They invited her to their parties and behind the velvet ropes of their exclusive clubs, onboard their yachts and their private jets. Like her mother, she was active in human charities, and over the years I would see her name here and there in connection with one foundation or another. She became great friends with the British royals, and used to appear with Princess Diana on behalf of this cause or that event. She was probably one of the most photographed women in the world."

"And you?"

He shrugged. "My life continued much along the course I outlined for the prince that day in his library. I took several degrees. I studied with the best scientists in the pack. I continued my research into their history. I had access to their laboratories and libraries. In return, I would occasionally be asked to do some small thing—transpose a number here or delay a test result there, deliver a package or a message. I never noticed that any of my efforts had an effect on any outcome—but then I suppose that was the point."

"How did they contact you?"

"Sometimes through a secret e-mail account, sometimes by telephone on a scrambled channel."

"And you never questioned their orders?"

"Of course not. I knew what our mission was and to question the methods would have been pointless."

"Besides," supplied Rolfe helpfully, "they only asked for small favors."

"Yes."

"And Lara? Did you ever see her again?"

He drank, his eyes on the opposite wall. "Not for a long time."

"But you kept up with her, so to speak. You knew where she was and what she was about?"

Emory looked at him for a moment. "If I asked, would you push aside your hair, and show me the back of your neck?"

He looked mildly surprised, and then laughed softly. "No. I would not. Not because I care one way or the other, but because it is much more enjoyable for me to watch you speculate. Now we both will want to see how this story ends, won't we?"

Emory frowned into his wine. "I know how it ends."

Rolfe reached again for the knife and sliced a bit of cheese. He popped it into his mouth, the black eyes sparking with mirth. "My dear fellow," he said, "you can't begin to imagine how it ends. Truly you can't."

Renegade

PART TWO

GOTTERDAMMERUNG

November, 1999

173

Renegade

From an essay by Emory Hilliford, age 7
Palazzo Fasburg, Italy

Aristophanes was a Greek story teller and a loup garou who lived a long time ago. He helped civilize humans. He told a story about how humans and loup garou used to be all one person, with four legs and four arms and two heads, all mixed up together. But they were so strong that they made the gods afraid. So the gods cut all the loup garou and the humans in half, so they wouldn't be strong any more. That's how we all ended up with only one head. And ever since, the humans and the loup garou have been looking for a way to get back together.

I think the gods were stupid.

Emory Hilliford
Human

CHAPTER EIGHTEEN

Ten thousand years ago the African plain was thick with herd beasts, lush with edible grasses and fruits, sparkling with clear pools and waterfalls. Species lupinotuum ran free in packs so large that when they moved the earth thundered and the air grew dim with their dust. They hunted, they feasted, they played, they grew. For uncounted generations this corner of the earth suckled and protected them, until, eventually, they outgrew its shelter and moved on.

Now the herds were thinned and often confined to wildlife parks to protect them from human scavengers. The grasses were still tall and lush, but the pools were shallow and far between. The land could not support a pack anymore, even a small one. But still there was something in the soul of their species that pulled them, in its own way, toward their origins. When their feet touch the ground there, it felt like home. When they scented the air, it smelled of new earth and hot wild blood. When they gazed up into a sky littered with stars, they knew they had seen those stars before.

It should not have been surprising then, that after a search of almost thirty years, they should find the creature here. In the place they all once had called home.

They watched with night scopes from a distance of a mile or so away. He stalked a leopard in naked human form, his movements as economical and precise as theirs might have been in wolf form. He circled the creature silently, narrowing his approach, and when he moved in for the kill the animal must have caught his scent; it turned and sprang into the air over his head. In a flash of white limbs and blurred movement he snatched the cat from the air in mid-flight, snapped its neck with a single shake, and tore open its chest cavity in one single smooth movement, and without so much as the crack of a twig to break the silence of the night. He spread open the carcass on the ground beside a stream, and settled down to eat.

The two who watched him from afar lowered their glasses, and moved in silently.

It all happened quickly, smoothly and as flawlessly as it had been planned. They were the best hunters in the pack. They had their orders, and did not make mistakes. Two of them in wolf form flowed down from the hill from either flank, as silent as oil and as swift as snakebite. They lunged and pinned the creature to the ground before the hunk of bloody lung he had just torn off could pass his teeth. Almost in the same movement, with a single breath, two more hunters, these in human form, splashed across the stream. One aimed a tranquilizer gun and released a dart filled with enough paralytic to fell an elephant. The other swung a titanium-fiber reinforced tiger net in a perfect arc that sailed across the stream and wrapped itself around the prone body just as the two wolves who held him bounded back. Flawless, efficient. They had spent thirty years training for this moment and now it was done.

The two wolves circled warily, their nostrils twitching with the scent of warm fresh meat that emanated from the cat's body, their eyes never leaving the naked, wire-muscled, human-formed male who lay unconscious and tangled in the netting before them. His mouth and hands were bloody from his feast. The soles of his feet were black. His eyes were closed, his chest unmoving.

The two in human form were dressed identically in form-fitting black and carried black packs across their backs. One of them slipped his backpack off his shoulders and began unpacking sterile tubing and a lightweight portable ventilator. "Get that net tight around him," he said, "but leave me room around the face to work. We've got four minutes to get this trach tube in before he's brain dead." Then, casting a quick, distasteful glance at the creature in the net, he added, "Poor mad devil. Might be best for him if he was."

"We have our orders," said the other, moving in close to grasp the cinch ends of the net. "Bring him in alive or not at all. He looks dead. Are you certain—"

He peered through the tiger netting that wrapped the man's face, leaning close for just an instant, and suddenly the eyes popped open. They were bright blue, alert, and unsurprised. He said politely, in English, "Gentlemen, good evening."

And before the hunter could gasp his surprise or recoil, before his colleague could pull the trigger on the dart gun that would deliver another 100 mg of curare into the creature's neck, he thrust a hand through the reinforced tiger netting as though it were made of spider webs and grabbed the hunter's throat. The two wolves roared and sprang, the dart hissed silently into its target, and the hunter fell back, blank-eyed, clutching the bloody hole in his throat.

The creature clothed in man skin, now with enough curare in his system to kill four humans or two werewolves, collapsed again to the ground. His eyes were fixed open, but his lungs stopped expanding, his heart stopped pumping, his muscles loosened. And as his fingers uncurled, the length of the hunter's esophagus dropped from them, spattering into a pool of cat's blood.

CHAPTER NINETEEN

Lara was at a party at one of those fabulous glittering beach houses in Malibu when she met Nicholas Devoncroix for the first time since the summer on Tyche. It might seem odd that in all this time they had not crossed paths, even in passing, but anyone who had been paying attention could quickly see they didn't exactly travel in the same circles. Human princes and kings took her on their jets and their yachts, to their ski chalets and their private islands. When Nicholas met with humans it was in soundproof board rooms under heavy security. Paparazzi camped outside her Paris townhouse and her New York apartment, and followed her from club to luncheon, from limo to red carpet. She always dressed outrageously for them, in red-leather corset and diamond-studded tongue, perhaps, or spiked boots and a feathered bikini, and they cheered their approval. When Nicholas was

179

photographed, it was usually in dark glasses with his head turning away from the camera. Nicholas climbed Mount Everest; Lara climbed the steps of the Kodak Theater. Nicholas controlled an empire, but Lara controlled her own destiny.

Or so she thought.

The world of humans embraced her, and she immersed herself in it, for it was the only place she was at home. Of course she consorted with her own kind from time to time—among the fast crowd with whom she usually ran they were somewhat ubiquitous, and many of them found her as amusing as the humans did—but Nicholas Devoncroix was not one of them. That was why it was so odd to find him in Malibu, California, at the kind of party even his minions would not generally deign to attend.

The house was one of those three-story glass and steel monstrosities that seemed to suck the starlight from the sky and the sound from the surf with its pure, unadulterated pretension. There was a swimming pool on the roof and two others, surrounded by a jungle labyrinth of paved patio, tropical plants and hot tubs, on the ground overlooking the beach. The music was so loud it pulsated, and the entire place reeked of sex and bitter sweat and drugs, as such places usually did. Lara had only agreed to come on a whim, and already she was growing bored. Crack cocaine of course had no effect on her species, and she had long since grown tired of pretending it did. Heroin and other opiates were equally useless, except as surgical anesthetics, and the way humans behaved under their influence was not in the least amusing. As for the so-called sensory enhancing pleasure drugs that so proliferated gatherings such as this, not one of them could come close to mimicking the sensory state that Lara enjoyed when perfectly sober.

She had been known to get roaring drunk on brandy on occasion, however, and she did enjoy the pleasant buzz from a good strong cigarette. For the most part, though, Lara had begun to conclude that Californians give universally dull parties. There was never enough to eat and the wine was always below par. She was just taking her little pearl-studded phone out of her purse to call for a car—she couldn't even remember the names of any of the humans she had arrived with, although she was fairly certain at least one of them was quite famous in his own way—when there was a little frisson of electricity in the air, a shimmer of sharp scent like the taste of ozone after a summer storm, and Nicholas Devoncroix stood in the teakwood arch of the glass paneled doorway.

He was an extraordinary looking creature, tall and slim with flame blue eyes and sharp, cool features. His entrance into a room would have drawn attention even had it not been for his natural electrochemical magnetism. He wore a black silk tee shirt with the long sleeves pushed up above the elbows and white jeans. His pale hair, which he kept long about his shoulders in the traditional fashion, was gently tousled by the sea breeze. And as he stood there, gazing around the room in a leisurely manner that could not be mistaken for anything other than arrogant, all eyes turned, as though under compulsion, toward him. Conversations skipped a beat. Drinks were lifted and forgotten. Laughter died. Such was the effect the most powerful of their kind had upon humans.

It was only for a fraction of a second of course, and then the humans resumed their activities, feeling foolish perhaps, and only a little uneasy as he began to move among them. Lara dropped her phone back into her purse, curious.

There were only three or four loup garoux at the party, and all of them were just as riveted, and as perplexed, by the sudden appearance of the heir designee as Lara was. One of them, a music producer with several multi-platinum records to his credit, sidled up to her and murmured, "Well, well. To what do we owe the honor?"

She gave him a brief scowl of annoyance and turned away, reaching for the fizzy drink she had recently set aside. "I'm sure I wouldn't know."

She sipped the drink and moved toward the balcony but kept Nicholas Devoncroix in the corner of her eye.

It wasn't, of course, that Nicholas was a recluse; not by any means. He was well known to enjoy expensive parties and the most exclusive clubs, and he always had at least one gorgeous loup garou female hanging off his arm. Three years ago, at a huge pack ceremony Lara had not bothered to attend, he had been anointed leader pro-tem of the pack, which meant that over the next several years he would co-rule with his father, learning and proving himself, while the power passed gradually and peacefully into his hands. In that capacity, he spent most of his time earning the trust of the industrial and political leaders, the financiers and innovators who quietly ran the world on behalf of the pack. He was occasionally seen at a state dinner, or in the company of other famous and influential leaders, both human and loup garoux. He did not, however, socialize casually, particularly with humans and particularly not at a party like this. It simply wasn't protocol. And, for someone who was already positioned to take over the pack that more or less controlled the financial, technological and political destiny of the world, there was very little point in it.

Lara wondered idly whether he would come over to her. It would be a deliberate snub if he did not, although she had certainly done her part to snub the pack and all it stood for over the years. Nonetheless, as a matter of good manners, Nicholas was required to greet and inquire after the families of each member of the pack who was present. The intricately tangled web of human diplomacy is only a shallow imitation of the protocols that govern the lupinotuum.

Lara went out upon the balcony, where the sea breeze played with her hair and tickled her skin, and the ocean, two stories and some hundred yards away, created a pleasant susurration in the distance. Not far off shore a boat was anchored, all dressed up with tiny white lights like a Christmas tree, and beyond it a fishing boat with a big search light on the prow crossed the horizon. Even the sea was never quiet off the coast of California. The night was studded with the glow of windows in every direction, and the light hurt her sensitive night-vision eyes. So she chose instead to rest against the rail, fix her gaze on the distance, and look at nothing at all.

There was a man with a beard and glazed-over eyes sitting on the floor in the corner, stroking a Maltese dog. But for the glitter of its marble-like eyes — and the smell, of course — one would have been hard-put to determine the dog was real. On one of the wooden chaises, two human women were locked in an embrace, and from another, a man absently sipped a drink while filming them with a small video camera. The clatter of activity from inside spilled through the glass doors. Lara tried to follow Nicholas's scent, but the ocean breeze made it difficult to do so.

And suddenly it wasn't.

She knew that he had come onto the balcony first because of the prickling in her skin, a hundred million tiny hairs being pulled toward his electrical charge. Then his scent infused her: the smell of thunder, rain on hot stones, kinetic energy. There was no other scent in the world like it, and no real words to describe it. Among their species, the very presence of that scent excited nerve endings, quickened senses, stirred blood. It was genetic.

He let the glass doors close on the cacophony inside and came over to Lara. The little Maltese in the corner bared its teeth and then whimpered and ran away. The man with the glazed eyes continued to stroke empty air.

Lara turned to face Nicholas Devoncroix. As he did her hair, charged with the electricity of his presence, floated in strands away from her shoulders and toward him, just as it had done the first time they had met as children all those years ago. She caught it back impatiently with one hand.

"Miss Fasburg," he said politely. "Your health?"

He didn't really want to know about her health of course. It was just a greeting. She tried to meet his gaze but instinct kicked in and she bowed her head as dutifully as any other pack sycophant. She really had no choice. His sexual chemistry was vivid, and that low-level thrum of his energy could act like a hypnotic on an unsuspecting female. The sensation caught her off guard, and then made her defensive. And then, because she was annoyed with both herself and with him for making her feel that way, she extended her bowed head into a low, court curtsey, her hand uplifted to him in the manner of old.

She replied, "Excellent, thank you." And, with a smirk hidden by her bowed head, added, "Your Majesty."

184

He did not take her extended hand, and she was left to straighten from the curtsey without the benefit of his assistance – which was no small feat in four-inch Manolo Blahniks. His face showed no humor whatsoever.

"And your family?"

Lara was beginning to regain her equilibrium, both physically and emotionally, and she reclaimed the drink she had left on the rail. "I really couldn't guess."

He said, "I saw your mother in Paris last week."

That surprised her. "Did you?"

"She expressed a certain …" he made a deliberate pause over the word, "concern, regarding your welfare."

It was all she could do not to stare at him. "Why?" What she was thinking was, *Why are you still talking to me?*

His expression was utterly phlegmatic as he answered, "Apparently there was a photograph of you posing nude atop some pyramid or another. It seemed a bit dangerous to her."

The photograph to which he referred was actually one of Lara's favorites. It had been taken at Chichen Itza, and she was captured in the process of stepping off one of the high steps into the clear blue Mexican sky. The photographer had wanted to make a statement about sacrifice, and apparently he succeeded because the photograph won a very prestigious award and went at auction for a great deal of money.

Of course Lara had excellent balance and she couldn't imagine the princess had really been concerned for her safety. If anything, she would have been pleased.

"And there was that distressing video of you and the Brazilian millionaire …"

Lara tried to think which one he meant.

"And the rumors about your intentions with the young Sheik have concerned us all, as I'm sure you can imagine."

Lara stared at him. His delivery was perfectly flat, his expression utterly composed, yet she caught the very faintest trace of humor around the corners of his eyes and inhaled a whiff of it from his skin. And she couldn't believe it: he was teasing her.

She said, "Did you really see my mother?"

He inclined his head. In better light, she might have detected a smile. "At a reception at the Libyan embassy. I was negotiating oil rights. She was looking beautiful. She sends her love."

Lara was for a moment at a loss for words. She took a sip of her drink, trying to compose herself. Her heart was fluttering with confusion, and of course he could hear it. She said, in a moment, "What are you doing here?"

"I had business with the host."

"Oh." She glanced around. "Who is the host?"

He seemed amused. "One of your cousins, actually."

"Oh," she said again, and felt a little foolish. This was not a familiar feeling for her, and she blamed Nicholas Devoncroix for it. "What kind of business?"

His look told her she had gone too far. The heir designee does not explain his business to anyone. She shrugged, and half turned back toward the rail, sipping the drink which had, unfortunately, gone flat.

He glanced around until he spotted the spiral staircase that wound to the ground floor and nodded toward it. "This noise hurts my head. Walk with me."

Surprise speeded her pulse, but she kept her composure otherwise. "Why?"

He lifted an eyebrow. "Because I am your pack leader and I command it."

Lara caught a soft laugh in her throat. "Not yet, you're not," she told him. "And not my pack."

He replied without missing a beat, "Because I'm bored and would enjoy the chance for an intelligent conversation."

She turned and regarded him thoughtfully for a moment. She smiled slowly. "Now," she said, "you have my attention."

They went down the winding steps, through the jungle garden and past the pool that glowed with such surreal underwater lighting it looked as though a space ship had landed there. Now and then they passed humans having surreptitious sex against a wall or brokering deals of one sort or another; drinking, eating, smoking, laughing too loudly and talking too loudly. The whole of it could easily give one a headache after a time, and Lara was as glad to be away as Nicholas was.

They crossed the wooden boardwalk and when they reached the beach Lara slipped off her shoes and carried them by the straps. Nicholas kicked out of his loafers and left them in the sand, but she loved her Manolos. Besides, they'd cost over eight hundred dollars, US.

There were still humans on the beach, even at 1:30 in the morning, but they were few and far between, and the sound of the surf and the taste of the spray drowned out their presence nicely. A subtle moon cast blue-green shadows on the distant foam, and the sea looked like a great black sheet of cellophane, gently rolling this way and that.

Nicholas said after a time, "What do you see in them?"

Lara's nerves went taut. She felt like a child in a schoolroom. "In who?"

"Humans."

She laughed a little, and hoped her relief was not too evident. For some reason she had thought he had brought her down to the beach to say something of importance; now she realized that he was simply looking for idle conversation. She began to relax. "In general, or is there one in particular you have in mind?"

He slanted a glance toward her. "You are as impudent as ever, I see."

Lara shrugged. She barely remembered having two words with him from that long ago summer, but if she had given the impression of impudence, it was not one she regretted. She said, "We'd all be somewhat the worse off without them, you know. Something a prospective pack leader might be well advised to keep in mind."

"I find them tiresome."

"I find them fascinating." *And*, she wanted to add, *they adore me. It's good to be adored.* But she didn't say it. She wasn't *that* impudent.

He said, "I have a diamond mine in South Africa that appears to have paid out. A human has offered me twice its actual value. Should I sell?"

Lara was interested. She loved word puzzles. "Has it really paid out?"

"No."

"Then absolutely you should sell. Take the money, invest it for the pack, and in a generation or less, when human technology has been unable to detect what you already know is there, you'll buy it back at half what you were paid, reopen it and make your fortune. Meanwhile, the human company will have paid the taxes, fought the wars to keep it safe, and done all of those other boring but necessary things that crop up when matters of great value are involved. Really, Nicholas, I may adore them, but I'm not an idiot."

He laughed. It was an oddly thrilling sound to her ears. "So I see."

She felt oddly out of her body, walking along the beach with him, chatting as though they were old friends, and yet rarely had she been so fully in it. The wind played with her hair and tossed the folds of her little silk dress this way and that and brought with it the taste of sea and salt. She was richly, acutely aware of the cold wet sand between her toes and the flow of Nicholas's hair around his shoulders. Every now and again she would become aware of his scent, so sharp and powerful and completely out of place in her comfortable human world. It was intoxicating.

And puzzling.

He said, "Of course, there is a flaw in your reasoning. Human society is infuriatingly unpredictable. In a generation's time they may have blown up the mine, been invaded by a foreign power, or sold it to the highest bidder a dozen times over. They might have closed up the entrance and built a city over it, or filled it with poison gas, or used it as a nuclear test facility. Or they might, of course, have accidentally stumbled upon its hidden resources. And then where would I be?"

"Regretting you'd ever taken the advice of a human-lover you picked up at a Malibu party, I suspect." She shrugged her shoulders. "Which is why you are pack leader and I am not."

He stopped unexpectedly and scooped his fingers through the wet sand, bringing up a handful of sea snails, still alive in their shells. His sense of smell was really quite extraordinary. He closed his fist on the bounty, cracking the shells, and popped the tender meat of one in his mouth. Then he surprised her by scooping out another and offering it to her on the tip of his finger.

There is quite a bit of ritual and protocol within the pack that surrounds the giving and taking of food, particularly between those of vastly differing status. It might have seemed like a casual gesture; it was far from it.

Lara took the little bit of cold meat on her tongue. It tasted like salt and sex, and the particles of sand from Nicholas's finger. He watched as she swallowed, his face planed by moonlight, his eyes shadowed. He cracked another shell, ate the contents, and discarded the remnants. They started walking again.

"I don't visit the ocean often," he said. "I'm put in mind of that summer we spent in the Greek isles, with your family. It was the last time I saw you, I think."

They had strayed close to the tide line, and a froth of cool water covered Lara's toes, splashing Nicholas's white jeans. She said, without looking at him, "You did me a kindness then. I never thanked you."

And he replied simply, "I never expected it." He added, "I confess I'm curious though. Who was it who did that to you? No one ever spoke about what happened. My father would have seen them punished."

There was a particularly savage custom regarding First Hunt called "hobbling," in which the youngest, weakest and slowest members were cut off from the rest of the pack and bound, forelimb and rear limb, to the prey, and left to fight or run until they either escaped the bonds or killed the herd beast. It was the finest kind of torment, to be bound to the screaming, panicked animal, dashed against boulders, flung to the ground, battered senseless, all the while tasting blood and breathing hot terror, unable to escape, unable even to gain purchase with teeth or claws, until finally the poor beast died of fright or the victim managed, somehow, to rip out its guts and chew her way free.

Of course the practice was considered barbaric and had been outlawed for centuries, but no one would pretend that it didn't still go on. Those who were smart enough and fast enough would never know the terror and humiliation of First Hunt hobbling. Those who were not could only hope no one ever found out.

Lara had really never had a chance. She was a natural target for the crueler young loup garoux, and she lacked the confidence to even try to escape them. She had never truly believed Emory could protect her, and as soon as the hunt started it became more important to her that he should not witness her humiliation than that she avoid it, so she tried to hide in the confusion. She was captured immediately, of course.

Nicholas had found Lara, so badly battered that she was barely conscious, and freed her from the corpse of the beast. She lost consciousness with the effort of transforming to human. She had always quietly admired the honor in him that caused him to say nothing about the manner in which he had found her, but then their own peculiar brand of honor was the hallmark of the Devoncroix. To have brought the matter to light would have humiliated her parents and his hosts, and brought further discord between the families. And there was no point in ruining everyone's holiday.

She said with a shrug, "What difference did it make? Besides, all I wanted to do was forget."

She never did, of course. She still had nightmares.

Another wave sloshed closer, soaking his jeans up to the

191

ankle. "Was it from your family or mine?"

Lara laughed a little, uncomfortably, and slanted a glance up at him. "Yours, of course. And it was two of them — your nephews, Anson and Nieles. I think they only meant it as a game," she felt compelled to add. "They didn't intend any disrespect to your father."

"Ah, I should have guessed." His tone was mild. "They were incorrigible little brutes, even then."

She couldn't help remarking, "A characteristic for which the Devoncroix are somewhat renowned. No disrespect, of course."

There was a spark in his eyes, and a small, speculative smile played with his lips as he glanced at her. "Of course."

She said, feeling bold, "Why are you here?"

He walked with his hands clasped lightly behind his back, his head tilted upward toward the stars so that his hair was combed back from his face, his strong neck exposed. He had the air of someone who knew his own appeal, and wore it easily. He said, "We're launching a new satellite next week. Some of the technology is being developed in California, and it's behind schedule."

"I see."

"And also, to attend this party."

"I should imagine you could attend any party you cared to."

"Yes, but you are never at any of them. Why is that, do you suppose?"

Lara was a little taken aback. "Probably because I've never been invited."

That seemed to amuse him. "I shouldn't be surprised. You've become quite notorious among the pack, you know."

She affected modesty. "I try."

"That wasn't necessarily a compliment."

Lara laughed. "I didn't imagine it was. The Fasburgs have forever gone their own way in the world and the Devoncroix have forever disapproved, and I don't see why that should change now."

He said, "Perhaps. But I didn't say I disapproved."

Once again, he caught her off guard. She didn't know what to say. They walked in silence for a few steps.

"Do you ever see that human your father was so fond of?"

"No." But her throat constricted a little, involuntarily, with the word. Even now, even after all this time, the thought of him hurt. "I believe Papa keeps in touch."

"He was an odd sort. He has started recording some of the history of the pack for us. Bizarre stuff, most of it. "

Lara said nothing.

He turned then, and surprised her by grasping her neck from the back in one strong hand, drawing her close to him, dipping his face to hers. She was too shocked to protest as he inhaled her scent and then, with absolutely no warning whatsoever, turned her face to his. He tasted her skin with his tongue, and her lips, and then her teeth, and the electric thrill that crackled in her hair sang through the nerves, hummed sweet and high in her ears, melted muscles and sinew. Of course she opened her mouth for him, of course she tasted his tongue on hers and of course her blood went hot and wild.

He murmured against her neck, "You are exquisite. I want to taste you naked. I want to run with you."

And Lara said, quite steadily, "You are presumptuous."

"You arouse me."

"Hardly a noteworthy accomplishment, in your human

form."

He raised his eyes to hers, jewels in the dark. And he smiled. He turned and started walking again. Lara kept the pace.

Nicholas maintained his easy gait, watching the stars, and his tone was casual as he spoke. "I see your photograph from time to time, I hear the stories of your outrageous behavior. I have been somewhat fascinated. I wanted to meet you. And now I have."

He stopped then, and turned toward the sea. "Do you see that boat out there?" He nodded toward the twinkling lights of the yacht she had noticed earlier.

Lara nodded.

He slipped his shirt over his head and dropped it to the sand. "It's mine." He unsnapped his jeans.

Lara murmured, "Of course it is."

He surprised her with a grin, and stepped out of his jeans. "Good night, Lara Fasburg. You have been as interesting as I thought you'd be."

Lara watched him wade naked into the surf chest deep, and then dive into the black water. He left her in a rather poetic reversal of her most vivid memory of him from all those years ago, swimming out to sea.

And she still wasn't entirely sure why he had found her in the first place.

Wrapped in a silk robe with a towel around his neck, Nicholas took his wine onto the deck and settled into a chair from which he could watch the play of lights onshore. The sea breeze dried his hair and the remaining moisture from his skin. A steward brought a platter of fruit and dark chocolate and set it on the teak table at his elbow. Absently, Nicholas selected a cherry, sucked out the pulp, and crunched the pit with his teeth.

"Success in your mission?"

A tall, dark haired werewolf stepped out of the shadows and helped himself to a morsel of chocolate. His name was Garret Landseer, and he was one of the few people in the world Nicholas trusted. They had been born three days apart, raised together as cubs in the nursery at Castle Devoncroix, and had grown up besting each other at every challenge until Nicholas, simply by virtue of being who he was, had proven himself unbeatable. And in doing so, had won Garret's loyalty forever.

"In a manner of speaking." Nicholas's tone was preoccupied. "She knows nothing of the human."

Garret was Nicholas's oldest friend and only confidant. He was also a pack security expert, and this news troubled him, but only mildly. "That is disappointing. The situation would have had a much swifter resolution if we had had a direct line to him."

Nicholas sipped his wine. "True enough."

Garret watched him carefully in the dark. "There must be a Fasburg connection, there's no doubt of that. No one else in the pack has connections with a human so highly placed, and no other human has such access."

"So it would appear." Nicholas found another cherry. "I found her ... interesting."

Garret settled himself into a chair within reaching distance of the chocolate. "And how did she find you?"

Nicholas lifted his glass. "Resistible."

Garret paused with the chocolate partway to his mouth and slanted him a companionable grin. "Shall I have her killed, mon liege?"

Nicholas sipped his wine. "Fortunately for her, lack of judgment in a female is not a capital offense. Besides, I intend to give her another chance."

Garret bit into a chocolate, still amused. "Perhaps I should warn her."

Nicholas said thoughtfully, "It makes no sense, you know. Petty sabotage, minor theft ... nothing that would do any real damage to a project or gain any advantage for the saboteur. Why would anyone risk the wrath of the pack for such absurdities?"

Garret said, "It's a common practice to target low-risk projects when testing espionage techniques. Perhaps they are looking for weaknesses in our security. Perhaps it's a trap. "

Nicholas was silent for a moment, watching the sea. "Perhaps it's a distraction."

Garret looked at him alertly, waiting for him to continue, but he did not. He said, "Have you brought this to the attention of your father?"

Nicholas's brows came together in the dark. "The situation is mine to deal with." He did not say what they both were thinking: it was possible that the entire intrigue had been arranged by the elder Devoncroix as a test of efficiency. It would not be the first time. The transfer of power within the pack was a matter of immeasurable consequence, which was why it took place over a period of decades rather than months or even years. No measures were too extreme to ensure that the heir designee was prepared in every way to uphold the enormous responsibility of his office.

Garret said, "While you were away, we received a new alert. Unauthorized activity on Channel 4 spiked at forty percent."

Channel 4 was code for their most secure communications

network. It was used primarily in times of crisis, when the pack Council or the pack leader determined it was necessary to keep information secret even from the most highly placed pack members. No one was authorized to use Channel 4 without Garret's knowledge. Or Nicholas's.

"Origination?"

Garret said, "Castle Devoncroix."

Nicholas nodded slowly, and sipped his drink. "So. It has gone that far."

"Yes." A silence. "What would you have me do?"

Nicholas watched the sea, and the lights from shore that glinted on its ripples, and the big ugly over-bright house where Lara was.

"Wait," he replied, at length. "We wait."

CHAPTER TWENTY

L ara saw Nicholas again in New York, two weeks later. She was attending a concert at Lincoln Center, and he was drinking champagne in the lobby. The great marble hall was crowded with elegantly dressed and richly perfumed bodies, many of them loup garou. Their voices echoed and blended and bounced off the high ceilings and walls in a cacophony of anticipation, like the sound of an orchestra tuning before the performance. Lara's senses were wonderfully dazzled by it all—the smell of humans, the richness of loup garoux, the thrill of music, the swell of excitement—and yet the moment she stepped into the building his scent isolated itself from all the others, his heartbeat separated itself from the hum of the others and the signature of his presence registered itself in the cilia of every cell in her body. Instinctively she turned in his direction.

In a hall that was thick with people, he stood in a clearing of about three feet in diameter. His formal wear was by Armani, his blond hair tied back at the nape, his expression cool and disinterested. When he saw her, he lifted his glass in a small salute. She turned to murmur a few words to the group with which she had arrived, and she went over to him. The strobe of a photographer's light followed her.

"Don't you find that annoying?" was his greeting to her. He lifted his hand, and before it had fallen again to his side someone pressed a glass of champagne on her.

Lara accepted the champagne with an admiring lift of her brow, and replied. "If you mean the photographers, I barely notice them anymore. Why do you ask? Is there a law against your being photographed?"

"Only the law that governs good taste," he replied with a bored glance around the room. Almost immediately, several of the photographers decided they had met their quota for the evening and turned to leave. "You look lovely," he added, when his eyes returned to her.

"I know." She was wearing a floor length red Dior gown with diamond spaghetti straps and silver Jimmy Choo's. Her hair was swept up to display simple diamond dangle earrings, one carat each.

She sipped her champagne. "I understand Anson and Nieles were transferred to the Sudan last week."

"They were growing soft in Paris."

She regarded him steadily. "I don't need you to fight my battles for me, Nicholas Devoncroix, particularly at this late date."

He replied, "It's hardly my intention to do so. I won't have a coward in my company, and what they did to you was both cowardly and brutish. I'd like to take you to dinner."

"I have concert tickets."

"The concert is only fair. I've heard it."

"I'm with friends."

"Do you mean those humans?"

She smiled. "I should introduce you."

"Thank you, no."

"And I thank you for the champagne." She took a last sip and placed the glass in his hand. He looked surprised. "I've looked forward to this concert, so I will decline your invitation to dinner. But if you like, we could meet afterwards for coffee. There's a quaint place called Milieu that overlooks the Park."

He frowned. "I'm not familiar with it."

"No doubt because it's solely owned and operated by humans." She smiled sweetly as she turned. "Send your car."

Nicholas did in fact send his car for her, and the driver navigated his way through the cold November streets without Lara having to give directions. A dewy rain clung to the windshield and refracted the lights of the city into colorful shimmering sparks. The strains of the concert still sang in her head. She settled back in the car in her long white suede coat with its high fur lined collar and cuffs and sipped the brandy that was provided from the bar. Nicholas did not join her.

She surrendered her coat at the restaurant and asked for a private table. Because they knew her she was immediately escorted past the big windowed main dining room with its charming views of the lamp-lit paths and horse-drawn carriages of Central Park, past the art-deco walls and clinking silver and chattering voices to a room with a fireplace and a half dozen tables, only three of which were occupied. The tablecloths were black, the place settings were white, the napkins red. There was a red rose in the center of each table. She chose a table near the fireplace and ordered a large hot chocolate with mounds of whipped cream. She was licking the first dollop of cream off the back of her spoon when she felt the familiar prickle along the back of her neck and Nicholas slid into the chair opposite her. The other diners cast quick, almost covert glances at him, and then resumed their meals.

He glanced around. "An interesting choice."

She scooped up another spoonful of sweet heavy cream. "No one you know ever comes here," she pointed out. "And I think you have something to say to me that is not meant for the ears of the pack."

A mild lift of his brow. "Do you indeed?"

"I know the limits of my allure, Monsieur Devoncroix. Your embrace on the beach was to scent my truth, not because you found me irresistible." Absently she stirred the chocolate, watching him. "What I can't understand is why you thought I would bother lying to you, and on what subject. However, if you followed me to New York, I suspect you may be ready to continue your interrogation."

"You do flatter yourself, my dear." He lifted his finger for a waiter, and ordered a coffee. When they were once again alone he leaned back in his chair and regarded her with relaxed amusement. "I did not follow you. As it happens, I live here."

"You live many places."

"As do you."

"Fifteen years have passed since our last meeting, and suddenly we meet twice in the same month, and on different coasts. I repeat, I know the limits of my allure."

His expression grew serious. "There's been a complex breach

of security in my office. Coded data is being transferred between a high-clearance IP address and one of our research facilities here in New York. We suspect the human Hilliford is somehow involved."

She flicked her tongue around the rim of her cup, clearing it of cream, and then took a sip of the chocolate. "That seems odd. I thought he had clearance to do his own research inside the pack. Why should he bother to be covert about it?"

Nicholas said, "Don't be naïve. The only entrée into the pack he has at all is through your father, and that is limited at best."

"Then it appears to me you should be talking to my father."

"I intend to. But you wanted to know why I sought you out. That is why."

"A waste of effort on your part. All I know of my father's interests are what I hear in passing."

The coffee arrived in a sleek silver half-pot with a matching cream pitcher and a bowl of raw sugar in glistening crystals. The waiter filled a square glass cup and set it before Nicholas. Nicholas dismissed him with a nod.

Nicholas said, "I take it then you have not heard anything that might shed light on my current dilemma."

She sipped her chocolate. "It seems unlikely. I have very few acquaintances in the pack and, as I said, I don't keep up with figures from my past."

He watched her steadily. "And if you did know something that could be of assistance to me, would you tell me?"

"No."

"Why not?"

She laughed softly. "I barely know you. What I do know I don't like. Our families have been enemies for generations. I have no interest in helping you and there's nothing in it for me. Shall I go on?"

He tapped his lips lightly with his forefinger, hiding a faint smile. "You are surprising."

"Only because you haven't been paying attention."

"As a matter of fact," he assured her, "I have been paying a great deal of attention to you of late." He took up his coffee.

"Should I be afraid?"

The smile deepened at one corner, and there was actually a twinkle in his eyes. She had always believed him to be humorless, and this caused her to feel slightly unbalanced.

He said, "I have heard you don't run."

"That would be a phenomenon, wouldn't it?" She gazed over his shoulder at the fire and sipped her chocolate. "We must run or die."

He was silent for a moment. Then he said, "I would like cake. These human chefs of yours—can they bake?"

It was her turn to smile. "Extraordinarily."

They ate cake stuffed with walnuts and sweet butter cream, and afterwards they walked outside into a night that smelled of wet fuel and cooked food and stale garbage and, faint and far away, evergreen. Nicholas touched her shoulder in a gesture that struck Lara as rather human, and they crossed the street to the park.

It was late, and it was raining lightly, and because of that the human population that generally frequented the park was greatly diminished. There was a policeman on a horse a mile or so away, the steady clopping of its hooves muffled by the damp. A shadow darted across the hazy puddle of light from a street lamp. The scent of loup garoux in their natural forms was distinct. As the hour grew later, it would grow stronger. On nights like this, Central Park was a favorite place to run.

"My father tells of a time when we once hunted here," Nicholas observed. "The park was kept stocked with small game."

"I suppose there weren't any restaurants here then."

He glanced at her to see if she was joking but her face gave no indication. Misty rain beaded in her hair and she turned up the collar of her coat. The fur caressed her cheek.

He said, "I would like you to come to Alaska." The words surprised him, but when they were spoken, he found he did not regret them.

She replied, "I have been to Alaska, for your Ascension ceremony, as a matter of fact. I did not find it to my liking."

"You were a child."

"You said unkind things about my looks."

"Did I?" He seemed genuinely puzzled. "I can't imagine. Your human form is very appealing."

"So I am told."

She tucked her hands into her pockets, and they turned in unspoken agreement onto a shadowed path that led down a set of shallow steps away from the glare of artificial lights and into a natural night that was easier on their eyes. A carpet of damp leaves was heavy underfoot, smelling of humus and decay. The click of her heels was muffled here, and his footsteps were almost silent.

He said, "How did you come to be who you are, Lara Fasburg? I am curious."

She smiled in the dark. "I had no choice. I was never any good at being anything else."

"Don't be facile."

"But it's true. I had no talent for music or drawing or invention or architecture or engineering. The pack values excellence and I never bothered to learn to be excellent at anything. Human standards are much lower. All they require is that you possess a pleasing form and an amusing lifestyle, and they will make you a hero. I find I quite like being a hero."

"You have a peculiar sense of humor."

She was thoughtful for a moment. "This is the flaw in the way the pack is structured. You—and your family of course, and your mighty corporation with all its various holdings and its outrageous wealth—you control an empire that is largely composed of humans, that is almost completely dependent on humans both as consumers and as your work force, and that exists, if you are completely honest, largely for the sake of humans. Yet you know nothing about humans. You hold them in contempt, and you segregate yourself from them."

"Untrue. I dined with a human only yesterday."

"And probably left him with the bill."

"Of course."

She lifted her shoulders in an exaggerated gesture of exasperation. "I despair of you."

He smiled, watching her from the corner of his eye. "You could teach me tolerance."

"I haven't the time."

"Then run with me."

The words were unexpected, and they caused a catch in her heartbeat, a flush of pleasured excitement that started in her core and crept outward to her fingers, her toes, forming dewy drops of heat where her fur collar touched her neck. To run with a member of the opposite sex was the boldest kind of flirtation, and an invitation from someone as sexually potent as Nicholas Devoncroix was not an easy thing to refuse. She said, shifting her gaze away in confusion, "You surely don't mean now."

"Why not?" He turned his face up to misty rain, scenting the air. She could feel the surge of energy from him as he did so. "It's a fine cold night and my human form begins to chafe."

She couldn't stop the quick pounding thrill of her pulse, as though her body were reacting to an invisible caress. Perhaps it was. She tightened her shoulders and thrust her hands deeper into her pockets. "For one thing," she told him, "I am very fond of this gown."

"My people will take care of it."

She cast a quick suspicious glance around and sensed nothing, no one. "For another, I'm not quite certain how I feel about running with someone who has people follow him around for the sole purpose of taking care of his clothes."

"I arouse you," he observed. Of course he could feel her heat, smell her excitement.

She did not look at him. "Hardly a noteworthy accomplishment in my human form."

He swung gracefully in front of her and caught the collar of her coat lightly in his hands. In the dark she saw only his eyes, but her senses roared with his presence. "Then," he said, "let's dispense with it."

With a gentle tug, he slid the coat off her shoulders, and down her arms. Her skin prickled instinctively in the cold. She removed her hands from her pockets, and the coat puddled around her feet.

She said, with her eyes fastened on his, "You waste your

charms on me. Why?"

"Because they are not wasted. You intrigue me." He took off his coat and tossed it aside, and his eyes never left hers. Heat and scent, raw and sexual, billowed from him.

She said, "I will not run with someone I don't trust." But she breathed deeply of him, feeling a little drunk with the sensation.

He took her earrings, one in each hand, and slid them deftly out of her ears, dropping them into his pocket. "I don't think I'm the one you mistrust."

He thrust his fingers into her hair, plucking out the pins one by one. Even in the dampness, her hair crackled to his touch, strands of it floating toward him, entangling in his fingers.

Lara caught his wrists and pulled his hands away from her scalp, holding them hard in the space between her face and his. She said lowly, "Do you see these hands?" Her eyes glittered in the night. Cold rain glistened on her face and trickled over her bare shoulders. Her fingers were iron, and his pulses throbbed beneath them with raging life. "It was hands such as these that built this park and the skyscrapers that look down on it. Hands such as these painted the Mona Lisa and wrote Eudora's vow. And these legs ..." she stepped forward, thrusting her knee between his legs, her ankle winding around his, her thigh hard against his. "These two strong straight legs are the legs that dance *Romeo and Juliet,* not the legs that race mindlessly across a plain. This is what we are at our best, Nicholas Devoncroix." She released his hands abruptly and stepped away from him. "The rest is mere savagery."

His blood roared in her ears. The feel of his skin and the hard sinews of his arms still burned her fingertips. His eyes were a quiet fire that consumed without burning. She watched as his fingers loosened his silk tie, and the buttons of his shirt. His voice was low and still. "Run with me tonight," he said, "and tomorrow I will dance with you."

If ever there was a moment when she might have walked away, it was then. Her heart pounded. Her breath dried up. And she did not walk away.

His clothes fell away. The night sparked with the sharp charred ozone smell of him and her skin tingled and burned in response. Anger and desire and a sweet helpless hunger for the wildness that was him, and that was her, clutched at her center and seared through her veins. He stepped into her; he took the straps of her gown between his fingers. His eyes were the only lights in the night, and they burned blue-black.

"Who are you, Lara Fasburg?" he said softly. He snapped the straps between his fingers, and the fabric slid down her body like a lover's hands, caressing each curve.

She stepped out of her gown, and the diamond straps glittered like raindrops on the ground. The air grew thick with the clashing molecules of the coming storm and drawing it in was like breathing honey. He stepped back, holding her with his eyes, and when he moved, his hair whirled and lashed around him as though borne on a violent wind, and it glowed with a blue iridescence that cast shadows on his skin. She kicked off her shoes. She heard the high sweet note of music trilling in her ears, and she knew it was the sound of his blood surging through his veins, of his power transmuting liquid to fire, melting capillaries, bursting vessels, transforming that which was once corporeal into something much more than mortal. Oxygen leached from the air and into the light and power that was his Becoming. She felt the glorious ache of magnificent force building in her womb,

208

tightening her spine, bursting through her lungs and swelling in her breasts and sparking through her fingertips.

He turned to her, he fastened her with his lightning eyes. He lifted his arms and with a flash of white gold color and a thunderous explosion of dizzying hot scent he leapt into the Change. Never before had she known what it was like to be brought into the passion of the Change by a werewolf as powerful as Nicholas. The intensity of the pleasure was shattering. She was caught in the swirling, roaring tide of his magnificence; wonderfully, willingly, rapturously ensnared, and she surrendered with a cry of ecstasy to the supremacy of her nature.

In this form there was no complex reasoning, no conflicting emotions, no careful thought patterns. There was only muscle and movement and instinct and the grand and glorious wonder of the senses. The taste of rain on the tongue, the roar of heartbeats in the ear, the rush of cold air through the nostrils. Claws digging into turf and stones flying underfoot. Night streaming by. Running, running, breathing, smelling, feeling. The silken luxury of her own fur, the wind cutting through it and caressing her skin with its sharp cold bite; the unparalleled luxury of another's footfalls beside her, turning when she turned, leaning when she leaned, racing and slowing, matching breaths, matching heartbeats in a harmony of movement so perfect that it was called the dance of the gods. This was what it was like then. This was what it was like.

They ran down dark and forgotten paths where humans seldom trod. They ran through small streams and tangled bushes. They inhaled the night, the rich smoky scent of their own kind, the hot spurting blood of small game. They raced and they leapt, they tussled and rolled in the wet grass; they used their teeth and their claws and their steel-band muscles. They let themselves sink into the glorious unfettered essence of what they were. They forgot what it was like not to be wild.

He was by far the stronger and the faster, and because he was who he was, he eventually forgot to temper his pace to hers. He let his muscles fly and his adrenaline soar. He circled and charged her and she, drunk with the glory of the beast that too seldom burst free, charged him back. She caught his throat with her teeth and he, in a brilliant ballet of grace and power, spun away and sank his teeth into her shoulder.

It would have been, with another, a harmless gesture of playful challenge, but for Lara it was the resurgence of a nightmare, a jolt of shock and pain that triggered something so deep within her she could not have fought it had she wanted to. And she did not want to.

She gave a scream of shock and pain and twisted away, snapping viciously at his face. She caught him just below the eye and tore away a flap of skin. Blood gushed. She charged at him again, beyond reason now, beyond restraint, mad with memories, mad with rage, helpless against the beast within her that had no choice but to fight back.

There were rules of combat and rules of the run; even had there not been common sense would dictate the inevitable consequences of attacking another werewolf near the eyes. The instinct for self defense was powerful and immediate. Nicholas flung her hard to the ground and pinned her with his weight, his eyes blazing and his face dripping blood and his teeth bared only inches from her throat.

There is always with them a moment before the killing strike in which logic returns, often for no more than an instant, but it is an instant in which the choice must be made with the forebrain, not with instinct. This protective mechanism prevents accidents and regrets in a species so powerful it could easily destroy itself in a matter of decades were its passions not so governed.

Nicholas recognized her, and the relatively minor nature of his injury, and his instincts were checked. Yet he may also have wondered, in that flash of cognizance, whether she had done it on purpose, and why, for when he sprang away it was with a roar of fury and a burst of light and color, and he was in his human form when he lunged at her again. Lara's change was less graceful, and she stumbled to the ground.

He hauled her to her feet by the arm. Her skin was still hot from the change and rain sizzled where it struck her skin. Her black hair was wet and tangled over her face and between the strands her eyes gleamed fiercely.

"You take a chance, Lara Fasburg." His voice, not fully returned, was low and guttural and his fingers on her upper arm were tight enough to have broken the bone of a human. Blood mixed with the rain that streamed down his face, and his nostrils flared with fury.

In the distance there was the sound of taxi cabs and the clatter of manhole covers. Human voices muttered nonsense behind their windows and their heavily screened balconies and their neon-lit places of night business. Elevators pinged. Doors slammed. Locks clicked. The air was fouled with human sweat, human shampoos, human breath, the greasy miasma of human food and human garbage, one barely distinguishable from the other. But here in this dark cove there was only the thunder of blood and the taste of rain, the smell of lightning and harsh

211

triumph and sex at its most primitive.

She pulled her arm away in a gesture that was not so much contemptuous as defiant. Her small breasts rose and fell with each quick breath. She tossed her hair away from her face and her eyes held his with a low hard light. "You wanted to know who I was," she said on a breath. "Now you do."

She leaned into him and licked the blood from his wound, but already it had begun to heal. He caught her head between his hands, he turned her face to his. He tasted his blood on her tongue. Waves of pleasure surged between them, and they sank together to the ground.

By the morning the wound on his face had completely healed, with not so much as the trace of a scar to suggest the memory of the night.

He would never bear her mark.

CHAPTER TWENTY ONE

The Present

O ur Lara," observed Rolfe, bemused, "is quite the puzzle, isn't she?"

"Some might say so." Emory pushed his hair away from his forehead with the heel of his hand. His skin felt hot even to his own touch, and he was tired and oddly weak. He wasn't surprised, but it was inconvenient. The water pitcher had been refilled, and he poured himself a glass. The effort made his biceps ache.

"So were they mates, then, Lara and Nicholas?"

"No. I've explained to you before, it's common for the loup garou to share sexual intimacy without feeling passion for each other. They were never mated."

"Because she was already mated to you."

"That's absurd." He sipped the water. "And impossible."

"Then explain to me how you know the details of what happened that night in Central Park which, if I have my chronology right, was some days before the two of you were reunited."

Emory said flatly, and without blinking, "She told me."

Rolfe considered that for a moment, and then leaned back in his chair, resting his cheek on his index finger. "So were you the spy Nicholas sought?"

"No," Emory said. "Not then. I had done nothing but give lectures three days a week to a theater filled with students in Montreal for the past year. In my spare time I worked on my book."

"Which one?"

"I don't recall."

"It was *An Analysis of Molecular Genetics*. You never finished it."

"That's right." He revealed no expression.

"You're very bright, Professor, no one denies that. But surely you don't expect me — or anyone, for that matter — to believe that at your age you had mastered molecular genetics which, in fact, would have been your third specialized degree."

He said, "That's right. As I told you, I had access to the best scientists in the pack, and to technology that was decades away from being shared with humans."

"And who decided when this knowledge was to be shared?"

"They did."

"They?"

"The pack scientists."

"So you were a puppet of both the pack and the so-called Brotherhood."

"Yes."

"You had no sense of loyalty whatsoever to your own race."

Emory said, "I believed I was doing what was best for my own race."

Rolfe regarded him with a thoughtful, faintly self-satisfied smile his face. "I'm curious. Was it your idea to study genetics?"

"It was the prince who suggested it. I was a good student."

"Of course. He made certain you would be. You were a bold and imminently successful experiment, weren't you? He must have been proud. Did it ever occur to you to wonder why he chose such a specific path for your education? "

"Occasionally. It didn't matter. I would have done whatever he asked."

"Except," Rolfe pointed out softly, "when you did not."

Emory put down the water glass and leaned his head against his hand, his fingers spread over his jugular. Rolfe's attention quickened.

"Are you taking your pulse?"

"Yes. It's slow."

"Do you need a medic?"

"No," Emory said. "Not yet."

"Because we have drugs that can work uncanny miracles on human physiology," Rolfe assured him. "You would be amazed."

Emory dropped his hand, and cupped it again around the water glass. "I know. Already I have told you more than I ever would have done of my own volition."

Rolfe smiled. "Excellent. And you will not lose consciousness? We are so close now to the end that I'm afraid I would have to do something drastic if you did. So promise me, please, a proper denouement. Tell me you will not die yet."

"Oh no," Emory said softly, on a breath. "Oh *hell* no. I am not done yet. Not by a long shot."

"So tell me," demanded Rolfe, and the glint in his eyes was almost childlike in its enthusiasm, "who was the spy? Who was it that Nicholas sought?"

Emory drank the water, sank back in his chair, and let his shoulders relax. "It was Alexander Devoncroix," he said. "His father."

CHAPTER TWENTY TWO

A colleague was excavating in Guatemala and he had
invited me to examine some of the artifacts they had
uncovered in a mass grave outside a temple site. I
agreed because it was warm there, and Montreal in November
was not the most hospitable place to be. I planned to spend my
winter hiatus in Guatemala, and was just locking up my office for
the duration when a package arrived by special messenger.
Inside there was an airline ticket for New York that departed in
three hours. There was no note of explanation, no business card,
no receipt. Just the ticket.

Occasionally a summons came like that—an airline or rail
ticket, an address on a scrap of paper, a telephone number to call.
I always felt a little like James Bond on those occasions, and I
won't deny the appeal of that kind of covert drama, even though
the most dramatic part of my so-called missions was usually the
summons.

Later of course I realized that none of these missions had ever had any significance at all. They were toying with me, testing me, preparing me. And the moment toward which it had all been directed was at hand.

A driver was waiting for me in New York. It was cold and rainy, and the sheen of headlights turned the wet asphalt into a black mirror. Exhaust fumes steamed the air in the car line. Masses of people moved past me, tugging their wheeled suitcases and muttering into their cell phones. The driver took my leather duffel and led me to a limo with tinted windows. He opened the back door for me and I got inside.

I looked into the ice blue eyes of Alexander Devoncroix.

Twenty years earlier he had filled me with awe; he had lost none of his power to intimidate with time. His thick silver hair was pulled back from a face that was a little more angular than it once had been, and eyes that were, it seemed to me, even sharper. He sat perfectly erect in the car, his hands lightly folded over one knee, and the stillness of his posture only increased the force of his presence. Near him, the air seemed thinner, details sharper, colors brighter, even in the dark. It was also more difficult to breathe.

I remember thinking very clearly in that moment: *the gig is up.*

I am not sure what, exactly, I was so certain was finished, nor why I was so certain it was over. It all had something to do with the luxurious interior of the car, the rich mahogany appointments and cordovan leather seats and the way Vivaldi's *Four Seasons* was playing so passionately in the background in a startling, almost clichéd imitation of the scene in the Michael Douglas movie from a decade earlier, *Wall Street*. I wondered disjointedly whether it had been done on purpose and for my amusement,

218

because that would be the kind of irony the Devoncroix would enjoy.

I was wearing jeans with a scuffed leather jacket and a pair of cowboy boots I had gotten in Calgary six years ago and wore so often that the heels were worn down. My hair was shaggy and unkempt and I wasn't entirely certain I'd shaved that morning. When I stepped into the back of that limousine and looked into Alexander Devoncroix's eyes I felt thoroughly outclassed, completely out of place.

I had been in luxurious limousines before of course. The manner of my upbringing made such things common place, and I was hardly intimidated by wealth or its trappings. By the same token, I was accustomed to dealing with the loup garoux in all their arrogance and innate sense of supremacy; even their peculiar body chemistry that so often catches humans off guard and causes them to stutter or forget their train of thought rarely affected me anymore. Yet at that moment, with the pure rich notes of Vivaldi in my ears and the most powerful creature in the world sitting not two feet from me, I knew for an absolute certainty that I did not belong in this world. And all these years, they had only been amusing themselves by allowing me to believe that I did.

I must not have been very good at hiding my reaction because he said pleasantly, "I take it you were expecting someone else. How is the prince, may I ask?"

I found my voice, easing myself into the seat facing him. "I spoke with him in March. He was building a hotel in Bali."

Alexander Devoncroix nodded. "I understand it is to be quite spectacular."

I was silent as the driver came around, started the car, and pulled away from the curb. The privacy panel was engaged. Alexander's eyes never left me. He said, "I have followed your research with interest. Except for that nonsense about Queen Eudora and the Fasburg, of course, it was quite thorough, and always entertaining. I admit, you surprise me."

He waited for me to object to his assessment of my research. As brash as I was, I knew better than to attempt to defend myself. He was the leader of the pack. One did not argue with him.

Headlights flashed upon the tinted glass, etching blue and yellow shadows across his face. He went on, "There were of course some details of our history to which you did not have access. I have brought you here to share them. The driver is human. We can be assured our conversation will not be overheard. We have perhaps twenty minutes into the city. Please make yourself comfortable, help yourself to the bar if you like. "

I said, "Thank you." My voice was a little hoarse, which was not surprising. I could barely draw a full breath. "I'm not thirsty."

The car glided along as though it was on ice. Vivaldi: *Spring*. No other sound.

Alexander Devoncroix said, "I recall when I first met you as a youth you credited me with disposing of the last members of the Brotherhood of the Dark Moon. Of course you have by now realized that I did no such thing." His gaze was steady; my heart was thunder. "Many have tried, throughout the centuries, to eliminate them, but without success. They are, you see, the essence of us. And like us, they cannot be destroyed. They merely change form. They have always been enemies of the pack, but in so many ways the pack could not exist without them."

I wondered whether he had brought me here to die. There

are less than a handful of crimes in their system of justice that merit the death penalty, but treachery against the pack is one of them. I had known that when I took my vows.

He said, "In the centuries following its betrayal by the human priest, the Dark Brotherhood began to deteriorate, quite predictably in my opinion, into something it was never meant to be. They despised and rejected humans, and in many cases, even their human forms. They chose a lifestyle that was wild and brutish and diametrically opposed to the integrity of the pack. Fortunately, they were widely scattered in small enclaves and clans around the globe and, without strong leadership or organization, the threat they posed was minimal. My own brother was the leader of one such enclave," he said, his expression unchanging, "and it was his ambition to unite the Brotherhood into a force that would dominate the earth. Had he succeeded, you and I would be having a very different conversation now. Most unfortunately for him, he trusted his schemes to a human accomplice, and he was betrayed. He was condemned to live in exile, and died quite mad. But before he did, he sired a child." There was now only the slightest hardening of his voice. "The child was half human."

Vivaldi continued to play. Headlights continued to scroll past. Time stopped.

I said, "That's not possible."

His eyes were like stone, chips of lapis glinting in the shadows. But his tone was calm, almost conversational. "You've no doubt discovered in your investigations that the Devoncroix bloodline contains a genetic anomaly. It is what has enabled us to survive, even thrive, in times of physical adversity and why our line has remained intact for almost as far back as history can

221

trace. Many believe it may also be the origin of the Scourge, which killed so many infants during the time of Eudora and still, from time to time, steals our little ones from us."

I said, trying hard to focus, "They call it the Devoncroix Effect."

He nodded. "Because we are strong and prolific breeders, the Effect is widespread throughout our species. No doubt it will eventually be associated with many other characteristics, abilities or peculiarities that have not yet been isolated."

My throat was so tight I had to speak or choke. "I don't understand—"

"In other interspecies' cross-breedings," he spoke over me without raising his voice or changing his matter of fact tone in any way, "or attempted clonings, the product of the match rarely reaches maturity, and is always sterile. This did not prove to be the case with my brother's offspring. The child, neither human nor loup garou, reached maturity and mated with one who carried the Devoncroix Effect in even stronger measure than did she."

My lips felt numb. I was not certain that the words, when they came, were even intelligible. "The result?"

"That," he replied, "is what you are about to see."

He was lying of course. I was convinced of that. What I could not explain was why. Perhaps it was a word puzzle, or a test of some kind. Again, I could not think why Alexander Devoncroix would concern himself with testing me, and to be honest, the not knowing was more alarming than the consideration—however quickly it might be dismissed—that his story had some basis in truth.

And so I asked, with a voice that was still hoarse and stiff and starving for air, "Why? I'm nothing more than a history keeper, a parrot of the science your people have taught me. Why tell me this? Why bring me here? What do you want from me?"

In the darkness, Alexander Devoncroix smiled. The coldness of it sent a chill down my spine. "Why, my dear young man," he said, quietly, "I believe you already know the answer to that."

As the silent black limousine made its way through the rain-bright streets of Manhattan, Nicholas Devoncroix stood in the mahogany lined dressing room of his penthouse suite and gazed at the pair of diamond earrings that glittered in his palm. They made him smile. His valet had found them in the pocket of the trousers he had worn the night before and had displayed them, quite properly, on the low wide chest that bisected the room. Nicholas dropped the earrings into the pocket of his slacks. He would return them to her tonight. He had promised they would dance.

Nicholas was enchanted, and he recognized the fact on a perfectly cognizant intellectual level. He had always been intrigued by the inexplicable, the unique, the outrageous, and his idle fascination with Lara Fasburg had begun years ago. She was untamed, and he admired that. She was ridiculous, and that made him laugh. She was dangerous, and that attracted him.

The constraints of his destiny were such that he must be ever aware, ever cautious, ever thoughtful. His passions were guarded, but volatile and intense. In Lara he found his opposite. Any liaison would be both reckless and addictive. He suspected, because he knew himself that well, that he would pursue it anyway.

There was a birthday party for a human of some repute that Lara had been invited to attend at the Plaza Hotel. Yo-Yo Ma was performing, and Nicholas found him entertaining. There would be dancing.

He slipped on his jacket and started for the door when his hand-held communications device vibrated in his pocket. It was a combination computer, telephone, camera, Internet connection and GPS tracking device that was fifteen years or so away from being made available to the human population. He glanced at the screen and saw the incoming message was from Garret. He pushed the button that would transfer it to voice.

"I'm on my way out," he said.

"You asked to be notified of any usual activity."

Nicholas started to open the bedroom door, then hesitated. A loup garou of his status was rarely alone; secretaries, guards, assistants and service providers were always moving about the apartment, and his private quarters were the only ones that were soundproof. He said, "Go ahead."

"Your father arrived in town this afternoon."

Nicholas frowned impatiently. "Then I'll be sure to ring him for lunch."

"So did the Fasburg."

The frown faded into thoughtful surprise.

Garret asked, "Is there to be a summit of some kind?"

"Not that I know of. Perhaps he's only here to see his daughter."

It was a feeble conjecture, and Garret was politely silent for a moment. Then he said, "The human Hilliford is here as well. He arrived less than an hour ago and was met at the airport by your father in a private car."

224

Nicholas tightened his jaw. There was no pretending that was not unusual, and it was beginning to look more and more as though his father was setting him up. He considered his options for barely a second before he said, "Follow them." And he disconnected.

The limousine drew to a stop in front of a Fifth Avenue brownstone with a high hedge and an iron gate. Two carriage lights illuminated the short cobbled walk, now shiny with rain.

Alexander said, "You are about to enter one of the finest genetic research laboratories in the Americas, and to meet three preeminent scientists in the field. They have been given to believe that the specimen you are about to see was engineered in a highly classified experiment conducted by one of our teams in Hungary. In fact, he has eluded us for over thirty years, and was captured in East Africa less than thirty-six hours ago."

The driver got out and walked around the car. I said, "Why not tell them the truth?" My lips still felt numb.

He looked at me with silent tolerance, and I slowly answered my own question. "Because if it is engineered, you control it." And the leader of the pack was always in control; no one must ever suspect otherwise.

The stubborn, insistent unpredictability of nature was one thing, unfortunately, that not even the greatest empire on earth could control.

The driver opened the curb side door, holding an umbrella. Alexander Devoncroix got out, eschewing the umbrella. Raindrops glistened in the lamplight on his silver hair. I followed.

"Wait for us," Alexander told the driver, and started up the walk.

225

He inserted a key card into a slot in the stone column beside the gate, and it swung open to admit us. The building was less than a dozen strides away, surrounded on either side by a well-manicured lawn planted with small trees and neat flowerbeds, now mulched over for the season. There was no sign or plaque anywhere to suggest this was anything other than a luxurious private residence. The door was reached by a set of wide stone steps that led to a portico. The lock clicked open when Alexander inserted the key card again. The security seemed rather lax for a scientific research facility, but then I realized that it was fully staffed by loup garoux. Given the acuity of their senses and their more than able capacity for defending what was theirs, even locks were a bit redundant.

Alexander surprised me by handing the key card to me. I met his eyes for a moment, but did not question. I tucked the card into my pocket.

Inside there was an elegant reception area clad in pale silk wallpaper with cove ceilings and tear-drop chandeliers. There were bookshelves styled with leather classics and marble busts of the poets, Louis Quatorze furniture and reading lamps. At the far end of the room was a door that swung open with a soft buzz when we approached.

I stepped into a stainless steel and black granite laboratory of the quality I had come to expect of their kind. Their computers were small and sleek and deadly fast; decades away from those commonly used by human researchers. There were electron microscopes with robotic arms and gene sequencers that could analyze and deconstruct hundreds of millions of lines of data in seconds. Except for a female at one of the microscope stations, an older male who was scanning a computer screen, and another tall, sharp featured male who was coming toward us, the room was empty.

"Routine operations have been suspended for the next several days," Alexander explained. "All but the most essential staff has been temporarily reassigned. You know Tobias, I believe."

As the loup garou reached us I realized that I had, in fact, met him before. He was a thin and angular fellow with a high widow's peak and jet black hair, and eyes that were now burning with the fever of excitement. He was the most brilliant biochemist I had ever known. His opinion of me was one of barely concealed contempt, which meant I was several notches in his esteem above the other human researchers with whom he occasionally came into contact.

He barely acknowledged me with a glance, and spoke to his pack leader in a rush of enthusiasm that was so unlike his usual persona that I blinked in surprise. "Sir, it is remarkable. Truly a phenomenal accomplishment. I've never seen anything like it. Since this morning we've isolated two new chromosomes that are unlike anything I've imagined were possible." And now his demeanor fell. "I am chastened and chagrined to confess I did not believe such technology existed."

Alexander said, "I will examine your data. You will also make all of your results available to Dr. Hilliford, who is the only human alive capable of understanding it." I thought I detected a slight steeliness in his voice as he added, "I shall require a full report from him. Should his report differ in any detail from yours, I will want to know why."

The resentment in Tobias's gaze was palpable when he looked at me, for it was a common practice for their experts to withhold data from me when I studied with them and I was always on guard against it. He turned back to his leader and said, "I understand, sir. I will instruct the others."

Alexander gave a curt nod. "And now we will see the specimen."

I thought, with a rather wild incredulity, *He's really going to carry this through!* because up until that point I was still trying to convince myself that this was all an elaborate hoax, a cruel joke perpetrated upon the human who dared to think he could infiltrate their ranks. But as we left the laboratory, as we walked down that long corridor past cold storage and isolation labs and sterile labs and finally pausing before a closed steel door with a television monitor and a closed circuit alarm—at some point during that walk, and just before Tobias used his own key card to unlock the door—I thought again, more calmly, *He's really going to carry this through.* And I made room in my mind for the possibility that this was not a hoax after all.

The lock clicked. We walked inside a very cold room that was bathed in a blue light. On a stainless steel table in the center of the room was a naked male. Tubes and wires fed into the monitors that supported and recorded his life functions and his brain activity, and those sophisticated machines blinked and hummed and glowed with his internal rhythms. I moved closer.

He was a slender, muscular male of apparent good health in his early thirties. His hair was thick and blond and shoulder length. There were no apparent injuries or disease processes. His genitalia were well formed and intact. There was no body hair evident anywhere, not even on his arms or legs. His chest rose and fell with the pressure of the ventilator and his teeth, as much as I could determine around the endotracheal tube, were strong and straight. There were calluses on his hands and feet. I knew

228

that if he opened his eyes, they would be Devoncroix blue.

He was real. He was alive.

Tobias said, "We're maintaining a medically induced coma. Nonetheless, his brain activity is far above what one might expect, approaching near consciousness."

Alexander's voice was a little sharp. "Make certain you continue to administer the paralytic on schedule. He must be kept contained."

"Of course." Tobias sounded offended.

I stepped close to the table. I wanted to touch him. I looked at the monitors. I tried to make sense of the numbers, but I could not. Finally, I reached out and touched his hand. It was warm, despite the coldness of the room, and the skin was supple. He was alive. He was real.

I said, unable to step away, "What is his name?"

Tobias didn't seem to know. Perhaps it had not occurred to him that a creature such as this should have a name. It was Alexander who answered.

"David," he said. And then he added, "Devoncroix, of course."

CHAPTER TWENTY THREE

The paparazzi snapped the photograph in front of the middle arch of the Palm Court. Lara, in a strapless black Chanel sheath with a Hermes silk stole draped elegantly from her arms, smiled up into the eyes of Nicholas Devoncroix, whose hand was protectively on her shoulder and whose face was bent toward hers. The tenderness of his expression said it all.

The captions would read: *Catch of the Century! Billionaire Bombshell!* And in the more respectable publications: *Business mogul Nicholas Devoncroix squires media darling Lara Fasburg around New York. Can a major merger be far away?*

They made their way through the reception line and bade their best to the guest of honor. A former American president and an astronaut were there, as were several Rockefellers and Kennedys. Nicholas was no stranger to any of them and neither, somewhat to his surprise, was Lara. They said the proper things.

They drank champagne and ate caviar on toast.

Lara's hair was long and loose about her shoulders. In a rare private moment, Nicholas smoothed it back behind her ear with one hand, and smiled when he saw she wore no earrings. "I have something that belongs to you," he said. He took the earrings from his pocket and, measuring the proper placement with a glance, deftly pierced the flesh of her lobes with the posts and snapped the earrings into place, one at a time. Her pierced lobes had naturally healed during the previous night's Change, and a small drop of blood glistened on his index finger when he moved his hand away. He held her eyes, his gaze explicit with memories of the night before, as he brought his finger to his tongue and licked the droplet away.

"You are a beast," she told him, but she could not repress the smile that deepened the corners of her lips. She touched one dangling diamond lightly. "But thank you for not losing them."

He took two flutes of champagne from a waiter and passed one to her. "Did you know your father was in town?"

She lifted an eyebrow. "Really? How peculiar. He detests New York." She sipped her champagne. "Where is he staying, do you know?"

"I believe he keeps a suite at Trump Towers."

"I think you may be right. I'll make certain not to wander in that direction until he leaves."

"I take it you're not close." As he spoke the hand-held device in his jacket pocket vibrated. He took it out and glanced at it briefly. There was a single line on the screen: *142 Fifth Avenue.* He felt a measure of relief steal through him as he replaced the device, and later he would understand that he was relieved only because he wanted to be. That was the address of one of their research laboratories. No doubt the human Hilliford had begged a favor from the pack leader who had, for whatever reason, always been more than tolerant of him, to gain admission to the laboratory. It was curious, but not alarming. There was no mystery here.

Had he been less distracted by Lara's scent, her voice, the loveliness of her skin and the chemistry of her nearness, he might have considered further, thought more carefully, asked more questions. But he did not want to concern himself with treachery and espionage on this fine night in these elegant surroundings with so many possibilities dancing in his head. And there are always *what ifs*.

"Not for ages," Lara was saying. "I told you, I don't keep up with figures from my past." She regarded him brightly over the rim of her glass. "This is convenient for you, however, isn't it? Now you can interview him about whatever you were dithering on about last night. What *was* it again? Remind me."

He regarded her with cool amusement. "I'm sure I don't remember. But I will say I'm relieved to learn your father hasn't contacted you. I was worried he had heard of our liaison and intended to challenge me on it. I'm sure he wouldn't approve."

"We have no liaison, Nicholas Devoncroix, and if we did my father's opinion on the subject would be the least of your concerns. However ..." She tilted her head speculatively as she looked at him. A small dimple appeared at one corner of her lips. "We would make an interesting couple, wouldn't we?"

"Indeed we would." He glanced around the room, as was his habit, and inclined his head to someone he knew. He looked at her again. "Tell me one true thing, Lara Fasburg," he said. "What is it that you want?"

The question seemed to take her aback. "From you?"

"No. In general."

Her eyes skipped over his face, and away. She sipped her champagne. She glanced around the room, and then at him again. "I would ask the same of you. What do you want from me?"

He answered the question easily. "For the present, your time. Your company."

"Until you grow bored."

"I don't plan to grow bored for some days yet. I think you may have a good deal to teach me."

"I'm flattered."

Her skin gave off the subtle scent of confusion, and genuine surprise. There was such an unexpected innocence to it that he wanted to stroke her throat, gathering that scent on his fingertips to memorize. He wanted to kiss her eyes closed, and taste her. The impulse, and the fact that he did not, in fact, act upon it, made him smile.

He said, "Now answer me."

She sipped her champagne. She cast her eyes to the side, and then back to him, bravely. Her scent now was oddly shy, faintly sweet. "I want," she told him, lifting her chin a fraction, "to be adored. It is all I've ever wanted."

He said, "Then you must be thoroughly content."

She focused her gaze briefly on her glass. "You would be surprised." Then she met his eyes again, and said, "Thank you for last night."

He inclined his head in gentle understanding. "We were not meant to live apart from our own kind."

She said softly, "Yes." And the sadness in her eyes made him

233

want to do something to banish it, and to make certain that look never came again.

He said, "Look, the dancing has started." He put aside his champagne and stepped back, holding out his hand to her. "Do you waltz?"

A slow and comfortable smile curved her lips. "Divinely," she assured him. She placed her hand in his, and he led her away.

CHAPTER TWENTY FOUR

Subject: David Devoncroix
Gender: Male
Age: 30 years
Species: Unknown

With every heading of every report I always stopped there, unable to read on for a moment, staring at the line. *Species unknown.* Species actually unknown. Not a myth, not a trick, not a trap or a lie. Species unknown.

I inserted the needle into his vein and drew my own blood sample. I placed the drop on the slide and the slide under the microscope. I examined it for myself.

I watched as tensile strength tests were performed using electrodes to stimulate his muscle groups. I saw his fingers close around a six millimeter titanium alloy bar and snap it in two.

I watched as Tobias used a scalpel to open a long wound on his arm, exposing fascia and muscle and bloody bone, and I watched as the ooze of blood was replaced with clear serous fluid, as inflamed tissue grew pink, as open edges sealed themselves, as smooth pale skin erased the scar of the wound. I had never seen a loup garou spontaneously repair a wound without changing forms. The entire process took less than a minute.

I examined his PET scan, CT scan and functional MRI. I saw the areas of the brain that exist only in lupinotuum, the increased olfactory receptors and the foreshortened auditory nerves that give them such enhanced senses of smell and hearing. I saw the brilliant, almost terrifyingly constant neural activity that lit up the lobes of his brain even in a deep coma.

I asked the most obvious question.

"Can he change forms?"

"It seems unlikely. One of the base pairs in the chromosome sequence is altered. However ..." Tobias walked to the large transparent screen in the center of the room and touched an icon that brought up a video replay of the subject's electromagnetic body scan. He slowed down the replay so that I could read it. I could tell that the subject appeared to be generating a detectable and constantly shifting electromagnetic field that was similar to the ones I had noted in scans of lupinotuum. My theory has always been that this fluctuating electromagnetic field, which plays such a crucial part in their ability to shift their forms, is also responsible for the physical reaction most humans have when first encountering them — the inexplicable attraction, the disrupted thought processes, even the uneasiness.

I asked, "Have you tried to communicate with him?"

I felt Alexander Devoncroix's eyes on me. Tobias gave me a look of barely concealed disdain. "A somewhat challenging task,

236

since he has been comatose since he arrived."

I touched another icon on the screen and brought up the genetic analysis. I read until my eyes blurred, touching the screen faster and faster, shifting between one program and the next, one set of data and another. Of course my brain could not absorb it all. Of course there was no real analysis taking place. I just wanted to see it.

David Devoncroix, male, age 30: Evidence indicated that he possessed all of the strength, the super-enhanced senses and the intellectual acuity of the loup garou, but he had only one form—human. Since the one great disadvantage of the lupinotuum has always been that they require an enormous amount of energy—and therefore, resources—to maintain two forms, this was clearly an evolutionary leap forward. He demonstrated that remarkable ability to heal himself almost instantly that is characteristic of the loup garou, but could do this while maintaining his human form. Brain scans showed an unusual amount of electrical activity in the lower cerebellum, even while in an induced coma, so it's reasonable to assume he may have access to parts of the brain that are generally dormant in both human and loup garou, but I did not have enough time to conduct the tests necessary to quantify this. Blood and tissue analysis showed an immunity to every disease for which it was tested.

Human beings have forty-six chromosomes in a DNA strand. Wolves have seventy-eight. Lupinotuum have eighty-two. The specimen David Devoncroix had one hundred three.

In all animal and most plant life on earth chromosomes are aligned in pairs, one from each parent. When an anomaly occurs, it is usually in the form of trisomy, or a triad of chromosomes instead of a pair. The deformity is always obvious, both mentally

237

and physically, and often fatal. The specimen David did not display a trisomy in his chromosomal structure, but a single extra chromosome. And because the anomaly occurred in a section of the DNA where the Devoncroix Effect might have appeared, had it been present, one could not definitively say whether he had an extra chromosome, or was missing a chromosome, or what role this particular chromosome might play in his structure, if any at all. Perhaps this was the marker for his species.

Because he was, from all the evidence of my eyes and by every scientific definition, a new species.

"We have to wake him up." I wasn't even aware of having spoken out loud. My eyes were now glued to the microscope, and I clicked through to examine another tissue sample on the carousel. I could smell my own sweat, and hear the dry, erratic thumping of my heart. "We need to do cognitive function tests, neurological, stamina and coordination. It's going to take years to analyze his DNA, years ..."

The shadow of Alexander Devoncroix fell over me. "It's time," he said, "to go."

My head was reeling as I went out into the night, and I actually staggered a little at the bottom of the stairs. I had to grip the rail for balance and let the truth wash over me. Not just the truth but the wonder of it, the marvel, the outrageous simplicity of it. I thought about centuries of history, of miracles lost, gods fallen and greatness crumbled to dust. I thought about wars and slaughters and civilizations overtaken by jungle vines. I thought about Eudora the wild and beautiful queen, and the priest who loved her. I thought about a thousand years of evolution, ten thousand. All of it leading to this moment.

This moment.

The rain had stopped, but was replaced by a pale cold fog that smelled of wet asphalt and exhaust fumes. Taxi cabs made splashing sounds as they edged through the traffic. Alexander Devoncroix awaited me on the sidewalk when I made my way through the gate. The car was gone.

"I've sent your luggage ahead," he said. "Your hotel isn't far. We'll walk."

I fell into step beside him. "Our mistake was in thinking that cross breeding wasn't possible because of the lack of homologous DNA." My voice was low and tight, the thoughts coming almost faster than I could express them. "But we didn't account for shifting chromosomal patterns during the Change, and for homologous recombination which would have begun as a DNA repair process during meiosis and could so easily get out of control due to the accelerated healing mechanism that kicks in during and just after the Change." I drew a breath. "We didn't account for the Devoncroix Effect."

We passed beneath a streetlight. A young couple with their heads bent toward each other, talking softly, moved by. An engine ground its gears on the street. Alexander's expression was thoughtful as he murmured, "What rough beast, its hour come round at last, slouches toward Bethlehem to be born?"

I felt a chill. I shoved my hands into my pockets and kept talking. "I need time. I need blood and cell cultures. I need to look more closely at the extra chromosome. It's possible this isn't just an anomaly. But we need to wake him up. I need to, we need to communicate with him, to find out how his brain functions, how he learns, what—who—he is."

Alexander Devoncroix replied simply, "I know what he is."

And that was when I knew that he had not brought me here to study the miracle that was David Devoncroix. He had not brought me here to analyze data or offer an opinion. He certainly had not brought me to act as a consultant to three of the most brilliant scientists of our time. I grew quiet inside, slowly but certainly. My thoughts were still whirling, but they were silent. My focus was on him. Waiting.

We crossed an intersection. People hurried past us. Brilliantly lit store windows cast their reflections in the puddles on the street. It was only mid November, but some of them already had Christmas decorations up. Spindly bare tree limbs in planters by the curb were wound with white lights. A restaurant door opened, emitting the fragrance of garlic and fresh bread.

Alexander said, "Do you know how many banks we own?"

I shook my head, my throat dry.

"The vast majority of them around the world, I assure you, and the ones we do not own are dependent upon us for their resources. The human moguls who believe they control the planet's mineral resources do so only at our discretion. We have worked hard over the years to build a synergistic relationship with your people, young man, because when you prosper, we prosper. In this way we have brought civilization to the edge of the greatness upon which it stands today. But this you know. You have written books."

He glanced at me. I said nothing.

"We have brought your people space flight, microtechnology, satellite communications, robotic surgery and pharmaceuticals that, in a single generation, have lengthened the average human life by twenty years. You will no doubt agree that the modern world, though deeply flawed, has been better off with us than without us over the past century."

A woman in a smart wool cape and battered running shoes hurried past us with a shopping bag full of purchases. I said hoarsely, "Yes."

"We have achieved our present status as masters of commerce and invention through greed, cooperation, enlightened self-interest and an absolute conviction of our own infallibility. Yet our culture is a singularly volatile one, steeped in the birthblood of violence that we choose, each day, to resist. It is important that you understand this. We choose to keep the peace. We choose to build rather than destroy. We choose the greater good over our own instincts moment by moment, day by day. This is not our nature. It is our choice.

"And yet throughout our history the savagery resurfaces at random moments. Pack leaders are overthrown. Philosophies are discarded. Cultures vanish. Civilizations are abandoned. The struggle to maintain the balance is never an exact science. And so I ask you now, having studied us from the unique viewpoint you have as an observer of our society, and not a participant in it: how do you think the pack will react when this new creature is made known to them? A mutant human-loup garou hybrid, a monstrous accident of nature, sprung from the noblest and strongest line in the pack, blood and flesh of the pack leader ... what will this mean to them, do you think? What will they do?"

I took a nature course once that required me to spend a spring in Denali National Park, observing and recording the activities of a particular pack of wolves. The breeding female, the mate of the alpha, gave birth while I was there to five cubs. Two were deformed. One had a crippled foreleg, stunted above the

241

wrist. The other had a bob tail. I watched her systematically kill, then eat, her malformed offspring. This is not unusual in nature, and I had expected it. What I had not expected was that within the week the pack would turn on the alpha and his mate, killing them and abandoning the remaining cubs to starve. Perhaps they sensed a weakness or disease in the pair that would contaminate the pack. Perhaps the incidents were unrelated.

But nature is often consistent in these matters.

I said, "The pack can't know. No one can know." There was a low desperation in my voice which only became sharper with the heaviness of his silence. "You convinced a molecular biologist and two geneticists that he was the result of in vitro engineering. You can convince the rest of the pack."

"As long as he remains an inert specimen, perhaps. But sooner or later he will be brought out of the coma, or he will overcome it spontaneously. As you have observed, his physiology is unpredictable, and remarkable. He is also quite sentient. He knows his own history, and he is capable of sharing it. We do not know what else he is capable of. But the mere fact of his existence will throw the pack into chaos."

The background noise receded into a distant murmur and clatter. The clack of our footsteps on wet pavement was loud in the silence. That, and the thump of my heart. Hard. Heavy. Terrified.

David Devoncroix. A creature formed from the impossible. A strand of DNA captured in the act of transforming itself, binding to a strand with a mutant gene. Recombinant chromosomes attempting to repair a perceived break in the chain, because that was what nature did: it survived, it adapted, it evolved.

It destroyed.

"The balance of nature is a delicate and beautiful thing," Alexander said, "and for those who are sworn to uphold it, capricious."

I sucked in my breath sharply, but dared not look at him.

"This hybrid," he went on steadily, "represents the most dangerous threat to the natural balance in perhaps all of history. He cannot be allowed to survive. You will shortly receive an order to make certain of this."

We stood across from the Plaza Hotel. Its lights illuminated most of the block, its flags flapped in the breeze. Cabs lined up and departed. The white horse drawn carriages queued around the side of the building, drivers wiping down the damp seats with towels. Traffic lumbered by. My blood roared in my head.

I turned at last to face Alexander Devoncroix. We stood on one of the most brightly lit street corners in New York, and every detail of his face was visible — the ice hard eyes, the small creases at the corners of them, the pores, the sharply shaped lips, the quiet flare of his nostrils as he drew in breath. I said, very distinctly, "How do you know what orders I may or may not receive?"

There was a very faint smile. "Because," he replied, "I am the one who was sent to give them to you."

CHAPTER TWENTY FIVE

It would surprise most to know that joy, for Lara Fasburg, was a rare and deeply elusive thing. There were moments when joy danced just outside her reach — a taste of wine that was exceptionally fine, a glimpse of breathtakingly clear cerulean ocean against a shimmering white beach; a dewy morning or a single pure, perfectly executed note from an opera. But years had passed since she had felt a true and thorough contentment, the steady glow of joy that spread quietly through her core and into the most unapproachable parts of her brain and out through her fingertips and her lips and her smile. Sitting beside Nicholas Devoncroix listening to the cello concert beneath the canopy of greenery and twinkling lights was such a moment. She could feel his heartbeat. She could smell his pleasure, and it was a heady thing. His warmth, though they did not touch, enveloped her. The music thrilled her. The clash of human perfumes and chafing dishes and rich buttery foods delighted

244

her. Joy. She felt joy.

And yet she was aware of a subtle anxiety skirting the edges of this unexpected, almost dizzying sensation of elation. It nagged and taunted her, warning her nothing this lovely could last, and of course it couldn't because her father was in town. Her father was in town and he never came to New York. Her father was in town and Nicholas suspected him of some covert activity against the pack. Her father was in town and so was she, and so was Nicholas, and there was no such thing as coincidence and moments of joy, so rare and hard won, never lasted for her.

The concert ended and they applauded the maestro, leaving their chairs for the long white skirted tables that promised an array of delectable dishes. Lara laid her hand firmly upon Nicholas's arm. She felt his muscles and his electricity, and the thrill of his nearness tingled on her skin. Fine strands of her hair crackled toward him and caught on the silk sleeve of his jacket. She did not bother brushing them back.

She said, "I want to tell you something."

He looked a question at her, politely.

"I am not my father," she said.

He smiled. "I'm quite certain I wouldn't have made the mistake, but thank you for clarifying the matter."

Her fingers tightened slightly and so did the corners of her eyes. His smile faded into simple curiosity. "I am not my father," she repeated firmly. "It's important that you understand that. If you have business with him, conduct it. If you would spend time with me, do so. I will not be used. I am not my father."

Nicholas looked at her thoughtfully for a moment. "I have no business with your father tonight," he said. "Tonight I want nothing more than to spend time with you. And you are far too clever to be used by me or anyone else, as you've already proven."

She looked up at him, searching his eyes for permission, and he stepped close. She leaned briefly into him, inhaling his truth. She let his scent wash through her and leave her weak with delight.

She said, a little unsteadily, "Your chemistry is strong and sometimes muddles my head, but you bring me pleasure, Nicholas Devoncroix."

He touched her hair, and she could hear the tiny sparks of static that crackled there. "I'm glad," he said. "For, as odd as it seems to me, you bring me pleasure too."

"Excellent." She smiled, and tucked her arm through his, covering his hand with her own. "Let's go to Paris."

"Marvelous idea." He turned her toward the serving table. "Do you mind if we have dinner first?"

She stopped and looked up at him, her eyes bright with a secret insistence. "Let's have dinner in Paris. Can you get the Concord?"

He looked surprised, and then intrigued, and then he laughed. "Of course I can," he said.

CHAPTER TWENTY SIX

W hy do you look so shocked?" Alexander Devoncroix was smiling at me, coolly. "I was at your initiation ceremony. I have known of your calling for years, and in fact helped plan it. Ours is an ancient and powerful name, you see. It means, quite literally – "

"Cross of the dark gods." I heard my voice, as from a distance. I felt my fingers, of their own volition, slowly rise and touch the cross-shaped brand on the back of my neck. A taxi passed by with a rush of air and the sound of splashing. A crowd surged past us. In the distance a doorman's whistle sounded muffled by the mist.

"I told you about my brother," he said. "I didn't tell you how he died. The poor mad devil attacked me and would have killed me, had I not done him the mercy first. I think before he died I saw gratitude I his eyes." He was no longer smiling. "I know it was in his thoughts, as I took them into myself at the moment of

247

his death. I knew what he knew, I saw what he saw, I felt what he felt. I could not have walked away unchanged."

"You did not destroy the Brotherhood of the Dark Moon," I said. How calm my voice sounded. How reasonable. "You united it."

"My brother was a powerful werewolf, and ambitious. But there was one even more ambitious than he, and his influence reached far, almost as far as mine. Defeating him would serve no purpose. Allying with him would serve us both. "

"Prince Fasburg." Not a question, but a statement. A simple truth.

He inclined his head fractionally. "He, and his family before him, have ruled the Brotherhood for centuries. We have not always agreed on strategy, but we have always agreed on purpose. The dominant species must prevail."

And with David Devoncroix, formed of the best—and perhaps the worst—of both human and lupinotuum, the dominance of the species was no longer clear.

Alexander went on, "We have no evidence that the hybrid responds to any known poison and as you see his healing reflexes are almost instantaneous. It seems to me that the quickest, and kindest method, would be an electric charge to the heart or the brainstem, or perhaps a simple injection of an air bubble into a vein while he is still comatose. You should of course disconnect the monitor alarms first, so as not to disturb the others. It should take less than a minute, and you will be well away before anyone realizes what has happened. You should go immediately to the Trump Towers, where the prince will see to your safety. He expects you before midnight."

I had a sudden flash of a wild, bloody night, of holding one of their own battered and broken against my chest, of the Devoncroix in their summer whites drinking martinis and nibbling hors d'ouvres; cigarette smoke on the Mediterranean air and the voice of the prince: *If you stay, you do so knowing full well what we are ...*

I said hoarsely. "He is your own flesh and blood. You cannot mean to kill him."

Alexander replied simply, "I cannot kill him, nor can any other member of my race. If we did, he would live on – all that he is and knows and has been and felt – with the death memory, just as my brother lives in me. We cannot allow that to happen." His eyes were as calm as a glacier lake as they fastened upon mine. "Now you will understand why, throughout history, there have always been human members of the Brotherhood."

Of course. For all of my great obsession with studying them, for all of my grand conceit in imagining I could in some measure belong with them, I had never put together those simple pieces. They could not kill another member of their own species without suffering the gravest of consequences. And humans made excellent assassins.

Alexander Devoncroix nodded a glance across the street. "Here is your hotel. You should go to your room, and prepare yourself. You cannot return to the lab smelling of fear."

Again my voice spoke, although it seemed to be a thing disconnected to me, uncontrolled by me, not even recognized by me. Yet the words were delivered with great care. "The world has waited a hundred thousand generations or more for this moment," I said softly. "The loup garou and the human united at last into a single being, an entirely new species. Neither your race nor mine has the right to destroy it. I can't believe you would ask this of me. I can't believe you would expect me to agree."

There was a quirk of his eyebrow, perhaps from amusement, perhaps from surprise. "My dear young man," he said, "you have enjoyed every advantage our pack has to offer for most of your life—wealth, privilege, education, access to places and information few humans could even dream of. Surely you did not imagine that you would not one day be called upon to pay the price?"

I smelled roses. I saw Lara's face, so close to mine, her hair all tangled up with wild roses, her eyes torn with sorrow. I heard her voice, desperate and broken with sorrow: *What they offer is not a gift, and the price, when it comes, will be a terrible one.*

I was on the sidewalk again, traffic blaring in my ears, lights spinning around me. I cried out, "I am a scientist! You—Prinze-Papa—all of you gave me the gift of science and this is science's greatest miracle! I won't destroy it! I can't do this, you know that I can't!"

Alexander Devoncroix held me with his gaze. His eyes were the color of super-heated steel. He said quietly, very lowly, "You have no choice. You will do this thing or it will be done by another, and in a far less intrusive and humane manner. You refuse, and you betray not only the Brotherhood, but both our races. I took the same vow as you, young human. Hear me as I say it to you again: A Brother will do nothing to disturb the balance. What nature has created, we must preserve."

I heard his words. I felt his gaze boring into my brain like two steel bars. I tasted my pulse in my mouth. And slowly I began to understand what the leader of the pack had just commanded me to do, and why only I, the human in whose loyalty Prince Fasburg had such sublime confidence, could do it.

What I did not understand was how.

I am not sure how long I stood on the street corner after he left me. I remember thrusting my fingers through my hair, digging my nails into my skull as though with the effort I could erase the memory of the last hour from my mind, turning around in a slow circle, looking for sky. But there was no escape. And I still smelled roses.

Somehow I made it across the street. I remember moving through the vast lobby like a ghost, out of time and out of step with the rest of the world. I saw the Oak Bar. I did not go there. I saw the front desk. I did not go there. I saw the arched glass panels of the Palm Court. I saw the sign that said "Private Party." I walked close to the glass. And I saw her.

I think I heard a man in formal dress say, "Excuse me, sir, but may I see your invitation?"

I didn't turn around. I placed my hand hesitantly, tentatively upon the glass. Despair and desperation flooded me as I opened my hand and pressed it there. I leaned forward until my forehead was also touching the glass, and I wanted, simply, to weep. I thought, *Lara, help me.*

She looked up.

Excerpt from **From Dawn To Dusk: A tale of Two Species,** *by Emory Hilliford, PhD:*

It can be argued that it was because of his vows, not in spite of them, that the human Louis Phillipe Montclaire turned his back upon his sacred calling and took the making of history into his own hands. He succumbed in the end to his own weakness, his obsessive love for all things werewolf. Even the rage of the queen he adored, even the threat of execution, even the vow he held most sacred, could not dissuade him from following what was, in his own mind, a higher moral imperative, and saving this race of magnificent creatures from extinction. His betrayal was the beginning of the end of the Brotherhood of the Dark Moon as it once had been; his actions had proven that humans could not be trusted and the grand goals of reuniting the two species in harmony and progress were all but abandoned.

The cure for the disease that had decimated the pack was a simple airborne virus that spread rapidly from werewolf to werewolf, was completely asymptomatic, and imparted an immunity to the killing birth defect both for the werewolf who carried it, and to all his offspring. The virus was so infectious that only a single culture of it existed, and it was entrusted to the care of a human holy man, Louis Phillipe Montclaire, for the simple reason that he had every cause to want to keep it safe. The virus that could eradicate the Scourge from the lupinotuum must first be incubated in the human body, and it was deadly to its host species.

Louis Phillipe knew he would die at the hands of the queen's guards, and he infected himself with the virus before he came to visit the queen. Through his blood

252

he spread the virus to the guards, to the queen, and to everyone with whom they came in contact. Among his race, he was the first to die. But over the next half century one half of the human population of the earth would be destroyed by what he had unleashed. What werewolves called a miracle, humans named the Black Death.

CHAPTER TWENTY SEVEN

L ara's hand was upon the arm of Nicholas Devoncroix when she felt Emory's closeness, and heard his need inside her head. She thought, *No please, not now ...* with a great rending despair, and she thought, *My love, my love, you've come to me!* with a surge of wondrous welcome so intense it left her dizzy. It was all at once, in the briefest of seconds, and then she turned and she saw Emory's face against the glass, and she felt the throb of heat in her palm where once she had lost a layer of skin, and her throat went dry and she had to turn her head away because she could feel the dark fingers of destiny about her and joy never lasted for her, never.

She looked up at Nicholas and she said urgently, "I never lied to you. Take my truth. Know it. *Please.*"

He half-smiled in confusion, wanting to believe it a joke, but he must have smelled her desperation, because the smile faded. He took her shoulders and leaned in to her, inhaling the scent of

254

her truth just as she had done with him only a moment earlier. Her diamond earring brushed his cheek. She whispered, "I could have loved you, Nicholas Devoncroix. I could have."

He straightened and looked into her eyes. What he saw there caused alarm and suspicion to quicken in his, and then he looked over her shoulder and saw the human standing at the glass.

His nostrils flared, his face went tight, and so did his hand upon her wrist. But she pulled away, a look of terrible desperation upon her face, and he let her go.

He let her go.

CHAPTER TWENTY EIGHT

T he door opened onto the music and the gaiety of the party, and she came out into the corridor. She was wearing a tiny black sheath that made her skin look like porcelain and her hair floated around her when she moved. Her eyes were as deep and bright as a sunlit sea, but there was anxiety in them, and breathless joy, and question, and fear. All the things that I felt.

She came close to me. I didn't dare touch her. She smelled like roses to me. She drank me in with her eyes: my hair, my face, my lips, the scar beneath my eye. My throat, my torso, my legs, my worn-down boots. And she drank me in with her senses: my shock, my terror, my desperation, my joy, my simple joy at being near her again. She whispered, "What is it?"

I wanted to touch her. The tiny scars on my palms ached for her. I swallowed hard. It took all the effort at my command to make my voice work. "I never wanted to do this. I never wanted to come here." It was a lie. All my life I had wanted nothing more than to come here, to stand here, to be here close enough to smell her, to see the gentle rise and fall of her chest, to draw her into my embrace.

I could see panic rising in her eyes. She searched my face desperately, trying to know my thoughts. "What? What has happened?"

"You're the only one who can help me," I said. "I wouldn't ask if there was another way. I need you to come with me. I'm so sorry, love. I'm so sorry."

Her eyes were awash with tenderness, yet laced with regret — the same dark and lonely regret that I was feeling. She said softly, "You surely have always known that all you ever had to do was stretch out your hand and I would place mine in it." And she took my fingers in hers, and closed her own about them. I felt her power surge through me. I felt the joy of completion. I felt the calm of certainty. I felt a hundred thousand things that had been denied too long. I felt whole.

I drew in her fragrance and lost myself in it. I pulled her close, and I covered her mouth with my own. I tasted her, I melted into her, I opened myself to her, I let her hear my thoughts. I let her feel and know and understand everything that was in me. I felt her shock and her disbelief, and when she tried to pull away I let her, but she merely sank into me again, breathing quickly, trembling a little in my arms, searching my eyes.

"I can't compel you," I whispered. "I won't compel you. Please tell me you believe this is the right thing to do."

I saw her chest rise and fall. I felt the brush of her unsteady breath. I wanted to hold her for the rest of my life. I made myself stand still.

She said, with her eyes big and shocked and yet somehow wondrously calm, "I would believe it because you do. But even if you did not ... I would do this thing because I think ..." And here her voice faltered a little, and her brow came together uncertainly, as though she were trying to divine the right words. "We were meant for this moment."

I could barely draw breath, so great was my wonder, my love, my relief. How desperately I wanted to believe that. That all the pain, all the loneliness, all the wrong choices and great, brutish mistakes of my lifetime could be redeemed in this one moment, with Lara, for her and by her. *Let it be so,* I thought helplessly, *let it be so.*

I was that desperate, and that foolish.

There was another burst of sound and color, and Nicholas Devoncroix came through the door. Though he stood perhaps ten feet away, there was no doubt he had heard every word before he came outside. His smile was laced was cool contempt, but his eyes churned darkly with hurt and betrayal. He said, "I've often heard it said that the only thing more treacherous than a human is a female. I am disappointed in the one ..." His eyes fell upon Lara. "And gratified in the other." He looked at me.

Lara stepped away from me, although her fingers still touched mine. I could feel the rending of her spirit, the great churning of her anguish. She said nothing. It was enough that I knew what I had done.

Nicholas looked again at Lara. He said calmly, "I asked for your allegiance and you replied you did not know me. Let me show you who I am. I could take you from this human now, but I will not. I could seduce you with promises and tempt you with power, but I will not. I could call my guards and take you away

258

by force if I wished, but I will not."

He looked at me for a moment and his stare was like an ice pick in my brain; I could feel small vessels burst and hear a rushing in my ears and my eyes watered. His gaze returned to Lara. "He will take you into his intrigue and risk your life, your comfort, your security and all that you hold dear. I," he said in a voice that was very still, "will let you go."

He looked again at me. "I wish you both great happiness in your endeavors. But ..." His voice was like ice as he turned to leave, and the fury in his eyes pinned us both. "Don't get too comfortable with your success. I have never lost twice."

He started to turn, and then looked back at her. "By the way," he added quietly, "I could have loved you, too."

I saw Lara's hand swipe away tears as she watched him go, and it stabbed in my heart. I knew then what I had stolen from her, what I could never replace. But I had no choice.

I had no choice.

CHAPTER TWENTY NINE

I used the key card that Alexander had given me to access the building. The lights were still on and the door to the laboratory slid open when I approached. All three scientists were still working, and they barely glanced up at me when I entered. I spent less than three minutes downloading all the data I could onto a portable drive the size of a quarter and I dropped it into my pocket. No one questioned me. I was under the authority of Alexander Devoncroix, and to offer anything less than their full cooperation would have been worse than treasonous; it would have been disrespectful.

If my heart was beating faster than normal it would not have surprised them. My heart rate, sweat glands and adrenal function had been accelerated from the first moment I was brought into the lab by Alexander. I told Tobias I wanted to collect another tissue sample, and in my nervousness almost knocked an entire stack of sterile kits to the floor when I went to collect one. Tobias shot me a look of mild annoyance but was clearly too preoccupied with the slide he was examining under the microscope to spare me much attention.

I had noticed earlier that they were keeping David unconscious by means of a low-voltage alternating current that was delivered through the same external electrodes that monitored his brain activity. The IV drip delivered a steady dose of succinylcholine that acted as a smooth muscle paralytic. The first thing I did when I entered the room was switch off the monitor alarms. There was nothing I could do about the fact that his vital functions were monitored on every computer screen in the lab; I could only hope that random chance would be on my side for long enough for me to get him out of the building before one of the scientists abandoned visual analysis for a computer and noticed the discrepancy.

Two things allowed me to think I could do this: Alexander Devoncroix believed David was strong enough to require two forms of powerful sedation and constant monitoring, and I had seen the data for myself. I believed that the moment he was conscious and breathing on his own, he would be capable of movement and rational thought. If he could move under his own power, I could get him out of the building undetected and into the car that was waiting for him outside. I figured I had approximately three minutes, if all went well, before someone either glanced at a computer monitor or came to look for me.

I quickly disconnected the catheters and IVs, anxiously watching the monitors for signs that his lungs were trying to function on their own. I turned off the EEG monitor and, with it, the electrical current that had kept his brain in a deep coma. I plucked off the electrodes and when I did his body started to convulse on the table. For a moment of blind panic I froze, and then I realized he was choking on the ventilator tube. Quickly, and not very gently, I pulled it out. He coughed, and a fine foam of spittle flecked his lips. He was breathing.

And then he opened his eyes. They were Devoncroix blue, they were brilliant with intelligence, and they were mesmeric. There was a moment, as quick and as intense as a landscape caught in a flash of lightning, when I felt the full weight of what I had done, of who he was and what he represented and I felt myself poised, with him, on the brink of a history that could never be rewritten.

But it was only an instant, and then the part of my brain that could feel the time ticking away took over, and I took his shoulders, helping him to sit up. "Listen to me," I said, low and quick. "I am your friend. You've got to leave this place." I remember wondering distantly if he understood English. "I have someone waiting to take you to safety but we have to move quickly and you have to do exactly as I say."

I had worn a rain coat into the lab and had pretended to be too distracted to take it off when I came in; now I shrugged out of it and pushed his arms inside. "You should be getting the feeling back into your limbs by now. Try to stand. Damn." I realized then I hadn't brought him any shoes, and a man in a raincoat without shoes was bound to attract attention. I struggled out of my boots and pushed them onto his naked feet. They were too big for him and went on without too much trouble. Still I was breathing hard as I straightened up and grasped his arm to help him off the table. "I guess you need these more than I do."

He looked at the boots, and then at me. He said, "Thank you."

The sound of his voice caught me off guard; I don't know why. I stared at him. He stepped down from the table as though he was awakening from a short nap, tightening the belt of my coat around his nakedness, shaking back his light hair. The gesture struck me as absurdly mundane, the tightening of the belt, the straightening of the hair, and there was a moment, just a moment, when I wondered how I had come to be in this place doing such an outrageous thing, and how this could possibly be real. Some fleeting, uncaptured thought about Dr. Frankenstein flashed across my mind and was gone.

His eyes were quick and alert as he glanced around the room, and then moved unerringly toward the door. He stopped, his head cocked, listening to what I could not hear. "There is a disturbance outside," he said.

My heart lurched. The room was soundproof to my ears, but I didn't doubt his. I moved quickly past him to the door. "Stay here," I said, and ran, silent in my socks, out into the corridor.

I hadn't gone half a dozen steps when I heard it—the crash of glass, a roar of fury, a choked off death scream. There was a smear of blood on the wire-reinforced window in the fire door that separated the lab from the corridor, and beyond it was chaos. Shattered equipment, overturned tables, electronics crushed and sparking. On the floor was a tattered lab coat soaked in blood, and beside it the form of a dark wolf, its abdomen open and its intestines spilling from the wound in a glistening pile. Not ten feet from where I stood gasping before the window, two massive wolves were engaged in combat, and as I watched the throat of one was opened by the teeth of the other, and blood spurted in an arc.

I spun away from the door, and David was behind me,

watching the proceedings through the window with a detached interest. I grabbed his arm and pulled him with me, running toward the exit at the front of the building and the car that was waiting for him there. I felt it before I saw it: a gush of air and then a great black blur and as I turned blood spattered over my face and hair, in my mouth and eyes, and I saw David throw the attacker back against the wall as though he were nothing more than a child's plaything that had gotten in his way. I realized then that it was David's blood, not mine, on my face. The gash on his arm had already begun to heal itself but the sleeve of my raincoat was bloodied and torn. Hardly had I taken note of this than the creature sprang again toward us with a killing roar. I saw hard muscles and bloody teeth and wild yellow eyes, and I saw David's arm shoot out and snatch the wolf from the air mid-leap. With a casual twist of his wrist, he snapped its neck and dropped the body on the floor.

When I looked at David, he was gone. In his place was a brown skinned and sloe-eyed male with close cropped brown hair wearing my raincoat with its torn and bloodstained sleeve and my cowboy boots. That is what I saw. And then there was David again with his pale hair and Nordic features and brilliant blue eyes, and I said, I think I said, "Hurry."

We reached the elegant reception room with its blood-smeared silk wallpaper and broken-spined books and the body of the loup garou who had tried to defend this place crumpled on the floor. We pushed out into the foggy night, the cobblestones cutting my feet through the socks, and went through the gate. During this time I glanced at David on three separate occasions. Once he was dark haired and olive-skinned, and then, chameleon-like, he was limpid-eyed and brown and four inches shorter, and then he was strong-shouldered and bald with a wide flat nose and full lips. And then he was blond again, as I first had met him.

That is what I saw.

We reached the curb just as the dark sedan pulled up. Lara's eyes flashed with alarm when she saw me but she could smell the blood was not my own so I did not have to reassure her. I opened the back door and urged David in. "I don't know, something happened, I don't know what, just go, go."

And, because she was Lara and she loved me, she did not hesitate or question. She pulled out into traffic even as I was slamming closed the car door. I never saw David Devoncroix again.

Nicholas Devoncroix was with his father, furiously demanding that my activities be investigated, when the red security light on the pack leader's telephone began to flash. The two of them entered the scene of the massacre together, and when Nicholas found my scent there he let out a cry of fury, anguish, and desperate, raging impotence that shattered glass, that stopped the swing of clock pendulums, that pierced the heart of every loup garou within hearing distance. Alexander Devoncroix took his son away, and told him the truth at last. Perhaps he would have preferred to take the secret to his grave, but after the slaughter he had no choice. Nicholas was the heir designee to the pack; the truth was his birthright and its consequences were his to resolve. When Alexander was finished, David the hybrid, assisted by perhaps the only person alive who could navigate the

265

worlds of men and loup garoux with such effortless ease, had disappeared. A ragged dawn had broken, and the world that he knew — that all of us knew — would never be the same.

CHAPTER THIRTY

I went back into the building, and into the restroom at the back. I must have stepped in blood because later my socks were hard and crusty. I spent a long time vomiting into the bowl, then I washed my face and hair with lavender soap until the water no longer ran pink. The blood had soaked into my leather jacket, leaving dark stains that were impossible to remove. I didn't try.

The panic was gone from my chest, leaving only a certainty, and a heavy sorrow. It wasn't simply that I knew what I had to do; I had always known that. It was that I knew now I could no longer delay. I found a 4 ml syringe and drew up enough succinylcholine to kill three men, or one werewolf, and I tucked it into the lining of my jacket. I walked outside and hailed a cab.

When the doorman at the Trump Towers saw my wet, slicked back hair, my white cheeks and shoeless feet, he reached for the security phone. I told him that Prince Fasburg was expecting me and it probably says something about the kind of company the prince was accustomed to keeping that, after barely another moment's hesitation, he rang me up.

The prince had plenty of time to prepare himself for my arrival, so whatever surprise he might have felt on seeing me was not evident when I came in. It was after midnight, but he was on the phone, casually negotiating some deal or another. He was wearing a crimson dressing gown with a velvet collar and, with his long dark hair and the glass of brandy in his hand, he looked like a movie star of old. He had the courtesy to end his phone call when he saw me, and he greeted me with a small grimace.

"You reek of death," he observed. "Feel free to use my shower."

It was a luxurious suite, with a spiral staircase leading downstairs to a conference room, and another stair leading to an upstairs bedroom. The lights of New York glittered through the floor to ceiling windows like a fantastical wonderland. The plush ivory carpet was like down beneath my feet, and the opulent furnishings reminded me of home. His home, of course, not mine. Never mine.

I came into the room, my hands in my jacket pockets. "No thank you. I won't be staying."

He poured me a drink from a cut glass decanter, but when he held it out to me I did not reach for it. He returned the glass to the console and sipped his own drink, looking me over, using those extraordinary senses of his to fill in the pieces of the story he did not already know. His black eyes showed absolutely no expression, though his lips smiled thinly. "So Alexander wins our wager. Humans are indeed treacherous. What a pity he will not live to collect."

I said, "I'm sorry to disappoint you, Prinze-Papa."

He acknowledged my apology with a slight incline of his head. "I did expect more of you. But you are still the same idealistic fool who faced down the Devoncroix pack on hunt night to protect a weakling who could not keep up."

I struggled mightily to keep my voice steady. "That weakling was your daughter."

He sipped his drink. "And you were as much a son to me as any human could have hoped to be."

I said, "You been waiting all these years for this moment to take over the pack. Has it all been about ambition, then? Was there never anything else?"

"Among the loup garoux," he agreed, "there is rarely anything else." And his expression gentled, just a fraction. "But I did love you, little man, in my fashion."

"You sent the werewolf to the lab to kill me."

He looked momentarily regretful. "Had you succeeded in your mission, there could be no witnesses. Had you failed ..." He looked at the bloodstains on my jacket. "Well, you could not be allowed to fail."

"You miscalculated."

"So it would appear. And you, my dear young fellow, have been manipulated by the master."

"I would say we both have been."

"Perhaps." He sipped his drink. "I never doubted your ability to perform the task, of course. As enraptured as you were by my daughter all those years ago, you betrayed her trust and broke her heart for nothing more than the opportunity to impress me. You have betrayed your own people a dozen times over the years in order to gain honor among mine. Certainly you

269

possessed the ruthlessness that is necessary for a properly trained scientific mind. Of course, I believed that your obsessive fascination with the Devoncroix would add weight to your orders, which is why I chose Alexander to deliver them. And I believed that he was wise enough to know the danger we all would be in if the mission was not carried out."

"Alexander Devoncroix would never sanction the murder of his own flesh and blood. He gave the order as you instructed, because to have done otherwise would have alerted you that he was aware of your plans to use this incident to take over the pack. But he also knew that humans rarely do what they are told." And so he had led me to the Plaza Hotel, and to Lara, the only person in the world who could assist me in defying the Brotherhood.

And he had reminded me of my vow. *A brother will do nothing to disturb the balance. What nature has created, we must preserve.*

"It was a bold scheme," the prince agreed thoughtfully, and with a hint of admiration, "and risky. But it had those very elements in its favor — that and the factor of unpredictability. I did not suspect. I am now well taught. Next time I will be more vigilant."

"Alexander must have known from the time he aligned with you that your real ambition was to overthrow him."

"Of course he knew. It has never been a secret between us. But over the years we have maintained a balance of power ... until his mistake tipped the scales in my favor." He smiled and raised his glass briefly, just as though the night's mission had in fact been a success, just as though he did not know that even now the entire balance of power was in danger of collapsing around us all.

"The pack has been misled for centuries," he said. "It rightfully should have belonged to the Fasburgs from the time of Eudora, and so it would have done had it not been, oddly enough, for the intervention of a human." Again he smiled faintly and without humor. "You have always had such admiration for the Devoncroix, but surely by now you realize that it is the Fasburgs who are, and always have been, the civilized ones. The Devoncroix are savages who, at best, can only attempt to emulate our example. Shall I tell you now the truth about the legendary Eudora and the vow that changed the world? I am surprised your research has not already uncovered it. All the evidence was there. Perhaps if you had been less eager to believe the myth of the Devoncroix you would have seen it."

He walked over to the window and stood for a moment, looking out. "What a wretched place," he murmured. "Yet utterly suitable for a dynasty that was built on greed and excess."

He turned back to me. "The story is told that Eudora the queen arose from the bloodied body of her beloved human filled with angst and regret that his life had been so carelessly lost, and in consequence she sent forth the decree that no loup garou should ever again spill the blood of a human. Upon this act of great enlightenment, supposedly, a new era of peace and prosperity was ushered in and the modern world was built. In fact, the decree came later, much later, when Eudora's scientists discovered that, while the cure for the Scourge that was killing their children was found in the virus with which the priest had infected himself, its actual cause had a much darker origin. The Devoncroix, you see, were an ancient line whose power and fame among our people was a result of their prowess as hunters. And what they hunted, even in Eudora's time, were humans. Untold

271

centuries of wantonly consuming human flesh had resulted in the genetic characteristic that is now known as the Devoncroix Effect. It was this which was responsible for, among other things, the Scourge. So the good queen Eudora, herself somewhat of a connoisseur of human flesh, issued the decree not to save the human race, but to save her own. An irony that she should have been so desperately misunderstood throughout the centuries, wouldn't you agree? And an even greater irony that it was the Devoncroix Effect itself which allowed this monster to be created."

I remembered the chromosome in the strand of David's DNA where the Devoncroix Effect should be. I tried to make sense of it. I could not.

"Suppose it is not a monster at all," I said, "but only a natural stage of evolution. Or suppose even further that it is an evolutionary *correction*. What if the hybrid is the original species, and you and I are the mutants?"

His eyes widened with surprise and delight, as though he were impressed with my cleverness. "Excellent speculation, my boy, however irrelevant. But your reasoning is of course fundamentally flawed. One must guard against romanticism in the scientific mind. "

I said, "The Devoncroix hybrid was created by nature. It was not yours to destroy."

He said flatly, "It was an abomination. It would have weakened the species, and destroyed the pack. But more importantly, its very existence has done the one thing centuries of plotting, subterfuge and determination have failed to do: it has brought down the dynasty of the Devoncroix."

I said, very quietly, "Not yet it hasn't."

He simply smiled. "My dear young fellow, you surely don't believe that I would have allowed a plan of this magnitude to rest upon the whims of one frail human, do you? The pack has been infiltrated at the highest levels, an undertaking that Alexander made possible — inevitable, really — when he began the attempt to cover up the existence of the hybrid thirty years ago. Within the week both the pack leader and his heir designee will be dead, opening the door to a peaceful take-over by the only person with the power to do so: myself. The hybrid will be recaptured and destroyed before morning. His scent signature is unique in all the world, and impossible to mistake. There is nowhere he can hide we cannot find him."

I said, "Your purpose would be better served to bring him before the pack alive, and humiliate the Devoncroix with his existence. The pack would turn to you of its own accord. If you kill him, no one will ever know what is possible because of the Devoncroix Effect. His death will bring you nothing."

He looked amused and, at the same time, puzzled. "My dear young man, you don't understand at all. It's not the possibility that the creature could destroy the pack that concerns me, but that he could control it. Don't you know I've had the best scientists in the world — including yourself by the way, although you contributed to the data unknowingly — examining the possibilities since his birth was confirmed? There has never been another like him. His strength and his intelligence exceeds anything history has known, and that is without even confirming his sensory or transmutation capabilities. The loup garou would be helpless to challenge him, and the human population ... well, they would simply be helpless, wouldn't they? They would call him a miracle, as you have done, they would worship him as a

273

god, they would be completely in his thrall. If this hybrid were allowed to live it would be possible, for the first time in modern history, for a single personality to rule the world, unquestioned and unchallenged. Surely even you can see the danger in that."

For the first time my resolve wavered. Unaccountably, my mind flashed back to that moment in the lab, the way he tightened the belt of my raincoat and tossed back his hair. *What rough beast, its hour come round at last ...* A nonsensical image, but it remained.

And then I focused again. "It is not for you to determine the course of mankind. You took a vow."

He laughed. "And what do you imagine we have been doing all these years, my friend, *except* determining the course of mankind? The balance of nature is all very well and good, as long as the balance is always slightly in our favor. The Devoncroix hybrid changes all that. That is why he cannot be allowed to survive."

He finished his drink and set the glass aside. "And so now all that remains is this business between you and me. I'm sorry it has come to this between us, my little man, I truly am. I had such great hopes for you."

I realized then the strategy behind his moving across the room from me to stand in front of the window. The distance would be an advantage to him when he chose to Change, and to charge. I used every technique I knew to control my heartbeat, my breath, my temperature. I had had years to practice.

I said, "You have given me more than I can ever repay, taught me more than I could ever have imagined. I will be in your debt for the rest of my life, and beyond." I slipped the hypodermic out of the lining of my pocket and popped off the cover with my thumb. I kept my movements subtle and the syringe hidden inside my pocket, but I did not deceive myself into thinking I was being surreptitious. I walked toward him. "But you have interfered with the balance of nature. You ordered the death of a Brother. You know what I must do."

He smiled, sadly. "I have told you, my little man, you will never be faster than we, or stronger than we. I don't know what kind of poison you have brought—I don't recognize the scent— but you should know that even the deadliest of human drugs are delayed in our metabolism. Four, five, or six seconds—it is enough to snap your neck or crush your skull. You have very little chance of leaving this encounter alive."

I said, still moving toward him, "I know that. But neither do you."

It was over in an instant. I was six feet away from him when he whipped off his dressing gown and sailed it at me. I pulled the syringe from my pocket but the flash of his Change blinded me. The air was sucked out of the room in an explosion of color that tasted like burnt cloves and bitter almond and then I was knocked to the floor with a powerful force. The hypodermic flew from my hand.

I grasped his powerful shoulders, fur and sinew and muscle, and twisted my face away from his teeth. Behind me I saw the door burst open, and I saw the swirl of a fur-trimmed cape and elegant sequined shoes, and I heard Lara cry, "Papa, don't!" and he looked away long enough for me to break away from his weight, to roll for the syringe on the floor. But then he was upon me again, and I cried out as his teeth tore into my shoulder, raking open flesh and muscle. He grabbed me by the torso in his mouth and flung me against a wall. I felt ribs crack. I heard Lara scream.

The wolf was upon me again. I threw up an arm to defend myself but it was a pathetic gesture. He slammed me to the floor with both forepaws on my chest and his breath hot upon my face and when I looked into his eyes I think I knew for the first time that he really intended to kill me.

There was a scream, no, a roar, behind me, and a flash of color and the smell of burned roses. I tried to gasp, "Lara — don't!" But I am not sure the words were audible. It was a breath, no more, and then the weight was lifted from my chest. The great black wolf lunged to meet the smaller, more delicate one, but too late. She had the element of surprise; he had never imagined she had the courage to do it. The prince collapsed on the floor with a great ragged tear in his jugular spurting blood into the ivory carpet and Lara, her muzzle dripping red, staggered back.

I pushed myself to my feet, dragging in shallow, painful breaths, staring at her. She was fixed upon the corpse on the floor. Her whole body shuddered. I braced my arm across my broken ribs so that I could speak. "Lara," I managed, but that was all. My heart was breaking, my soul was shattered, everything that had ever made me what I was was nothing but a discordant symphony of jagged pieces. "Lara."

She looked at me, and there was a moment, just the briefest of moments, when I thought I saw the dark gaze of the prince reflected in her eyes. But then there was nothing there but anguish, and shame, and regret, and then she turned from me, and ran toward the window. I screamed at her, but it was no use. Glass shattered, curtains billowed, and she was gone.

CHAPTER THIRTY ONE

The Present

The hands on the Patek Phillipe read 8:30. The bottle of wine was almost gone, and the remains of fruit and cheese and bread were scattered over the silver platter between them.

Rolfe commented, "A dramatic tale to be sure, but please don't tell me Lara Fasburg leapt to her death that night in New York, because that would be too much. Really, I don't think I could go on listening if it were true."

Emory shook his head slowly. His gaze was upon his glass. "No," he said dully. "She didn't die. She sacrificed more than her life for me that night. She gave up her humanity."

And then he looked up, making an effort to return his voice to neutral. "They can leap and climb great distances with impunity, particularly when in the throes of the kind of adrenaline madness that overtook Lara after her father's death. I don't know how she survived that night. I did not see her again for some time."

"One has to love the dreadful poetry of it," Rolfe murmured. "The beautiful Lara, who wanted only to escape her savage nature in the world of humans, was forced in the end to descend into savagery to save the human she loved." And he looked at Emory alertly. "Of course you lied about your bond with Lara."

Emory said nothing.

"More than once," Rolfe pointed out. "That was unspeakably foolish. Did you think that denying you were bond-mates would somehow protect her?"

"Maybe I was trying to protect myself. One can't be too careful about revealing one's alliances these days."

Rolfe pursed his lips thoughtfully. "True enough. So what became of you that night after Lara deserted you?"

Emory gazed into his wine glass. "Their bodies, if left unpreserved, deteriorate in a matter of hours, and by the morning nothing remained of the murder but a blood-stained carpet and the shattered window. The mystery of the death of Prince Fasburg was never solved, though of course I was a prime suspect for many years. The princess died of grief within twenty four hours, as is customary when the mating bond is broken. The Dark Brotherhood believed it was I who had killed the prince. I let them think so."

"It was," agreed Rolfe, "the least you could do to protect your lover. And David, the cause of all this mayhem? How was he able to evade the trackers who were sent for him?"

Emory said, "Later, when I thought about it, I realized that the various appearances he assumed when I saw him were merely a way of disguising his scent signature. There was very little left for anyone to trace. Lara, of course, was adored and protected by humans all over the globe, and if she asked for a favor they did not hesitate. David was on a human's private jet bound for the Andes within twenty minutes of leaving the lab. He was well away by the time Lara came to confront her father and found me there."

Rolfe lifted an eyebrow. "The Andes?"

Emory coughed a little. He tasted blood in the back of his throat, and swallowed. "The loup garou have Sanctuaries in remote places around the world—places of safety and secrecy that have never been penetrated. My understanding is that such a place was his destination. Whether or not he actually reached it, I don't know." Emory leaned back heavily against the chair. "I'm tired. I need to rest."

"In a moment." There was no impatience whatsoever in Rolfe's tone. "You've done extraordinarily well. Just a few more details, if you please. Did you see Nicholas Devoncroix again?"

Emory was silent for a moment, as though debating how to answer. He stretched forth one hand, toying with the stem of his wine glass.

Finally he looked at Rolfe. His face, and his tone, was expressionless. "Yes," he said. "I saw him."

CHAPTER THIRTY TWO

I did my best to rid the prince's suite of any evidence of Lara's and my presence. I tied back the curtains to keep them from billowing through the broken window and I turned off the lights in hopes of delaying the inevitable moment when someone from the street would glance up and notice, if they had not already. I hid the wolf-formed body of the prince in the bathroom. I did this all in a state of shock; my mind numb, my body in agony. Occasionally there would be a flash of memory: the click of high heel on marble floor, a waft of perfume, the way the princess had smiled when she first embraced me. The spark of amusement in the prince's black eyes: *So, little man, will you come and live among us, and be one of us?* Lara, gripping my hand as we sailed from the church portico into the canal, laughing with triumph and clinging to each other when we surfaced. The smell of burned roses. I hardened myself, I batted the memories away before they could take hold. I knew if I didn't,

280

they would suck the last of the life's blood from me, and I had much to do before I could die.

I stole one of the prince's overcoats to hide my bleeding wounds, and a pair of his shoes. I left via the freight elevator and exited opposite the door I had entered. I was becoming light headed from pain and blood loss and I knew my shoulder wound needed stitches, but I didn't dare go to the Emergency Room. I knew a human doctor in New York; we had gotten drunk together once or twice at scientific conferences and I had kept just enough of his secrets to persuade him to open his office for me at one o'clock in the morning. I told him I'd been stabbed, and let him think it was in the process of trying to buy drugs. He looked disgusted and made it clear this was his last favor, but he wrapped my ribs and stitched my shoulder and injected me with penicillin, then sent me off with a handful of Percocet and a prescription for antibiotics. He turned me in the next day, of course, but by then it didn't matter.

I didn't dare go back to the Plaza. I spent the night on the streets, freezing and coughing and dozing intermittently under the influence of the painkillers. In the morning I went to the public library, and began the process of trying to find Alexander Devoncroix.

In the end he found me.

Alexander Devoncroix had offices all over the world, of course, and it did not take a great deal of technological savvy to finesse the Internet into giving up his Park Avenue address. By this time I was a fugitive from the police, and I could not guess how many of the prince's operatives had been ordered to kill me. My time was limited, and I did not dare risk wasting it. I waited until dark, and I made my way on foot toward Park Avenue.

The black limousine slid to a stop at the curb before I had gone a block. When the back door opened, I heard Vivaldi.

I got inside, guarding my stiff ribs and my throbbing shoulder. Alexander Devoncroix was in shadows, and I could not see his eyes. I heard the crisp snap of a newspaper and, as we passed slowly under a streetlight, he set the paper aside and looked at me.

I said, "All you ever wanted was to have the prince out of the way. Whether I disposed of him, or whether he killed me — and was subsequently executed for murdering a human — didn't matter. What happened to David didn't matter. The threat to the pack was never the hybrid. It was Prince Fasburg."

Alexander inclined his head. "My first loyalty is now, and has always been, to the pack. I think you understand that."

The painkillers had taken some of the edge off my rage, but had not dulled it entirely. My one fist tightened against my ribcage, and sweat popped out on my brow. "You have no idea what you've done. You don't even care."

"On the contrary. I know exactly what I've done, and I care a good deal. This is why I'm offering you the use of this car, young man, and suggesting very strongly that you put as much distance between yourself and this city as possible. I mean you no harm and it may comfort you to know I share your ideals. But you will be dead before dawn if you do not heed me."

I said coldly, "I am your last witness."

I thought I saw him smile in the flicker of streetlight. "I am the leader of the pack. You pose no threat to me. The only one who did is dead, and the hybrid is safe and well away. We will deal with him when we must. You have done us a service. But my tolerance extends only so far. If you need a passport or funds,

I can provide them. Otherwise, I suggest you find the first international flight you can and be on it."

I said, "The pack has been infiltrated. There are assassination plans in place for you and your heir."

If the information surprised him he would not, of course, reveal it. He pressed a small button on the console, and in a few moments the car pulled to the curb. He said, "I've enjoyed our association, Emory Hilliford. I'm sure you understand that it must now come to an end."

The door opened, and he turned to get out.

I was weary to the bone, cold and hungry and aching, and I was not sure I had the strength to even form the next words. But I had to ask.

"How did you know?" I asked. "How did you know I wouldn't kill him?"

He merely smiled. "Why, Dr. Hilliford," he said, "I've read your books."

He got out of the car, and I never saw him again. Within the hour, Alexander Devoncroix was dead.

I pushed my way through the gathering of mourners in the anteroom outside the chamber of the Park Avenue mansion where the leader of the pack and his mate lay in state. The word had been put out that they had been struck down by a human driving an automobile while crossing Central Park. I did not know at that time whether it was true or not. But I knew it had not been an accident.

The air was thick and sour smelling and the faces I passed were sharp and white with narrowed eyes. The well-dressed bodies were restless and bristling, uneasy in their human forms and bound to them, it seemed, by only the thinnest threads of consciousness. The leader of the pack was dead. They were without anchor, without purpose, barely tethered to life. I could feel the outer edges of a thousand years of civilization begin to crack and peel away.

Two guards were on either side of me and another behind. Though I had come of my own volition, I never would have gotten that close to Nicholas Devoncroix in this time of crisis without them. I do not know what I would have done had he refused to see me. I did not know what I faced when I stood before him.

We stopped before a tall, ornately carved door. One of the guards opened it and stepped back. I went through alone.

The room was a study of some sort, with a desk and a computer, some formal furniture drawn up before a fireplace. The fireplace was dark and cold. It was four o'clock in the morning and the room was lit only by two lamps whose yellow pools of light did not meet. Nicholas Devoncroix stood before the window alone, looking out.

In little over five hours the New York Stock Exchange would open. Already the Tokyo market was battling to right itself. Telephones were ringing in human offices, on human nightstands, in human coat pockets all over the world. Among the lupinotuum the news would have been almost instantaneous. They would have fallen to their knees with the impact of loss. Planes would lose their pilots, machinery would lose its operators, cars would lose their drivers for seconds, perhaps even as much as a minute at a time. The newspapers would be filled with reports of unrelated incidents around the globe. Among their species, the attachment to the pack leader was a mysterious but indisputable phenomenon, and his loss was a physical thing.

Shops would close, industry would be suspended, banks would not open, companies would lock their doors as thousands upon thousands of lupinotuum followed the trail of their grief to Castle Devoncroix. In Paris and London and Rome and Los Angeles, the loup garoux, in a desperate attempt to ease their anxiety, would take to the natural forms, running madly through the parks and beaches and eventually the city streets. There would be mayhem, mass terror, colossal losses.

Except of course, that the natural transition of power had been designed to prevent precisely such a disaster. The reason that the streets of New York did not now run red with blood was because Elise and Alexander Devoncroix had spent almost a century preparing for this moment.

"You have courage, human," Nicholas said without turning. "I will grant you that. But as I recall, a lack of reckless courage was never one of your failings."

I said, "I am sorry for your loss." The words seemed at that moment small and frail and human, and they fell into the shadows and were swallowed up.

Nicholas spoke with his back to me, his gaze upon the darkened streets below. "You were with my father tonight."

"You know I didn't kill him."

"How do I know that? Because you say it's true?" His voice was conversational, almost matter of fact. I did not respond.

He turned then and walked toward me in a leisurely fashion. His expression was calm and perfectly composed, but his eyes were dark with grief, and had a hard glitter. He stood before me for a moment, and then, with no warning whatsoever, he drew back his arm and backhanded me hard across the face. I

285

staggered back and tasted blood, but I knew he could have easily broken my jaw had he wished to.

He repeated, so lowly and with such intensity it was almost a growl. *"How do I know that, human?"*

I wiped the blood from my split lip, holding his gaze. "I was meant for another assignment," I said deliberately. "You know the one I mean."

I surprised him enough to cause his eyebrows to draw together briefly, almost infinitesimally, with a flare of quickly suppressed rage. He stood less than a foot from me. I could feel his breath on my face. He said, in a near whisper that reverberated around the room, "Your stench was in every corner of the laboratory. I know what you were meant to do. I know what you did. I know what you are."

Suddenly his hand shot out and grasped my throat, slamming me back against the wall so hard that I saw stars. His fingers closed around my trachea like a vise, squeezing off my breath until my airway was the size of a straw. Instinctively and futilely I clawed at his hand. Wheezing noises came from my throat. His voice came to me through the roaring tunnel of pressure in my ears.

"Do you know why you are still alive, human? There is one reason and one reason only. Honor."

Abruptly he released my throat and air came flooding back. I coughed and my broken ribs stabbed. I could still feel the iron imprint of his fingers on my skin.

He stood staring at me for another long moment, while the rage and the contempt in his eyes faded, slowly, into something cold and oddly resigned. "Half a millennium ago," he said, "my ancestor issued an edict declaring a truce with your people." He turned away from me, moving across the room. His voice sounded tired. "By this time tomorrow that edict will be revoked. Count yourself fortunate you found me tonight."

For a moment I didn't understand what he meant. And it was another moment before I could speak. "You can't mean … you can't mean to reinstate the Edict of Separation. It was overruled by Eudora's vow! Your father never would have sanctioned this. You know he wouldn't!"

"And you of all people know I have no choice!" he practically spat the words. "Until we can determine what deviance of a mismating allowed this …" he struggled with the words. "This monster to be spawned, it could happen again. I will be on a plane for Alaska to deliver the edict to the Council before noon tomorrow. I will protect the pack."

I pushed away from the wall. "You're playing into their hands." My voice was hoarse and shallow of breath. I fought to make my words clear, pronouncing them through teeth gritted against the pain. "This is exactly the kind of chaos they wanted to ignite."

He looked at me sharply, eyes narrowing. "Who?"

Of course I did not have to say it. He knew precisely who I meant.

I said simply, "Don't do this thing. Don't let history remember you this way."

His eyes never left mine as he said very quietly, "Look around you. Look at what has been wrought in less than forty-eight hours. The leader of the pack is dead at the hands of a human. Three of the most brilliant minds this world has ever known have been slaughtered while trying to protect an aberrant freak of nature that never should have been born. You are wanted for murder by humans and treachery by your comrades. Who knows where this night will end for either of us? And all because one of my race once loved a member of yours. Don't tell me how history should remember me, human. My history was written long before I was born."

I said, "I came to deliver a warning. I tried to do the same for your father, and I was proven right. The pack has been infiltrated at the highest levels by members of the Dark Brotherhood. Some of them are human." I did not flinch from his gaze. "I should know. Don't get on that plane."

I turned and made my way to the door. I had no idea how far I would get, whether I would be allowed to leave the city, the building, or even the room. By that time it didn't matter.

I had almost reached the door before he spoke. He said, "Where is Lara?"

I could not meet his eyes when I answered. There was too much pain, such a great ocean wave of pain and shame. So I spoke without turning. "She has killed her father and gone feral. She did it to save a human. You are right. Our history was written before we were born."

I left him then, and he let me go. There was nothing more I could do. I had reached the end of my story.

The next day, Nicholas Devoncroix got on the plane.

CHAPTER THIRTY THREE

The Present

Rolfe remarked, "An interesting study in contrasts, that Nicholas. Brilliant and ruthless by all accounts, but forever a victim of wayward, impulsive emotions. What a pity he was cut down so soon. I would have liked to have known him."

He took up his glass. "What is this Edict of Separation?"

"It's a pack law that, among other things, forbids social interaction with humans. It removes the penalty for killing humans, and enforces a strict and permanent separation between the species. It hasn't been in effect since Queen Eudora. I think it was meant only to be a temporary measure, until all the evidence could be brought to light, but Nicholas died before he could revoke it, if that was ever his intention. It remains in effect to this day."

Rolfe nodded. "That explains a good deal, of course. How did you know there was a bomb on Nicholas's plane?"

"I didn't. That's the irony. I knew only that the prince had planned to assassinate the pack leader and his heir but I didn't have the resources to discover how. If Nicholas hadn't hated me so, if he hadn't been so anxious to invoke the Edict, matters might have turned out very differently for us all." He paused. "Or maybe not. We'll never know."

Rolfe said casually, "I have heard he's still alive."

Emory shrugged. "For years afterwards rumors persisted that he had survived the attack, but he never surfaced. Personally, I can see the appeal of the rumor. Even I like to comfort myself now and then by imagining that he might one day re-emerge, like the lost dauphin, the last of the great Devoncroix leaders, and put everything back to rights again. But of course what I'm really wishing for is the return of an era. And that is gone forever."

Rolfe tapped his index finger against his chin, nodding thoughtfully. "So it is. But you must admit, it was an empire built on sand. It was bound to fall."

"You may be right. The pack struggled to right itself valiantly for a time. There were battles for succession, brief victories, quick defeats. It was as Alexander said—the loup garoux are a volatile culture who have depended throughout history on two things for stability: a strong central leadership, and the balance of the Brotherhood. But now the Brotherhood of the Dark Moon was in as much disarray as the pack itself. They lost their ideals and their cohesion and devolved into little more than a gang of thugs. The pack made no effort to control them because, under the atmosphere of general lawlessness that ruled the pack, their activities often proved a useful distraction.

"Over the next several years commerce with humans began to disintegrate. Businesses reduced the wages of their human employees, and in some cases, their numbers. Pack funds, which once were so brilliantly and centrally managed, fell under the control of a dozen greedy despots. Banks began to struggle, and eventually to fail. Industries abandoned quality control on goods manufactured for human consumption, and research and development for new technologies struggled to find clear direction. An empire that took centuries to build does not collapse overnight, but after over a decade of infighting, disruption and moral disintegration, the center could not hold. And the loup garoux, fighting among themselves for their own greedy share of what was left, were content to let the humans clean up the mess. For the first time in six hundred years a generation of loup garoux reached maturity without reciting Eudora's vow."

Rolfe's smile was not so much amused as amazed. "And all of this even though the hybrid, who was both the Devoncroix's and the Fasburg's greatest fear, was quietly locked away in a remote Sanctuary in the Andes somewhere. Surely this is a fine example of being unable to outrun one's destiny."

"I suppose."

Rolfe regarded him speculatively. "Regrets, Professor? You fell very far from grace indeed, I should imagine. You were wanted by both the human authorities and your fellow brethren and both of your protectors were dead. I find it a wonder that you survived at all."

Emory said, "Oddly enough, I owe my survival to the same chaos and lack of leadership that brought down both the pack and the Dark Brotherhood. In the confusion that followed the deaths of Prince Fasburg and Alexander Devoncroix, I was able to slip away. Of course I have lived like a renegade since then, traveling from city to city, from country to country under one of a dozen sets of false papers. I have worked for tips as a tour guide in Egypt and slept on subways in Manhattan and bussed tables in London. I've lived this way for so long I'm not sure I know anything else anymore. I have many regrets. But they are not what you think."

"Indeed?" Rolfe topped off Emory's wine glass with a flourish, his manner inviting.

Emory took up the glass, holding it once again with both hands, and took a sip before resting his back against the chair again. He was thoughtful for a moment, considering his words. "I did have a few friends left among the humans in the scientific world, and without a body the American police were unable to press a case against me, so that many of my human colleagues never knew of my connection with the troubles in New York. Occasionally I would be able to get lab time, although I never dared stay too long in one place. I began to examine the slide I had stolen from the lab in New York, and to test the blood on my jacket. Human technology was years away from allowing me to read the data I had collected from their computers, so it was a laborious process. But eventually I isolated a peculiar organism in David's blood and began to understand, in part, how the Devoncroix Effect had been adapted to him."

Rolfe lifted an interested eyebrow, but Emory took his time, sipping his wine. "For centuries," he said, "scientists believed that the Black Death that decimated the human population of Europe was a bacteria-borne illness carried by fleas. But recent schools of thought suggest it was more likely a hemorrhagic virus of the Filoviridae type. Ebola and Marburg viruses belong to that group. David appears to be a carrier for a unique Filoviridae virus that can act as the trigger for hemorrhagic fever in humans, as well as for what is now called the Scourge in loup garoux – the sudden, inexplicable malformation and death of newborn cubs. The virus is spread by the exchange of bodily fluids – blood, most often, but occasionally semen, saliva and even sweat – and can be passed between humans and loup garoux, acting differently on each species as it incubates within the host. In the loup garoux, it will mean the stillbirth of ninety-five to ninety-nine percent of all offspring. In humans, it can remain inactive in the body for years, or even decades. Symptoms begin slowly, but once the disease process takes hold the victim will experience bleeding diathesis, neuromuscular degeneration, fever, a rapid disintegration of internal organs and a painful death. During this time he is highly contagious. Once the virus enters the bloodstream, in both species, it is there forever."

Rolfe maintained a respectful silence for a moment. "And when did you become symptomatic, Professor?"

Emory sipped again from the glass. "A month or two ago. There was no way I could have escaped the contagion; I was covered in David's blood the night we were attacked at the lab. I am entering the last stages, which will be far more rapid than the first."

"I see." His tone was speculative. "In the fourteenth century, it took three years to reduce the population of Europe by half. In this day of global travel, massive overcrowding, and random violence I would estimate the entire human population could be reduced by ninety percent in a fraction of that time. The loup garoux will be gone within a generation. Fascinating. Nature, it would appear, allows for but one dominant species at a time."

Emory added softly, "And nature always maintains the balance."

Rolfe smiled. "So it does." And abruptly, he was all business again. "Now tell me of the lovely Lara. She recovered her senses after that awful night, I take it. You are in contact?"

"I've told you, no. Because of me, she was forced into an act of patricide of the most heinous sort. She will never forgive me, and I wouldn't ask her to."

"Where is she?"

"Her family has property all over the world. I imagine she has been able to hold on to some of it. Certainly she has friends, both human and loup garou, who will protect her should she need it, and hide her if necessary. One rarely hears her name any more."

"It would appear she has fared the best of all, then."

Emory took another long and careful sip of his wine. "Unless, of course, you count the death of her lover, the murder of her father, and the betrayal of the one man to whom she swore her fealty for life."

There was a small glint of amusement in Rolfe's eyes. "Touché." Then, "The hybrid David. Where did you see him last?"

"Seriously, Rolfe, you really must pay attention. I told you, I put him into the back of a car with Lara in November of 1999 and I have neither seen nor heard from him since then."

Rolfe's gaze was steady, dark, and unfathomable. "Something happened to you recently in France," he prompted. "Tell me what it was."

Emory said nothing.

Rolfe glanced at his watch. "I have nothing but time," he assured Emory with a small smile. "Yours, unfortunately, is limited."

Emory drew a breath, released it, took a final sip of his wine, and set the glass on the table. "Each year," he said, "I make of pilgrimage of sorts to a little church in the Valley of the Loire." His tone grew reminiscent. "They say it dates back to the fourteenth century, perhaps even older. There is a huge palais at the top of the hill, the chimney tops barely visible over the trees. But the palais is private, its gates closed and locked, and no one ever goes there anymore. I like to go in the spring, when the roses are in bloom."

Rolfe prompted gently, "You wait there for Lara."

Emory kept his heartbeat still, his breath even. "She never comes."

"And this year?"

"This year as I sat in my customary pew in the empty little church in the quiet of the day, a priest, the rector of the place, passed by me, as he often does, and said to me, as he often does, "God bless you, my son." He clasped my hand in both of his and when he moved away, there was a slip of paper in my palm. It said, *Our friend has gone abroad. He said to tell you his time has come. And thank you.*"

Emory was silent for a moment, gazing at the glass before him. Then he looked at the man opposite. "I left the church. I remember standing at the bottom of the hill, looking up at the palais. The roses were spilling over the top of one of the garden walls. And that's all."

Rolfe regarded him thoughtfully. "And so," he said in a moment, "let us review. You did not kill David after all, as you told me when we began this interview."

Emory looked down at his glass, found it almost empty, and refilled it with the last of the bottle. "No," he said. He was tired. The muscles of his face sagged, and his voice was heavy.

"You lied."

"I did."

"That was foolish."

Emory sipped his wine, and almost managed to form his lips into a smile. "If you've learned nothing else about me today, you should have learned that I have been a greater fool for far less reason."

"Still, it's a pity." Rolfe sounded genuinely regretful. "I've grown rather fond of you in the course of our time together."

"Thank you," Emory replied. "I wish I could say the same." And he lifted his glass in a salute. "Although you do keep an excellent wine cellar."

"I am puzzled," observed Rolfe mildly, "over the great fuss that has been made over this hybrid, your David. You risked your life, betrayed your vows, and gave up your future to save him, as did the lovely Lara. You were willing to kill the only father you have ever known to avenge him, and now, it appears, you will in fact die for him. And to what end? You know nothing about him—except, if your report is to be believed, that he is capable of single-handedly destroying both of the planet's dominant species. What else is he capable of, I wonder?"

Emory did not reply.

Rolfe's expression grew mildly speculative. "He has been locked away in this Sanctuary for, what? Over a decade? I wonder what that must have been like for someone as accustomed to the freedom of the wilderness as he was. I wonder what that might have done to him."

Emory sipped his wine. "I'm sure I don't know."

Rolfe said, "Where is David?"

"I don't know."

"Your loyalty is admirable," Rolfe pointed out, "but very likely misplaced. He is dangerous, by your own admission. He is very possibly also quite mad. Of course he must be captured again, and contained."

"I'm sorry I can't help you."

"Ah." Rolfe smiled. "Somehow I don't believe that. So let me ask you one question that I believe you will have no trouble answering honestly. Why did you do it? I understand why the Devoncroix would want him out of the way. I understand why the Brotherhood would consider his very existence a threat. But why did you go to such lengths to save him? What good can you possibly think will come of it?"

And now Emory smiled, and gave a small shake of his head. "You really haven't been paying attention, have you? I'm an idealist. I believe in things greater than myself. It wasn't David I gave up everything to protect, it's what he represents. What he can be."

Rolfe inquired politely, "And what is that?"

"What the human race was meant to be," Emory explained simply. "What the loup garoux were meant to be. We've been at war with each other and with ourselves since creation, trying to fill the emptiness. But David is end of all that. He will bring us together. He is the best of both our species."

"Or the worst," suggested Rolfe.

"Perhaps." Emory conceded. "Either way, it's over. History has been changed, for both of us. And I have lived to see it begin.

I'll die without regrets. "

Rolfe said abruptly, "The note that the priest gave you — what did it really say?"

"I told you that."

"Was it, in fact, the priest who approached you, or was it someone else?"

"It was the priest. I told you."

Rolfe sipped his wine, his eyes unblinking, studious, unrevealing. "This," he said at length, "is why the loup garoux hold your species in such contempt. You are pathetic liars." He raised his glass again to his lips, found it empty, and said mildly, "Damn. That's the last of it."

His gaze shifted then, over Emory's shoulder, and Emory heard the door open. He half turned, and caught a glimpse from the corner of his eye of the man who entered. Tall, slim, long-haired and incredibly strong. He slammed Emory back against the chair and bound him, chest and arms, before he could summon much more than a token struggle. The strip of reinforced plastic that secured him to the chair was so tight it compressed his ribs, and he could feel the thrum of his heart against it. His breath was a little short.

"Good Christ," he said. "We're not really going to play this out, are we?"

Rolfe said, "I am a man of my word. And I count four lies you have told me. That translates into four fingers. Although," he added courteously, "I do appreciate the effort you have made to relate the remainder of your story. I found it both entertaining and enlightening, and it filled in quite a few blanks in recent and ancient history that have tormented me."

The tall man seized Emory's left arm and jerked it forward,

pinning his hand to the tabletop at the wrist. In his other hand he produced a heavy bladed knife with a bone handle, its edge honed razor-sharp. Emory's muscles stiffened in visceral resistance although he knew a struggle would only prolong the pain.

He said, "Is this worth the life of your children, then? The extinction of your whole race? I told you, I am infected."

"So you did," agreed Rolfe.

Once again the door opened behind him and Emory twisted his head around instinctively. His heart stopped beating in his chest, his saliva dried up in his mouth, his very blood seemed to stop coursing through his veins as Lara, bound and shoved by an unseen hand, stumbled and fell to her knees not six feet away from him.

She was dressed in white jeans and a pink silk blouse that was torn and stained and untucked. Her feet were bare. Her hair was loose and dull and tangled around her face and her back. When she fell her head snapped forward but she immediately jerked it upright again, revealing a bruised and bloodied left eye and a crust of dried blood near her temple. And a small pink scar bisecting her eyebrow. She looked at Emory.

She looked at him, and her eyes were filled with triumph and defiance and a furious determination for survival and when she looked at him his eyes flooded with tears and all he could think was, Lara. *Lara* .... But he couldn't say it. He couldn't even say her name.

Rolfe was watching him with mild amusement. "It was noble of you to try to conceal your bond from me, but completely unnecessary. I've known from the beginning. Without the bond she never would have known how to find you, would she?"

"Bastard." His voice was hoarse, barely a croak. He strained against his bindings.

Rolfe gave an impatient jerk of his head and the man released Emory's wrist and stepped to Lara, pulling her to her feet and shoving her into the chair at the head of the table, between Emory and Rolfe. Her hands were bound behind her back, as Emory's had been when he was first brought in, but the man with the knife released them. Before she could make use of them, however, he slammed his hand against her throat, bending her head back against the chair and rendering her effectively paralyzed. Her eyes went wide with shock and the instinctive effort to breathe. Emory struggled uselessly against his bonds.

Rolfe looked bored, and actually glanced at the hands of his watch. "One last chance, Professor, to tell the truth. This is an easy one. No prevarication, and I will allow you and your lover to depart in more or less the same condition in which you arrived. It was David who came to you in the church at the foot of the Devoncroix Palais in the Loire, we already know that. What he put in your hand was an instruction as to how to contact him should you need to. You've memorized and destroyed it. Tell me what it said now, and you both go free."

Lara's eyes blazed at Rolfe. "You know nothing about us, if you think it will be easy." She was gasping for breath, and practically spat the words at him. "You may prepare to breathe your last."

The tall man drew back his hand with an almost negligent gesture and struck her hard across the mouth. A bloody gash appeared where her beautiful lips once had been.

Emory shouted, "Stop it! She doesn't know anything!"

Rolfe smiled. "On the contrary. She knows everything." He

300

glanced at Lara. "You've had quite the career for yourself since you left New York, haven't you, Princess? Or perhaps you would prefer to be addressed as 'Commander.'" And he laughed softly.

Lara lifted her chin, her eyes cold. "I would prefer," she said, "that you did not address me at all."

"Your efforts are pointless of course. Effective change was never won through blind resistance, but through ..." and he gave a polite nod in Emory's direction, "allowing nature to take its course."

He turned briskly to Emory. "Now, here is the situation. Your lover's fate is in your hands, and it will be a simple matter for you to stop this. Please observe the way my friend Cameron is holding her." Once again the werewolf with the knife slammed his hand against Lara's neck, pinning her head back against the chair. Her eyes flared with fury and pain, but she was helpless.

"Do you know what becomes of a loup garou who is injured and who is physically refrained from Changing to heal herself? No? Well, she will eventually die, of course, or suffer the long-term impairment of her injuries. But long before that happens, she will endure the agonies of convulsions, she will lose control of her bladder and her bowels and at last, her dignity. She will rage and hallucinate and forsake all that made her uniquely loup garou, the top of the food chain, the dominant species on the planet. She will hate you. You will pity her. It will all be so sad I don't know if I can bear to watch. So how are your ideals holding up, now, Professor? I ask you for the final time, how can I find David Devoncroix?"

Emory's face was wet, his hair dripped into his eyes. He pressed against the plastic bond until he thought his ribs would crack. He said nothing.

Rolfe made a small moue of disappointment, and glanced at Cameron. Before Emory could so much as draw a breath for a shout, Cameron grasped Lara's arm, slammed her hand upon the table, whipped out the evil-bladed knife, and sliced.

Blood gushed and pooled in a dark river on the polished surface. Lara's scream, hoarse and wild and terrified, filled the universe. Her small finger, the nail perfectly buffed and polished and sculpted into a delicate crescent shape, skidded several inches across the tabletop and lay there, separated at the last joint from the body to which it had once belonged, in the growing, pulsing, black pool of its own blood.

It wasn't until he heard Rolfe's voice that Emory realized his own scream had melded with Lara's, that the sound he heard was not of her agony but his own, and when it died he was looking into the cold, cold eyes of the werewolf called Rolfe.

Rolfe lifted his arm from the table to avoid staining his immaculate shirt cuff with the slow trickling rivulet of blood, and the expression of his lips as he did so was of faint disgust. "Now, you see what you have done," he said mildly. He looked at Lara. "That's one."

Lara struggled against the cruel restraint of Cameron's hand against her throat. Her face was chalk white, her lips drawn back from her teeth, her muscles set as she fought the pain and her own body's natural instinct to Change.

Rolfe said, "Shall we try for two?"

Cameron, without releasing his crushing hold on Lara's trachea, produced the knife.

Emory threw himself against his bonds. He shouted hoarsely, "What do you want from me? I don't have his fucking cell phone number!"

Cameron grasped Lara's blood-slicked arm and once again slammed it onto the table. Emory screamed, "*No!*" and the blade came down again. Bone and flesh broke and the bloody shape of another finger lay on the table, severed from the hand. The sounds that came from Lara's mouth were guttural and animal-like and hoarse and gasping. She tossed her head from side to side against the chair, shuddering. Rolfe inquired mildly, "Shall we talk once again of ideals, Professor?"

Emory clenched his teeth together hard, his breath coming in puffs through flared nostrils. Sweat congealed around his eyes and dripped into the corners of his mouth.

Rolfe glanced again at Cameron and Cameron, dispassionately, lifted the knife.

Emory shouted, "Wait!"

Rolfe looked at him.

"Wait, stop, I'll tell you, I will!" Emory's breath was ragged, his words barely distinguishable. Lara bucked and struggled against her captor, whose hand was on her throat again, so tightly that no sounds came. Rolfe looked at Emory inquiringly and he spoke quickly, quickly before he lost his nerve, quickly before Lara could stop him.

"It was a computer code," he gasped. "An IP Internet address that connected directly to his handheld device. I can find him anywhere in the world with it. Get a pen. Write it down. "

Lara screamed, a furious, despairing, death-welcoming scream, and thrashed against Cameron's restraining hand. Rolfe did not spare her a glance. His gaze was steady upon Emory. "Tell it to me."

Emory, gasping and shaking, recited the numbers.

Rolfe, smiling very faintly, said, "Wrong, Professor."

303

And he said to Cameron, without once looking at him, "Thank you. You may leave."

Cameron's exit was swift and wordless, and Rolfe stood almost in the same motion, and moved to Lara. Emory's breath and his heart were thundering a counter-point cacophony, his whole body shuddering; he couldn't focus or try to form words and it seemed a long, time-elapsed moment before he understood what was happening, before that understanding translated to his consciousness and finally to his soul; before he accepted it. Before he understood.

Lara was white and drenched in sweat, trembling, her eyes rolled back, her teeth chattering, barely conscious. Rolfe swept behind her and bent low, his arm around her throat as Cameron's had been, his head bent over hers, embracing her, almost as a lover might. His hand moved downward over her bloodied, shaking arm, caressing it, owning it. And when he reached her hand he stretched the fingers forward, oiling them in blood, even the pulsing stump of the missing fingers, and he covered them in his own, stretching out his hand to clasp the severed digits that lay dead upon the table, covering them.

Emory could not see her face. Rolfe's shadow encompassed it. He could see her body stiffen, almost as in its death throes, and then, abruptly go limp. He threw himself once again against his bonds, sobbing. But Lara's breath was quiet and even. Her face had relaxed its rictus, her eyelids fluttering to open. And her poor, mangled hand, glistening with blood and stretched forth upon the tabletop, was curled into a quiescent posture, with all five digits attached.

This Emory noticed in the time it takes one wet, desperate breath to dry in one's throat, in the time it takes a universe to shift, in the space that lives between what is real and what is not. His brain had not yet analyzed what his eyes reported when Rolfe straightened up, and stepped away from Lara. Only it was not Rolfe at all. His hair was no longer dark, but blond and shoulder length. His features had changed. And his eyes were Devoncroix blue.

The color had returned to Lara's face, the bruises faded, the cut lip healed. Her breath was suspended between parted lips, her gaze fixed upon the creature who stood over her. She cradled her bloody right hand in her left one, flexing the fingers, all of them. She said a single word: "David."

He plucked a silk pocket square from his jacket and used it to wipe the blood from his hands, then, with a small expression of distaste, tossed it on the silver tray with the crusts of cheese and fruit rinds. "That, my dear professor," he told Emory with a quirk of his brow, "is the way to tell a proper lie."

He stepped over to Emory's chair and snapped the heavy plastic cable that bound him between his thumb and forefinger. Emory's upper body sagged against the chair as blood rushed painfully back into his limbs.

"Cleverly played," David told him. And then he added curiously, "What would you have done, when I tested your non-existent IP address?"

Emory couldn't answer. Even had he been able to draw enough breath into his throat to produce words, his brain could not form them.

A delighted smile touched David's face as he answered his own question. "But it didn't matter, did it? You wanted only to distract me long enough to give Lara a chance to Change. That was the plan from the beginning. Delightful." And he laughed out loud, pleased with himself.

Emory surged upward, blind with rage, and then Lara was on her feet, lunging toward him, capturing him in her arms and holding him fast, but there was no need. Of course David blocked any move he might have made with a single mild, uplifted hand.

Emory tore away from Lara's restraint, blood still pulsing in his temples. But he balled his hands into fists and tried to regulate his breathing and he shouted at David, "*Why*? Why did you do this? I've done nothing but protect you, I've risked my life for you, and so has Lara. *Why*?"

Emory felt Lara's hand on his arm, fingers digging into his muscles in warning, or reassurance. He seized her suddenly and drew her close, his hand in her sweat-dampened hair, feeling her heartbeat and her breath, close to his. The sagging wetness on her blouse was her own blood. And his breath was so harsh that it burned his lungs.

David regarded them both with a kind of detached fascination for a moment, and then he moved around the table. Idly, he picked up a fruit knife from the platter, traced its blade between his thumb and forefinger, and returned it. He said, "One day we will have dinner, the three of us, at one of the fine hotels in Paris or Rome, and we will discuss dichotomies and dualities, the nature of good and evil, and whether one can, in fact exist without the other. I'll tell you about my youth, my education, my view of the world, and what I really have been doing this past decade. What I thought about in all that time, what I discovered, what I decided, what I became. I will tell you secrets about myself, about what I am and what I can do, that no living being knows and we will bond in understanding, you two and I, on that night. But before that can happen, I have some other matters that require my attention."

Lara pulled herself away from the shelter of Emory's arms. Her voice was strong and clear as she demanded, "What do you want from us?"

He looked at them then with his power-blue eyes, his expression cool and calculating. "There are those, both human and werewolf, who would see me dead. Others who would capture me and attach me to their machines, or vivisect me for the amusement of their own tiny brains. Still others would pull me into their sect or cause or try to persuade my alliance against their enemies. I have a great many people working for me, of course, whole armies waiting to serve me, but none of them know the full truth of who I am, and without it their loyalty is transient at best. It occurred to me that it would be useful to have at least one person I could trust. So I found you in France, Professor, and I told you a secret. But a secret means nothing unless it can be kept. So I had to be sure it could be."

My God, thought Emory, but he could not speak it. *All of this ... my God.*

Lara said very steadily, "We saved your life. Wasn't that enough?"

He smiled. "You would think so, wouldn't you? But ..." He shrugged. "It's a new day. The old rules no longer apply."

He took out the phone from his jacket and pushed a button. "You may leave this room whenever you wish; no one will try to stop you. Someone will be waiting outside to take you to your transportation once I am well away. I should give him my full cooperation if I were you. My generosity is notoriously short-lived."

Emory said, "And then what?" His fingers were so tight on Lara's waist he knew he was hurting her but he did not dare let go.

David replied, "You will be returned to your lives, such as they are. And I will get on with mine."

"What does that mean?" Lara demanded, her voice thin and furious. "What can that possibly *mean*?"

David seemed amused. "My dear, don't be naive. I knew this day would come and I've spent a lifetime preparing for it. I have headquarters all over the world. I have financial, industrial and technological resources that even I haven't fully investigated yet. What that means is that I can do, in fact, whatever I like." And he tilted his head at her in a faintly mocking fashion. "I am, after all, a Devoncroix."

He came around the table and moved toward the door, glancing at his watch. "And now, if you'll excuse me, I'll say my good-byes. I have a full schedule, as I'm sure you can imagine. "

He glanced at Emory, and his expression altered slightly. For a moment it seemed oddly, almost impossibly, human. "You gave me your boots," he said. "That was kind of you. I don't forget a kindness."

For a moment, something in Emory wavered. And then, with a force of will, he made himself release Lara's waist. He stepped forward, his heart pounding hard. He knew the hybrid could hear it, and he didn't care. "With your permission, David, I would give you something more."

David tilted his head quizzically.

"My fealty," Emory said. "We may have our differences in philosophy, but I want you to know I still believe in what you can be. I will keep your secret." He moved to David, took his face between his hands, and kissed him on the mouth. He said simply, stepping back, "My life for yours."

David looked surprised, and then gently, almost reluctantly, pleased. "How odd," he said. "I didn't think there were any humans I wished to save. Now I may reconsider."

He reached out his hand and lay two fingers upon Emory's carotid pulse. Emory felt a surge of heat that seemed to crisp his skin, but before he could cry out with the pain, it was gone. Sparks danced before his eyes, then cleared. The air seemed suddenly purer, each breath more invigorating, his muscles seemed longer, his heart beat stronger. David's expression, as he stepped back, was oddly tender.

"Long life, Professor," he said, and turned to the door.

Lara whirled around. Emory caught her wrist and held it, hard. "Where will you go?" she demanded. "What will you do?"

He made an airy, expansive gesture over his head and replied without turning, "I go to discover this brave new world I've inherited. And to make as much mischief within it as I possibly can, of course."

Emory's throat was tight, his breath caught somewhere in his midsection. His words sounded odd and far away, as though coming from the lips of one already dead. "Don't make me sorry I saved you," he said.

David turned then to look at him, his hand upon the handle of the door, eyes brimming with amusement. "My dear professor, if you are not sorry already, you are far, far less bright than I gave you credit for."

They could hear his laughter long after he left the room, as it faded down the corridor, and even then, as they stood alone in the elegant blood-wrecked little room, they heard him laughing in their heads.

Lara stepped away from Emory slightly, to better examine his eyes. A thousand days and nights of longing and regret flashed between them, a thousand unsaid words, a thousand buried thoughts. But it was gone, as it always was, in an instant. She said only, "Were you successful?"

Emory drew a breath, and released it unsteadily. "I don't know." A bleakness came over his face as he added, "And worse, I'm not sure what to hope for."

She touched his arm lightly, and a rare tenderness crossed her face as she did so. "This is Castle Devoncroix," she said. "Are there things you want to see? I could show you."

He looked at her for a moment, almost managed a smile, and shook his head. "No," he said. "There's nothing to see here but ghosts now."

He walked forward and tried the door. It opened easily and they left together, not touching, and did not look back.

EPILOGUE

To my friends, human and loup garou, in the Alliance:

I have done my best, in this and other writings, to put forth a fair and accurate account of the events that led us to this moment in history. Times being what they are, however, information is unreliable and accuracy is difficult to maintain—almost as difficult as the task of compressing a hundred thousand lifetimes of history into a few pages. And because times are what they are, and my life, and those of my compatriots, are so uncertain, I take the risk of leaving behind this written record of the early days. The days when we still had choices and, for better or worse, made them as best we could.

From the beginning of time species Homo sapiens and species lupinotuum, a single atom split in two at the moment of creation, have been two halves of a whole yearning toward each other even as, by the very nature of their existence, they repel. Now, once again, they are joined. We live in the age of miracles, and on the cusp of Armageddon. I'm sorry to say that the two are not mutually exclusive.

I was not entirely forthcoming with Rolfe—or David—about many things, as you no doubt have guessed. The first years after the collapse of the Devoncroix Dynasty were chaotic indeed. The global pack and the unified Brotherhood both were scattered and in disarray, with various factions from each constantly on the brink of war with each other and with humans. There emerged from the chaos the need for purpose, sanity and vision.

Lara Fasburg, with the memories and the powerful intent of her father—one of the strongest, if perhaps most misguided leaders of the modern time—now integrated into her consciousness, has led what is now known as the Alliance since 2003. Our purpose is to protect humankind from renegade loup garoux, to maintain the balance of power as best we can, and to restore Nicholas Devoncroix to his rightful place as leader of the pack.

He is alive. I dare say no more.

My bond with Lara was weakened by the death of her father, it's true, but it did not entirely disappear. She risked her life for me when I was captured. I would have given my life to spare her pain. Few humans will ever know this kind of love, or the weight of this burden. I breathe for two, as does she. I think for two, as does she. I walk more carefully than I have ever done before, because I know one misstep could cost a life much more valuable than my own. I wish sometimes I had never known this responsibility. And I wonder how I could have endured these past years without it.

While it is true that I have lived much of my life under cover over the past ten years, I did so in service to the Alliance. I may have exaggerated my lack of access to technology during this time, for as soon as I discovered I had been infected by the virus in David's bloodstream, I — and all of the pack scientists within the Alliance — began researching a cure. Because this is a shifting-antigen virus, the best we were able to come up with is a mutant strain that has virtually no affect on the live virus but may one day, if we are able to continue the research, be adapted into a vaccine for those not yet affected . I know this because I inoculated myself with the mutant virus years ago. It may have slowed down the progression of my disease, but did not, clearly, halt it.

The mutant strain does, however, have one unexpected side effect. The tests we performed on the remaining samples of David's blood show that this virus is capable of causing an autoimmune response that destroys red blood cells faster than they can be replenished. The symptoms begin within hours and death follows quickly. This virus is easily transmitted through something as simple as a casual kiss. Like the one I gave to David.

As of this writing, we have been unable to determine whether David's unprecedented immune system was able to adapt to and destroy the disease I gave him, or whether it will, as our lab tests assured us, produce a fatal reaction that will eliminate the hybrid, and all the possibilities he represents, forever. I did what I thought was necessary at the time, just as I always have done.

All these years I never doubted the rightness of my decision in sparing him that night, despite the dreadful consequences that resulted. All these years I never minded fighting to restore what was lost for his sake. I believed in the evolution of nature. I believed in the potential of the future. I believed he was our destiny.

Now I am not so sure. About anything.

As soon as we discovered the virus David carried we knew that if he escaped the Sanctuary before a cure was found he would have to be destroyed. We knew this, but it had always seemed such an academic thing. And suddenly it wasn't.

Shortly before I was captured and interrogated by David, Lara received word from the Sanctuary from which he had escaped. All 131 residents were dead. Slaughtered. Artists, musicians, philosophers, seekers of peace whose only crime had been, perhaps, to bore him.

Twenty-four hours after David touched me and I felt life sing through my veins, my blood tested negative for the virus. I was cured. And my first thought, God help me, was *Had he cured me before my kiss had the chance to work its deadly magic on his blood? How powerful was he?*

How powerful did I want him to be?

To that, I have no answers. This is what I know.

The magnificent loup garoux have ruled over all of nature for over a millennium. They have been hunted as monsters and worshiped as gods. They have taken us into their palaces and anointed us with oils, and they have roasted our bones over their fires. And for the past six hundred years they have walked among us with a mixture of contempt and desperate affection, needing us and despising us, never quite able to forget the twisted, broken history we share. They see in us what they once were. We see in them what we might have been. And the seeing breaks both our hearts.

Eric Fasburg and his family were banished from the pack for treachery against the queen. Within the decade the disease that had been killing their infants was eradicated from the pack, and Eudora found a mate among one of her own clan. They lived to see the birth of eighteen children, one hundred ninety-two grandchildren, three hundred forty great-grandchildren.

It is estimated that between 1342 and 1345 one third to one half of the population of Europe was destroyed by the plague. Perhaps had Louis Phillipe, keeper of secrets, student of arcane knowledge, possessed the gift of foresight he might not have considered his sacrifice such a noble one. Or he might have, in fact, thought the trade equitable. The cost in terms of human life was enormous. But civilization was saved. Slowly, here and there in warm pockets of the earth, art began to blossom. Poets and thinkers put forth their ideas, a Galileo reached for the stars, a DaVinci unleashed his genius. Science and invention thrived, continents were explored, operas were written because once long ago a vow was broken, a choice was made; humans died, and werewolves lived.

I no longer indulge myself with speculations about the nature of right and wrong, or deceive myself into believing that I am capable of discerning what comprises a balance between them. I have made choices. I soon will make others. I suspect I will choose according to my nature. In the end, that's the best that any of us can do.

In the meantime, you would be wise to remember what happened the last time the gods went to war. Civilizations crumbled, the beasts ran wild and darkness ruled the earth. There can be no victors in such a scenario. They are still out there, our fine heroes, the magnificent species lupinotuum, genus hominid, warvulf, lycanthrope, lycos, werewolf. Their muscles are strong, their brains are large, their senses sharp, their synapses fast. They are still at the top of the food chain. And, as I was once assured by someone who should know, the old rules no longer apply.

I am

Emory Hilliford, PhD

Human

Assassin

ABOUT THE AUTHOR

Donna Boyd is the author of several dozen books, under a variety of pseudonyms, that include mystery, suspense, romance and women's fiction. A full list of her work can be found on her web site. She lives in a restored Victorian barn in the Blue Ridge Mountains with a variety of four-legged companions that may or may not include werewolves. You can contact her at www.donnaball.net.

Also in this series:
THE PASSION
THE PROMISE

Made in the USA
Middletown, DE
14 September 2017